DIVING STATIONS

(NICK HAMILTON 4)

EDWYN GRAY

WOLFPACK
PUBLISHING
— EST 2013 —

Diving Stations
Nick Hamilton Book 4
Edwyn Gray

Paperback Edition
© Copyright 2019 Edwyn Gray

Wolfpack Publishing
6032 Wheat Penny Avenue
Las Vegas, NV 89122

eBook ISBN 978-1-64119-479-2
Paperback ISBN 978-1-64119-480-8

Library of Congress Control Number: 2018967087

AUTHOR'S NOTE

British local time, i.e.: Hong Kong or Singapore time, has been used throughout the book

DIVING STATIONS

ONE

The Admiralty official who first suggested the posting probably received an MBE in the New Year's Honors List in
appreciation of his services to the Royal Navy and the
nation. And, if he failed to win an award, it certainly wasn't
the First Sea Lord's fault. Many civil servants were known
to have been knighted for less.

Not that Lieutenant Nicholas Hamilton DSO RN was
a bad submarine commander - his seamanship and courage
in dangerous situations were invariably highly commended
in his personal reports.

But he had a reputation for being difficult and at least
half a dozen flotilla commanders had breathed a heartfelt
sigh of relief when his tour of duty with them came to an
end. On the other hand, there were many submarine
captains who would have willingly shouldered the burden
of Hamilton's unenviable reputation in exchange for some
of the brilliant successes he had enjoyed in his brief career.

His exploits in rescuing the captured British merchant
seamen from the prison ship *Nordsee,* in the early weeks of
1940, had made him a national hero - although his ruthless

destruction of the Vichy French submarine *Gladiateur* had been hushed up for diplomatic reasons. Nevertheless, it had not gone unnoticed in the right places.

Yet for all his undoubted ability Hamilton was regarded as a nuisance. His habit of only obeying orders when they suited his own particular purposes infuriated his superiors; while his total lack of scruple worried the more responsible Admirals who took the trouble to think about such matters. And, despite the success of the unusual missions to which he had been entrusted, he had proved an inexplicable failure on routine patrols. In fact, he was probably the only captain in the entire British submarine service to have survived two years of war without sinking a single enemy ship in the course of normal patrol operations.

Even a three-month tour in the Mediterranean combat zone had failed to reflect an improvement in his record although, as the Sixth Sea Lord readily admitted in his more charitable moments, Hamilton had carried out two further special missions with complete success. But as these operations remain subject to the restrictions of the Official Secrets Act even today, more than thirty years later, the details have never been revealed to anyone outside a select circle at the Admiralty.

And so, when William Strong, the Deputy Under Secretary, suggested that the addition of a submarine to the China Squadron might be a good thing, the vice admiral responded with unusual enthusiasm.

'Send *Rapier* out to Hong Kong, eh? How soon can we do it?'

The Deputy Under Secretary was no stranger to the labyrinthine channels of decision at the Admiralty. Formal approval of transfers between stations could take several months. And, with the foresight of experience, he had arranged the pieces of his jig-saw with infinite care.

'Fairly quickly, sir,' he said. Strong had the usual civil service aversion to committing himself too precisely. '*Rapier* was pulled out of Malta two weeks ago for a minor refit at Alexandria. That means she's the nearest submarine to the Far East - assuming we route her via Suez.'

'I wouldn't have regarded that as a particularly strong recommendation,' Gresham observed doubtfully. 'The DNO usually prefers to create maximum chaos by finding the most inconvenient and impractical posting possible. In my opinion, the fact that *Rapier* is the shortest distance from Hong Kong is probably a disadvantage. Do you have anything better?'

'Well sir, in 1939 we had a complete flotilla of fifteen submarines at Hong Kong. As you know, they've all been withdrawn for service nearer home. And now, just when Japan looks like turning nasty, the C-in-C China hasn't a single boat available to defend the colony.'

'I doubt if that will cut much ice with the DNO either,' Gresham sighed. 'The 10th flotilla was withdrawn from the Far East because we had a shortage of submarines in the Med. And, since we've now lost at least half of the poor sods, I can't see anyone agreeing to release a much needed boat to a station that's not directly engaged in combat operations. Don't forget, they're even pulling out the old Yangtse gunboats to form an Inshore Squadron to cover the 8th Arm's seaward flank in North Africa. And that's *really* scraping the barrel.'

The civil servant nodded his agreement and remained silent for a few minutes - his eyes fixed on the large wall chart behind the admiral's desk. He still had his trump to play.

'Just supposing the Japs *did* launch an attack sir,' he said slowly. 'What do you reckon their chances of success?'

Admiral Gresham gave a short laugh. 'Not much, Strong. If we send a couple of fast battleships to Singapore, as the War Cabinet proposes, the Japanese will end up with a bloody nose. They haven't got a single well-designed ship in their Navy - and the RAF's Spitfires will run circles round their aircraft. They'd be on a hiding to nothing - and they know it.'

The Deputy Under Secretary made no comment. The admiral's views did not fit in with what he had heard from officers recently returned from the Far East, but he knew that Gresham was only reflecting the general opinion of the War Cabinet and the IGS. He wondered whether the US Navy entertained a similarly complacent underestimate of the Japanese war machine's capabilities.

'Of course, I'm not denying that we might lose Hong Kong in the event of hostilities,' the admiral continued. 'The land frontier with the Chinese mainland is virtually inde-fensible. But the Yanks certainly won't let them take over the Philippines and the Jap bombers haven't the range to operate against Singapore from their bases in China.' Gresham had fallen neatly into the trap the Deputy Under Secretary had so carefully prepared. Strong seized his chance without hesitation.

'But if they were to secure air bases in French IndoChi-na,' he pointed out, 'it could create a very different situa-tion.' He walked across to the map and indicated the distances involved. 'It's only about six hundred miles by air from Saigon to Malaya - and we know they've got bombers with that sort of range.'

The admiral looked up at the chart and shrugged. Why did these damned civilians always think they could run the war better than the service chiefs? 'The French wouldn't grant the Japanese landing rights. And,' he added defiantly, 'if they *did* the Royal Navy would soon go in and settle their hash!'

'I wouldn't be too sure, sir,' Strong warned him gently. 'Oran and Dakar didn't go down too well with our people. Even Jimmy Sommerville delayed action well beyond the set time-limit at Mers-el-Kebir to give the French a chance. *And* because he didn't fancy mass murder. If the Japanese decide to occupy Indo-China, we'll have no margin of time to allow admirals to come to terms with their consciences.'

'Very well, Strong,' Gresham yielded reluctantly. Much as he hated to admit it, he knew the Navy was opposed to further attacks on the French fleet. 'I grant it wouldn't be easy. But what has this got to do with Hamilton and *Rapier*?'

I wondered when you'd ask, Strong thought to himself. He smiled. 'Everything, sir. Hamilton has already proved that he'll attack the Vichy French without compunction. Don't forget he has destroyed one French submarine already.[1] And he has no scruples. He's the one man in the Navy who can be relied upon to attack the French, if for any reason the Japanese should try to occupy Indo-China with Vichy approval.' The Deputy Under Secretary paused for a moment and then added quietly, 'And there's another thing, sir. I doubt if any warships operating along the Chinese coast from Hong Kong would survive for more than a few days if the Japanese mounted a full-scale attack. And of all the officers in the Royal Navy, I would have regarded Lieutenant Hamilton as certainly the most expendable....'

Admiral Gresham rubbed his chin thoughtfully as he digested the civil servant's words. Strong's analysis of the situation was brutally practical. And it would certainly solve a number of problems at a stroke. He had nothing against Hamilton personally, in fact he'd never met the man, but when the safety of the nation and empire was at stake no cost could be too high. And having assuaged his conscience to his own satisfaction the Admiral smiled bleakly.

'I'll see the DNO straight away. As you say - it's worth a try.'

HAMILTON'S initial reaction to the projected transfer was one of angry disbelief. Like many Englishmen, he enjoyed the excitement of war. The tensions and stresses of combat, the ever-present danger, and the necessity of unrelenting vigilance brought him the satisfaction of being stretched to the limit, both mentally and physically. And war gave a purpose to life - a life made all the more precious by the fact that it might only be short.

As far as Hamilton was concerned, Hong Kong was no more than a peacetime station, where spit-and-polish and the dreary round of cocktails and social small-talk were more important than combat efficiency and a determination to defeat the common enemy. The Colony was ten thousand miles away from the *real* war, and he scarcely rated the Japanese invasion of China as being in the same league as the European conflict with Nazi Germany. In any event, Britain was securely neutral in that particular Asiatic power-struggle, and Hong Kong was virtually unaffected by the fighting on the mainland.

The admiral's day cabin was hot and stuffy and the task of persuading Hamilton to accept the transfer without complaint had tried the flag-officer's patience to the limit.

Rear Admiral Herbert could understand Hamilton's dismay. He was feeling none too pleased himself. Experienced submarine commanders and trained crews were desperately needed in the Mediterranean, and he could not understand the reason for the Admiralty's decision to reduce their already slender resources by sending a much needed submarine to the Far East. But, as one trained in the old school of docile obedience to orders, he had accepted the posting without argument.

He was, however, shrewd enough to discern the true reason behind Hamilton's reluctance to go. Despite his spectacular successes, the young lieutenant was anxious to prove his ability on routine patrols. And *that* could only be achieved in the face of the enemy. It was not merely a matter of personal prestige or glory. The DSO which *Rapier*'s commanding officer had won when he rescued the prisoners from the *Nordsee* was adequate proof of his skill and courage.[1] And his activities in the Kattegat and off the Belgian coast during the evacuation of the BEF had only served to add to his reputation. There were, the rear admiral realized, other equally important considerations.

Hamilton was a career officer and, with six years seniority as a lieutenant, he was keen to earn his half stripe. Most of his contemporaries had already been promoted over his head, and in recent months a growing number of RNVR officers had achieved the coveted third narrow ring on their sleeves. Herbert was no fool. He knew Hamilton's background was against him and could not help but sympathize with his frustration. Promoted from the lower deck - an upper-yardman in Navy slang - he lacked the polish and social graces of his brother wardroom officers and, despite his proven abilities, the Admiralty seemed determined to keep him as a 'two ringer' until the seniority rules made his ultimate promotion unavoidable. And while the delay continued, Hamilton was losing valuable experiences and seniority in the next rank - which he badly needed if he was to climb the ladder of promotion in his chosen career.

'I know how you feel, Lieutenant,' the admiral admitted carefully. 'And I have no wish to lose either you or *Rapier* from my command. But I have no doubt that the Admiralty in its wisdom knows what it is doing. And if trouble *does* break out in the Far East, you'll get all the action you want - probably a damned sight more. After all, *Rapier* will be the only British submarine in the area and you'll have the entire Japanese navy in your sights.'

'It's tempting, sir,'' Hamilton nodded. 'But frankly I can't see Japan taking the risk of involving either us or the Americans in a war. We'd wipe them off the face of the sea in a few weeks.'

'That's where you're wrong, Hamilton,' Herbert grunted. 'We haven't got enough ships out there to do anything but get ourselves sunk. If the Japs *do* come into the war on Hitler's side, we'll have to rely on the US Navy to do the fighting for us. And if the Tokyo High Command decide to play it safe and by-pass the Philippines, we'll be on our own.' The admiral paused thoughtfully at the prospect. The moment passed and he smiled. 'But I don't think it will ever come to that,' he continued reassuringly. 'And much as I hate to lose *Rapier,* you and your men are badly in need of a rest. And Hong Kong will be just the ticket.'

Hamilton knew Herbert was right. Reluctant as he was to admit the truth, he was physically and mentally exhausted from two years of unrelenting combat. His men, too, needed a break from the rigors of operational patrols and *Rapier* herself could do with a refit. A few months in the peaceful atmosphere of Hong Kong *was* what they needed. Bright lights, good food, and a respite from the ever-present threat of enemy air attack would do them all a power of good. And perhaps when they came back into the fray, the break would have added that extra spark of zest which would be rewarded by a successful patrol.

'I suppose you're right, sir,' he admitted grudgingly. 'Perhaps we do need a rest. But I'd like to request a posting back to the Med. after three months.'

The rear admiral stood up. 'I'll do what I can, Lieutenant. We've lost too many good skippers in the last few weeks - I'll have you back just as soon as I can find the right strings to pull.' He held out his hand. 'Good luck, Hamilton. And remember - once you're out in China, at least you won't have to crash dive every time you see an aircraft.'

'I'll try sir,' Hamilton grinned. 'But old habits die hard.'

Hamilton leaned his elbows on the rim of the conning tower bridge and stared ahead over the bows, as *Rapier* cut through the smooth green waters of the South China Sea. The mist of spray spuming back across the foredeck helped cool the stifling heat of the midday sun, and the men sprawled on the hot steel plating, grinned contentedly as the cold droplets of water spattered their tanned bodies. After twenty-four months of air attacks, the voyage across the Indian Ocean and down through the Bay of Bengal had resembled a luxury pleasure cruise. And with typical good sense, the skipper had relaxed discipline as soon as *Rapier* cleared Steamer Point at Aden to give his men a much needed chance to rest and relax.

The submarine had only stopped at Columbo long enough to fill her bunkers, and their call at Singapore had been too brief to permit shore leaves. But Hong Kong now lay less than two hours away over the shimmering horizon, and every man aboard was already planning how to celebrate his arrival.

The weather was good and the blue arch of the sky was clear of cloud, except for a few white wisps of stratus to starboard. The vast estuary of the Pearl River lay on its port hand and, somewhere below the heat haze on the northwestern horizon, the Portuguese colony of Macao slumbered fitfully - girding its loins and gathering its energy for another night of gambling, dancing, drinking, and whoring.

'Number One and Coxswain to the bridge.'

'Control Room, aye aye, sir.'

Turning away from the voice pipe, he paced the narrow circuit of the bridge area with his hands clasped together behind his back while he waited. He could hear the clatter of footsteps echoing inside the empty upper chamber of the conning tower, and stood away from the hatch opening as Roger Mannon and Chief Petty Officer Ernie Blood clambered through, out on to the deck.

Hamilton eyed his first officer coldly as he straightened up and saluted. Mannon had only joined *Rapier* a few weeks previously. He was young and eager. But the wavy gold rings on his uniform sleeves marked him down as an amateur and, in Hamilton's opinion, the submarine service was strictly for professionals. It took years of training and service experience to make an efficient submarine officer. How the hell could a volunteer reserve officer, whose experience of the sea comprised a few hours of coastal sailing at weekends, qualify for the exacting disciplines required for submarine service.

Not that he blamed Mannon personally. Roger was keen enough. But it somehow seemed totally wrong to share the wardroom with a chartered accountant, who knew more about balance sheets and company law than buoyancy tanks and the King's regulations. Admittedly he was learning. But that wasn't enough when the life of every man in the boat depended on the skill and experience of his shipmates; and Hamilton felt himself duty bound to check and recheck everything Mannon did - an additional chore that became an onerous burden in the tropical heat.

He nodded his head towards the slumbering men sunbathing on the foredeck. 'Get the sleeping beauties below, Cox'n. I want a tiddley ship when we enter harbor.'

'Aye aye, sir.'

'And then muster the fo'c'sle party in number six rig. I'll show the China Station that we haven't forgotten how to do things Bristol fashion, even if we *have* been fighting their bloody war for them over the past two years.'

Blood leaned over the conning tower coaming and hurried the off-duty watch below, in a voice that reflected his years of service as a gunnery instructor at Whale Island. Then, having checked that the foredeck casing was clear and the gun hatch closed, he made his way back to the bowels of the submarine to gather up the fo'c'sle party. Hamilton moved to the voice pipe.

'All hands to harbor stations!' He glanced at Mannon as he closed the cover of the speaking tube. 'Ever been through the peacetime drill for harbor stations before Number One?'

'No, sir.'

'Well, keep your eyes skinned and you'll learn something. It's a bit different from the sort of lash-up you've been used to with the Malta flotillas.'

'But not so exciting, sir.'

'It's exciting enough if something goes wrong,' Hamilton corrected him crisply. 'You've obviously never served in a ship that's been ordered back to sea and told to return and berth in a seamanlike manner. I once saw it happen to a Rear Admiral before the war. It took him a long time to live it down.'

Blood emerged from the conning tower hatch, his face gleaming with perspiration after a few brief minutes inside the steaming-hot submarine. 'Fo'c'sle party fallen in, sir,' he reported punctiliously.

'Thank you, Cox'n. Take over the helm.'

Blood relieved Finnegan at the wheel. It was customary for the coxswain, the senior petty officer, to take the helm on entering or leaving the harbor, and Blood enjoyed the responsibility of conning *Rapier* to her berth. When the boat was closed up at diving stations, his place was at the controls of the aft hydroplanes, where he was responsible for maintaining the submarine's depth - a critical duty during a torpedo attack. But although a dedicated submariner, Ernie Blood always preferred to be at the helm. It made him the most important man on the boat next to the skipper and he took a quiet pride in the fact.

'Steering zero-two-zero, sir,' he repeated as Finnegan passed over the course.

Hamilton glanced down at the chart. There were no landmarks in sight yet, but he felt confident of their position.

'Ease her to zero-one-eight, Cox'n. Full ahead both.'

'Zero-one-eight, sir. Full ahead both.'

'Aircraft approaching on port bow! Height 5000!'

Only a few weeks earlier, the look-out's warning would have cleared the bridge in seconds and *Rapier* would have quickly thrust her bows beneath the surface, like a fox going to ground. However, Hamilton showed little concern, despite the instinctive tensions of the other men on the bridge. Walking casually to the port side, he raised his glasses and scanned the blue sky to the north-west.

Three small black dots flying in arrowhead formation were approaching from the direction of the Chinese mainland; but they were still too far away to identify with any degree of certainty. He lowered his glasses.

'Probably our welcoming committee from Hong Kong. Maintain course and speed.'

Mannon continued studying the aircraft intently through his binoculars. The planes had appeared too far to the west to have come from the Colony, and there seemed something vaguely threatening in their purposeful approach.

'Do we have any two-engine machines on the China Station, sir?' he asked.

Hamilton shrugged. 'I've no idea, Number One,' he admitted. 'I suppose we might have some Blenheims or a few Marylands serving with the RAF. Why?'

Mannon didn't answer the question. 'They're changing course, sir. Heading towards us by the look of it.'

Hamilton raised his binoculars again. Mannon was too jumpy. And he didn't want the rest of the crew to be affected. Nerves could be highly contagious in a submarine. That was the worst of the Wavy Navy - good chaps in their own way, but no experience. He located the formation and brought his lenses into critical focus.

Rapier's skipper was the first to admit that he was no expert on aircraft recognition, but there was certainly something strangely familiar about these three. The silvered wings glinting in the sunlight seemed oddly unreal after the drab colors of European combat aircraft, and he wondered momentarily whether they were carrier planes from the US Pacific Fleet. He dismissed the thought as quickly as it entered his head. Despite the enormous size of their vessels, even the Yanks still had to find a way of operating twin-engined machines from carrier decks. He held the aircraft steadily in his binoculars and, as one suddenly peeled away from the formation, he saw the red blob of the Rising Sun on the underside of its starboard wing.

'Japanese,' he informed Mannon curtly. 'Nothing to worry about. Probably having a quick look-see to check we're not a Chinese boat.'

'But the Chinese don't have any submarines, sir,' Mannon objected.

'Perhaps they haven't, Number One. But a submarine running at speed on the surface is difficult to identify from the air. When you're looking down from five thousand feet it could be anything from a motor torpedo boat to a destroyer. Once they realize their mistake, they'll leave us alone.'

Mannon did not share his skipper's optimism. He had a strange feeling of foreboding about the approaching aircraft and raised his glasses to study them again. Selecting the leading plane, he examined it closely in search of evidence to substantiate his unease. What he saw was enough. 'They're opening the bomb doors, sir!'

'Are they, by God?' Hamilton did not seem over-concerned by the news. 'Yeoman! break out the Union Jack and spread it over the after deck.'

He glanced up at the conning tower jack and felt vaguely reassured by the white ensign streaming in the breeze. 'Coxswain! Stop engines.'

'Stop engines, aye aye, sir.'

The acknowledging bell of the telegraph repeater tinkled faintly from deep inside the hull, and *Rapier* almost immediately started losing speed.

'Is that wise, sir?' Mannon asked.

'In the circumstances and in my judgement - yes,' Hamilton told him. He disliked having his orders called into question, but he had enough sense to realize that the first officer meant well in his inexperience. Nevertheless, he made a mental note to speak to him later in the privacy of the wardroom. He did not believe in admonishing junior officers in front of the men. 'If this was a hostile boat, the last thing we'd do is to turn ourselves into a sitting target by stopping,' he explained. 'It's the most effective method I know of making sure the enemy will investigate before he starts shooting. And it'll give us time to rig up some sort of identification.'

The threatening roar of the aircraft engines was now clearly audible, but Hamilton remained outwardly unconcerned. Walking to the after end of the conning tower, he peered towards the stern. Drury and three hands were carefully spreading the flag across the deck and lashing the ends to the mooring cleats along the sides.

'It doesn't seem to be having much effect on the Japs,' Mannon observed doubtfully, as the bombers formed up in line-ahead formation.

'Perhaps they're color blind,' Hamilton grunted. He watched the three Mitsubishis carefully. 'Hard a'starboard, Cox'n!'

Ernie Blood spun the wheel and *Rapier's* bows swung to the right, so that she presented her stern to the approaching aircraft like a bitch on heat. Hamilton waited expectantly, but the huge Union Jack had no apparent effect on the intentions of the oncoming machines. As they levelled off at five hundred feet, he saw a cluster of black bombs fall away from the belly of the leading aeroplane.

'Everyone down!'

The first Mitsubishi swept over the top of the conning tower with the shattering roar of an express train screaming through a wayside station. The shriek of the falling bombs passed directly overhead, and the ear-splitting explosion as they struck the sea well clear of the starboard bow threw a fine spray of water over the submarine.

'Not even a near miss,' Blood commented scornfully. '*And* on a sitting target at that. Bloody Japs must be cross-eyed.'

By the time Hamilton had scrambled to his feet, the three aircraft were already climbing for height and banking over for a second attack. He released a string of obscenities to relieve his feelings. Mistaken identity was an ever present hazard at sea. But not even a half-blind idiot could have missed the enormous Union Jack spread out across *Rapier's* stern. For reasons best known to themselves, the Japanese pilots were making a deliberate and cold-blooded attack on a neutral warship. Well, if *that* was the way they wanted to play it...

'Gun crew close up to action stations! Full ahead both engines, Cox'n. Maintain course, but stand by to go a'port when I give the shout.'

'Helm, aye aye, sir. Standing by.'

Mannon watched the three Mitsubishi Otori bombers level off at two thousand feet at the end of their steep climbing turn. It was his first taste of an air attack, and he felt his stomach churning as the aircraft angled down into a shallow dive for the next bombing run. Hamilton's incisive command broke the spell.

'Hold fire until you're quite sure they intend attacking, Number One. I'll leave you to give the order.'

The sudden responsibility chased the fear from Mannon's blood. Hurrying to the for'ard section of the bridge, he checked the gun crew were at their battle stations, ordered the layer to follow the leading aircraft in his sights, and warned Morgan, *Rapier's* gunner's mate, to wait for the order. Then, seemingly unconscious of the fact that he was standing in the middle of the target area, he joined Hamilton and watched the formation coming in again, with the concentration of a spectator at a football match.

This time the bombers approached out of the sun directly over the submarine's bows. Two were flying in line-ahead, while the third hung slightly astern of its companions on their starboard flank.

'Watch the first two, Number One,' Hamilton snapped. 'And open fire as soon as they show themselves to be hostile. I'll keep an eye on the other bastard. I don't know what he's doing, but he's up to no good.'

Hamilton's instinct, born from long combat experience against the German *Luftwaffe* proved uncannily accurate. The third aircraft suddenly swooped to wave top height and swung towards the submarine. Bright yellow flames flickered from the nose, followed moments later by the *tak-tak-tak* of machine gun fire.

'Hard a'port, Cox'n! Stand by – *fire*'

The shrill whistle of the falling bombs merged with the staccato chatter of the machine gun and *Rapier* threw back a wall of spray as the bows slammed sideways. The sudden alteration in course caught the Japanese bomb aimers off balance and their bombs exploded harmlessly clear of the submarine, although the concussion kicked the boat sharply to starboard.

'Keep after them, Number One!' Hamilton shouted to Mannon.

Rapier's gunners needed no encouragement and blobs

of black cordite smoke trailed across the sky in pursuit of the bombers as they veered back into the sun.

'They don't seem too keen now we've started hitting back, sir,' Mannon grinned cheerfully.

'Don't get too bloody cocky, Number One,' Hamilton told him discouragingly. He put his mouth to the voice pipe. 'Control Room, send up the Lewis guns. Any internal damage?'

'Control Room, sir. Lewis guns on their way. No reports of damage. Did we get any of the bastards?'

'Not yet, Scotty - but we will.'

Taking advantage of the momentary lull, Hamilton carried out a rapid visual inspection of the hull for external damage. Several bullets had struck the side of the conning tower, but had done little more than chip the paintwork. Glancing up, however, he saw the white ensign had been ripped to ribbons by the Japanese machine guns.

'They're coming in again, sir,' Mannon reported anxiously.

'Stand by. Open fire as soon as they get within range, Number One.' He looked across at Ernie Blood. 'Everything under control Cox'n?'

'Fair to middlin', sir. It ain't exactly the first time, you know.' He stared up at the sky to check the position of the aircraft relative to the submarine, and then nodded his head to starboard. 'I've been watchin' that there boat, sir. Seems to be in a hell of a bloody hurry.'

Hamilton swung his glasses in the direction Blood had indicated, and saw a large launch some two miles away from the submarine's starboard quarter. It was one of the big TSD Chris Craft designs- the sort of vessel millionaires use for shark fishing off Florida - and, judging by the glistening white wave curling from its bows, it was running at a good twenty knots. He shrugged. It posed no threat to *Rapier*. Probably an innocent fishing party getting the hell out of it when they saw the shooting start. And who could blame them? It wasn't their war.

'Nothing to worry about, Chief. Just a fishing boat making for Macao.'

The throaty roar of the Nakajima Kotobuki radial engines climbed to a high-pitched scream, as the bombers hurtled down to renew their attack. *Rapier's* unexpected swing to starboard threw Hamilton off balance, and he clung to the rails as the deck tilted under his feet. A wall of water swept over the bows drenching the gun crew on the exposed foredeck with spray, but the sharp rhythmic bark of the quick-firer never wavered for a second. Often knee-deep in swirling foam, the gunners continued serving their weapon as if engaged on peaceful summer afternoon target practice in the Solent.

Rapier twisted like a demented eel, as Blood's violent evasive action threw the submarine from starboard to port and back again in quick succession. The angry chatter of Burton's Lewis gun compounded the noisy confusion of bellowing aero-engines and gunfire. It was almost impossible to think and Mannon could not help envying the cool detachment of the skipper and his coxswain, as they fought to keep the submarine out of danger. Now that the deck gun was in action there was nothing left for him to do, and to keep his brain busy, he concentrated on observing the movements of the attacking bombers.

Davidson, *Rapier's* gun layer and a veteran of the Norwegian campaign - where he had fought a squadron of Stukas almost singlehanded, until his armed trawler had been sunk under his feet - followed the Mitsubishi in his sights. A line of ragged smoke puffs punctured the sky - each closer to the target aircraft than the last.

The leading bomber wobbled unsteadily as shell splinters pumped into the fuselage and a thin wisp of glycol spumed from beneath the port engine.

'They're breaking off the attack, sir,' Mannon yelled excitedly as the three aircraft sheared away, swooped to wave height, and roared astern of the submarine with their throttles wide open.

Hamilton said nothing. The action of the Japanese pilots had only served to prove his point. He was sorry that Admiral Herbert was not present to witness the flight of the bombers when faced by determined opposition.

'Stop firing, Number One.'

'Check, check, check! Cease fire, Chief!' Mannon had a wide grin on his face as he turned away from the for'ard lip of the conning tower screen. 'We certainly made the bastards run, sir!'

It was his first taste of surface action. Now that the nervous tension had gone, the acrid smell of burned cordite was like nectar and the excitement left a feeling of intoxication.

Hamilton grunted disinterestedly. Keeping the binoculars firmly pressed to his eyes, he watched the departing bombers clawing for height before turning and regaining formation. Mannon would soon learn to curb his enthusiasm. There was no place for emotion in battle. Killing had to be a question of reflex. With the senses stunned by the noise and paralyzed by the sights and sounds of death and destruction, the professional must continue to function like a finely balanced piece of machinery. Too much adrenalin upset a man's judgement and led to mistakes. And even the smallest error could spell instant disaster to something as vulnerable as a submarine. Hamilton himself felt neither excitement nor elation at their apparent success. And his senses were still tautly alert, as he watched the aircraft fleeing towards the mainland lurking beneath the north-western horizon.

'Shall I tell the gun crew to stand down, sir?' Mannon asked.

'Negative, Number One.' Hamilton lowered his glasses. 'I want to make quite sure our friends have finished their fun and games first. Tell Morgan to bring up some more ready-use ammo.'

'Aye aye sir.'

The sharp crackle of cannon fire echoed across the sea and Hamilton moved to the port side. The big Chris Craft launch was zig-zagging wildly as it came under attack, and he could see the Mitsubishis circling over the fishing boat like hornets gathering over their nest.

'You murdering bloody swine,' Hamilton swore angrily. He turned to Blood. 'Bring her round to port, Chief. Steer for the launch. I'm going to sort these bastards out once and for all.'

Mannon hurried to join the skipper on the engaged side of the bridge. Now that the initial excitement of the bombing attack had subsided, the first lieutenant's old caution reasserted itself. *Rapier* was making fifteen knots and the launch, swinging in a wide arc to escape the Japanese bombers, was speeding towards the submarine as if seeking the protection of its guns. Picking up his glasses, Mannon carefully examined the twin-screw diesel cruiser.

'Do you think we ought to get mixed up in it, sir?' he asked doubtfully. 'The launch is flying a Portuguese flag.'

'I don't care if it's flying a pair of lace knickers, Number One, I'm not sitting by and watching an innocent fishing boat being shot up by a gang of trigger-happy Japs.' He moved to the front of the bridge and leaned over the coaming. 'Stand by, Mister Gunner. Open fire as soon as we're within range. And let's see some *proper* shooting this time!'

As Hamilton turned away, he heard Morgan admonishing his crew in his sing-song Welsh accent. 'You heard what the Skipper said, me boyos. You're not using a powder puff to dust their bloody arses. I want you to hit those buggers where it hurts. And if you don't, I'm going to get the three of you polishing the brass on that gun for the next six months!'

'Range 1500, Chief! Height 2,000.'

'Elevation 55!'

'Fused for 2000.'

'Breech open.... *Load.*'

The man at the helm of the launch certainly knew how to handle a boat. As the aircraft dived to renew the attack, he cut speed for a few moments and then, having timed his action to the last second, banged open the throttles of the twin diesel units and turned sharply to starboard. The pilot of the leading aircraft zoomed low across the bows, but the sudden alteration in course had spoilt his aim and he made no attempt to release the bombs. The second aircraft, following on his tail, tilted over on to its starboard wing in an effort to get in a quick burst with its machine guns. For a few seconds the silver fuselage was square in *Rapier's* sights.

'Fire! Reload... *Fire!*'

Morgan's second order proved unnecessary. The first shell exploded just below the center of the bomber's fuselage and the Mitsubishi folded in the middle like a piece of hinged cardboard. Flames burst out from behind the cockpit, the body snapped into two separate pieces, and the burning remains of the aircraft fell into the sea with a hissing splash.

'Good shooting, lads. Keep it up!'

Mannon said nothing. It had been a brilliant piece of gunnery and he didn't begrudge Hamilton's praise. But he could not help wondering how the hell the skipper was going to explain the destruction of a neutral aircraft to the powers-that-be at Hong Kong. A shout from Hamilton interrupted his thoughts.

'Number One! Tell Murray to radio HK for a rescue boat. And inform them we need air support.'

You'll be lucky, Mannon told himself, as he made his way to the voice pipe. He could well imagine the effect of Hamilton's signal at Naval HQ in Hong Kong. It was probably just the pretext the Japanese were waiting for to invade the Colony. The reply, he decided, would be an official raspberry - or worse. Lifting the lid of the speaking tube, he relayed the skipper's orders to the control room.

Rapier was less than a hundred yards away from the launch, as the two remaining aircraft came in with guns blazing to avenge the loss of their comrade. The sharp crackle of cannon fire echoed across the empty sea and the men on the submarine's bridge ducked instinctively But the Japanese pilots were no longer interested in the British warship. This time they wanted an easy victim that couldn't hit back. There was a sudden explosion, followed by a loud whoosh of flames as the cannon shells punctured the Chris Craft's fuel tanks. Within seconds, the motor cruiser was in flames from stern to stern and Mannon stared aghast at the awful spectacle.

'Stop engines,' Hamilton ordered calmly. 'Steer to windward, Cox'n. Stand by fo'c'sle hands to pick up survivors.'

Rapier's deck guns stopped firing and, as the rumble of

the diesels faded away, Blood moved the wheel to starboard. The two bombers had quickly left the scene and vanished into the blue void of the sky. The eerie almost unnatural silence was only broken by the soft slap of the sea against the hull plating, and the angry crackle of the fire as the submarine drifted downwind towards the burning launch.

'Half-astern both!'

The reversed thrust of the propellers brought the submarine to a standstill. Hamilton peered into the pall of black fumes obscuring the remains of the motor cruiser. The smoke and flames made it impossible to see clearly, but he could just make out a group of people huddled against the side of the wheelhouse. Why the hell didn't they jump? Snatching up the microphone of *Rapier's* loudhailer, he pushed the button and held the grille close to his mouth.

'Abandon ship... we'll pick you up.'

The metallic tones of the disembodied voice had no effect. Protecting their faces from the flames the survivors cowered in terror, as if they were more frightened of the submarine than they were of the fiery furnace on which they were marooned.

'Show 'em the Union Jack, Yeoman,' Hamilton told Drury. 'They think we're bloody Japs.' He moved to the front of the bridge. 'Throw out some lines, Morgan.'

'Won't do no good, sir,' the gunner shouted back. 'If they're Chinese they probably can't swim. We'll have to go in after them!' Morgan had served on the China Station in the early thirties and knew what he was talking about.

Hamilton dragged off his shoes, unbuttoned his shirt, and climbed up on to the narrow lip of the conning tower bridge screen.

'Take over, Number One. The gunner is going to need a hand getting those poor devils off.'

Mannon was given no time to protest. Hamilton balanced precariously on the lip of the coaming for a moment, and then plunged into the warm sluggish waters of the China Sea. Further forward on the foredeck plating, Morgan and two members of the gun crew followed the skipper's example and joined him in the water. Less than twenty yards separated the two vessels and it only took a few strong strokes to bring them up alongside the burning launch.

Hamilton felt the heat of the fire sear his face as he looked up and, treading water, he spat the sea from his mouth.

'Jump!' he yelled. 'Jump - we'll look after you.'

The bewildered survivors on the launch hesitated. Then, as if the sea threatened a worse fate than the fire, one of them held his nose and plummeted down into the water with a mighty splash. *Rapier's* gunner was alongside him almost immediately. A brawny arm encircled the man's neck, dragging his face clear of the water so that he could breathe. Then, rolling over on his back, Morgan began towing the spluttering Chinaman towards the submarine.

'Okay, sir, I've got him.'

Encouraged by the speedy rescue of his companion the second man jumped, disappeared beneath the surface like a stone, and was quickly grabbed by Davidson as his head bobbed up again. Hamilton trod water and waited. The third and last figure, smaller and lighter than the others, stepped towards the rail, paused for a moment to look at the flames, and then dropped with thistle-down grace into the sea. Hamilton swam towards the floundering survivor and grabbed for a handhold. To his surprise his hands encountered the unexpected softness of a woman's breasts and, without pausing to think what he was doing, his fingers instinctively closed over the twin mounds. The girl twisted away as she felt his hands on her body and, ignoring the dangers of drowning, she struggled to escape his grasp.

Hamilton grabbed her shoulders, ducked her down violently under the water to discourage further resistance, and started to haul her back towards the waiting submarine. He wondered how he was going to explain this unfortunate reflex action when he got her aboard but decided, on balance, to ignore the incident. Perhaps she would believe it was an accident if he said nothing....

A life line snaked down from the *Rapier's* bows and he grabbed it thankfully. Looping the rope under the girl's arms, he fastened it into a noose and told the foredeck party to haul her in. He followed behind in an easy crawl and trod water while the seamen lifted her gently aboard the submarine. Then, grasping Mannon's hand, he clambered up the slippery slope of the ballast tank and grabbed the clean towel Wilkinson was holding ready for him.

The gunner's mate reached the side of the submarine a moment later, with Davidson following not more than a stroke behind. Since both men were dragging a survivor, they were carefully lifted up to the foredeck casing. Hamilton felt slightly relieved to see that the other two members of the motor cruiser's crew were not women.

'Get them below, Number One. And tell the Doc to check them over.' He rubbed the towel rigorously over his head. 'Better put the girl in the wardroom - no point in giving the men any unnecessary temptations.' Glancing towards the bows, he saw that the girl had lost most of her clothing in the water. 'And find something for her to wear or I might get tempted too!'

Throwing the wet towel back to Wilkinson, Hamilton hauled himself up the bulkhead rings of the conning tower as the crew lowered the survivors down through the gun hatch. Swinging his leg over the coaming, he vaulted down and resumed his place on the narrow bridge. He looked around. The blue void of the sky was now empty of aircraft, and the smoldering remains of the motor cruiser rolled gently in the swell.

His hands still tingled where they had touched the girl, and he stared down at the foredeck casing in silence, as he recalled the brief glimpse of her slim body sprawled nakedly on the steel deck plating. He was anxious to meet her again, but knew his eagerness must wait. There would be plenty of time to make her acquaintance when they reached Hong Kong. But, all the same, he could not help wondering what she had being doing aboard the launch.

Dismissing the thoughts from his mind he walked to the binnacle to check the compass. The purple haze of Macao was faintly visible on the port horizon and the yawning mouth of the Pearl River lay ahead over the bows. It was sufficient to give him a rough and ready bearing.

'Half-ahead, both, Chief. Steer zero-one-zero.'

'Half-ahead both, sir. Course now zero-one-zero.'

'Number One!'

'Sir?'

'You look a bloody awful mess,' Hamilton informed him dispassionately.

Mannon did not dispute the observation. His once white shorts were streaked with green slime from the weed-encrusted ballast tank, and his face was grimed with cordite smoke. The skipper, he decided, looked even more of a scarecrow - although he had the tact to keep his opinion to himself.

'Do you want me to change, sir?'

Hamilton grinned. He was shirtless and shoeless and

his shorts were torn and sodden with sea water. His arms were covered with superficial cuts where the razor-edged barnacles adhering to *Rapier's* ballast tanks had ripped his flesh. And blood still trickled from his nose where the girl had butted him in the face during the brief struggle in the water.

'To hell with being tiddley, Number One. Let's show Hong Kong what a *real* fighting ship looks like. Damn the paintwork and the polished brass. It'll give the buggers something to talk about while they're putting on their starched shirts and getting ready for dinner tonight. And I hope it gives 'em indigestion.'

TWO

Despite the cooling draught from the deck head fans the cabin was oppressively hot, and Hamilton could feel the sweat trickling down his face as he stood stiffly to attention in front of the Deputy Chief of Staff. Not even the row of opened scuttles in the bulkhead behind the deck brought any relief to the airless atmosphere, and *Rapier's* commander looked hopefully at the enticing line of bottles on the captain's sideboard. He ruefully reflected that his flamboyant attempt to impress the Hong Kong garrison had been a dismal failure.

Rapier had attracted the usual crowd of onlookers as she entered Victoria Harbor from the direction of Stonecutters Island. But apparently blind to the battle-torn ensign and bullet-scarred paintwork, the citizens of the Colony had quickly lost interest in the new arrival, and the piers fronting Connaught Road were deserted by the time the submarine nosed its bows towards the dockyard. Even a narrowly averted collision with a passing cargo junk had failed to bring forth the anticipated rebuke from the harbormaster. If was as if *Rapier* was an unwelcome visitor - a harbinger of bad tidings or a carrier of plague - and Hamilton's justifiable pride in his ship and his men was ruffled by the chill of their reception.

Only the Port War Signal Station showed any interest in the submarine's arrival. A searchlight flashed berthing instructions which, as soon as acknowledged, were followed by a curt *Imperative and Personal* for the Captain to report to HMS *Tamar* once his boat had been brought safely to her moorings between the destroyers *Thracian* and *Thanet*.

Tamar, as Hamilton soon discovered, was no more than an engineless hulk, fitted with additional deckhouses to serve as HQ and receiving ship for the Hong Kong Station. In 1882 she had taken part in the bombardment of Alexandria, but now she was a mere shadow of her former glory - a relic of a bygone age when Britannia had truly ruled the waves. Arriving at the gangway, he presented his papers to the marine secretary on duty and was then escorted to a small cabin near the stern, which served as the office of the Deputy Chief of Staff.

Captain Reginald Snark, another relic of the past who had served as a junior gunnery officer on the battle cruiser *Lion* at Jutland, looked up as Hamilton entered. He then promptly lost interest in his visitor and busied himself with a store's list which he carefully marked off item by item. *Rapier's* commander knew it was all part of the treatment - a device to cut him down to size by demonstrating his insignificance in the august presence of a post-captain. He had suffered similar indignities before and he waited patiently. Snark ticked the last entry on the list, scrawled his initials dutifully in the left-hand margin and blotted the ink pedantically, before putting the document into his out tray.

Then leaning back in his chair and placing his fingers together under his chin in the best judicial manner, he surveyed the young submariner with cold blue eyes.

'You've got off to a bad start, Lieutenant Hamilton,' he said curtly and without the usual polite preliminaries.

Hamilton said nothing. It seemed ridiculous to make so much fuss about *Rapier's* near-miss with the junk on entering the harbor. But it was the sort of triviality in which senior officers delighted during peacetime, when they had nothing more important to think about. It was a pity, he decided, that Snark couldn't be posted back to Europe to discover the grim realities of a shooting war.

'You will, of course, have to apologize,' the captain continued. 'Providing, that is, the Governor is able to avoid more serious repercussions.'

Hamilton wondered what he was babbling about. Why the hell should the governor give a damn about a minor collision between one of His Majesty's ships and an old trading junk that had seen better days. And 'more serious repercussions'? No doubt some wily Chinese merchant was making an exorbitant claim for damages - putting on the squeeze as they called it in the Orient.

'I don't think you need worry too much, sir,' he said easily. 'I remember running down a Grimsby trawler just before the war. We invited the skipper to the wardroom for a drink, gave him a carton of best Scotch, and he went away as happy as a sandboy.' Hamilton smiled at the memory.

'Are you completely out of your mind, Lieutenant?' Snark snapped. 'This is a serious matter - an international incident of the first magnitude.'

Oh for God's sake, Hamilton groaned, inwardly. If this was the attitude of the Colonial authorities, no wonder the

Empire was going down the drain. The owner of the offending junk needed a good boot up the backside for sailing too close to the naval anchorage in any case.

'Naturally, I will apologize if the Governor wishes me to,' he agreed diplomatically. 'But it seems an awful lot of fuss to make over one damned junk.'

Captain Snark frowned. 'Junk? I do not understand, Lieutenant. I am referring to your ship shooting down a Japanese aircraft.'

'Well I certainly don't intend to apologize for *that*,' Hamilton snapped back.

Snark stood up suddenly, his face white with anger. 'You forget where you are, Lieutenant,' he said coldly. 'I do not tolerate insolence. You can make your excuses to the C-in-C in due course but, firstly, on the express orders of the Governor you will apologize to Commander Aritsu.'

'For defending my ship from hostile attack?' Hamilton found it difficult to believe his ears. What the hell was the Royal Navy coming to? 'With your permission sir, I would like to see the C-in-C immediately. I have no intention of apologizing to those murdering bastards. *And*,' he added tartly, 'I take my orders from the C-in-C not a civilian official.'

Snark chose to ignore the defiant challenge in Hamilton's final statement. 'Commander Aritsu does not see your action in that light. His complaint to the Governor indicates that your submarine deliberately opened fire on three Japanese aircraft without provocation.' He paused for a moment. 'I might add, for your information, Lieutenant, that the authorities here had been expecting some hotheaded young incompetent to do something stupid like this. And the Japanese have been waiting for such an excuse to give them the pretext for marching in and occupying the entire Colony.'

'Well, Commander Aritsu has got it all wrong,' Hamilton retorted curtly. '*Rapier* did not open fire until the aircraft had actually dropped their bombs - and we made every effort to establish our identity and avoid an incident.' He swallowed his anger with difficulty. 'Am I to understand, sir, that it is now an offence for a British officer to defend his ship in the face of an enemy attack?'

'In certain circumstances that could well be the case, Lieutenant,' Snark told him firmly. 'You must remember that Britain is not at war with Japan, and it is the government's earnest desire to avoid a confrontation in the Far East when our resources at home are stretched to the limit. The situation in China requires great tact and diplomacy - it is a tinder-box that requires only one small match to send the whole of South-East Asia up in flames. The C-in-C will acquaint you with the position when you see him.'

Despite outward appearances, Snark had also been a fighter in the past and he had a certain amount of sympathy for Hamilton. But, no matter how unpalatable they might be, orders were orders. He allowed himself a frosty smile, 'I can understand your bewilderment, Lieutenant. Coming from the war zone, this sort of thing must seem very strange. And, believe me, I don't like it any more than you do. But we are in the hands of the diplomats. We have our specific instructions and they must be carried out. The Governor has arranged for you to see Commander Aritsu tomorrow morning. Take my advice. Go across to the club, have a few drinks, and cool off. Your new colleagues will be happy to fill you in on the peculiarities of service on the China Station. And I have no doubt that you are more likely to listen to them than you are to me.'

You're too damned right, Hamilton thought to himself as he replaced his cap, saluted, and left Snark's airless cabin. No brass-hat was going to tell *him* to leave his ship unde-fended in the face of enemy attack. And he doubted whether the other officers would be any more successful in the task. After two years of combat operations, he was unlikely to be convinced of his errors by a group of officers who had never fired a gun in anger....

The Officer's Club was conveniently close to the guard ship and Hamilton picked his way through the traffic on the Bund and slowly walked up the sweep of the wide stone steps leading to the entrance. The cold bite of the air- condi-tioning was a welcome relief after the sweltering heat on the waterfront. As Hamilton removed his cap, a white- coated Chinese attendant bowed him obsequiously towards the main bar - an attractive, spacious room overlooking the harbor, with a long polished mahogany counter, a glittering display of inviting bottles, and deep comfortable club armchairs.

He settled himself on a leather-topped stool and lit a cigarette. The bartender, a retired chief petty officer wearing a row of ribbons from the Kaiser war on his white mess jacket, put down the glass he was polishing and came over to take his order.

'A large Scotch with ice.'

Bennett put his glass under the optic, measured out a generous double Haig, and deftly added two large lumps of ice. He put it down in front of Hamilton with a cheerful grin.

'New in, sir?' he asked.

'This afternoon,' Hamilton nodded. The bite of the whisky helped to calm his still ruffled temper. 'The trouble with this place is they don't know there's a war on.' He tilted the glass and swallowed the remains of the whisky in one gulp. 'Another double,' he told the bartender. 'If you ask me, the only way to look at Hong Kong is through the bottom of a glass.'

Bennett grinned tactfully and went back to the Haig. A small group of officers were gathered further along the bar, and he watched as one of them got up from his stool and walked across to the new arrival.

'You must be from the submarine?'

Hamilton nodded as the lieutenant commander held out his hand. 'Welcome to Hong Kong- my name's Otter-shaw, Harry Ottershaw. I run one of the gunboats- *Firefly*. We're berthed down by the Star Ferry Pier.'

Hamilton gripped Ottershaw's hand firmly. 'Nick Hamilton - *Rapier*,' he acknowledged by way of introduction. 'Just in from the Med. And I can't say I think much of your C-in-C's welcoming committee.'

Ottershaw perched himself on the empty stool next to Hamilton and grinned. 'We heard about your spot of bother with the Japs. I'm afraid the authorities don't like it when we start shooting back. I expect you got a rocket from Snark.'

Hamilton shrugged. 'I can look after myself,' he said defensively. 'But I'm damned if I'm going to apologize.'

Ottershaw smiled sympathetically. 'I'm afraid you'll have to, old man. Most of us have had to eat humble pie with the Japs at various times since we've been on the Station. It's all part of the way of life out here.' He glanced up as his drinking companions came down the bar to join him.

'This is Mike Grimshaw - another gunboat man,' he said by way of introduction. 'And Jock McVeigh. They've both been out here for so long they're practically natives. This is

Nick Hamilton, chaps, skipper of the sub we saw coming in this afternoon.'

Hamilton shook hands and called Bennett across to order another round of drinks for his new colleagues. As he turned away from the counter, he saw Grimshaw looking at the ribbon of the DSO on his breast. The gunboat commander frowned thoughtfully for a moment and then broke into a wide grin.

'Of *course* - I thought your face looked familiar. You must be the chap who rescued the prisoners from *Nordsee* last year. Your picture was splashed all over the newspapers at the time.' He raised his glass in salute. 'Good to have you with us. But what the devil are you doing in a dump like Hong Kong? I thought they only posted us old has-beens out here.'

Hamilton shrugged. 'I've been asking myself the same question ever since I received my orders. What the hell am I supposed to do with an operational submarine on a peace-time station - sit around and make myself look pretty all day?'

Ottershaw exchanged glances with his companions. 'You'll have plenty to do, old boy. We might not be directly involved in the war out here, but we manage to get ourselves shot at on most patrols. And it's not only the Japanese. Everyone seems to be trigger-happy in China.'

'Except the British,' Hamilton said pointedly.

'We call it restraint,' the lieutenant commander corrected him gently. 'But we have our moments. We're permitted to open fire on certain occasions. But most of the time our orders are to keep out of trouble and achieve our ends by negotiation.'

'Most of us felt the same as you when we arrived out East,' Grimshaw intervened. 'But you must live and learn.

It's a tricky problem. And as you'll soon discover, we're in no shape to take on the Japs in a full-scale war.'

Hamilton remained skeptical. 'They ran off soon enough when *Rapier* gave 'em a taste of their own medicine. What they need is a sharp lesson.'

'Aye - perhaps they do,' McVeigh conceded. 'But just watch out and make sure ye dinna learn one yeself.' Ottershaw glanced at his watch. He could see Hamilton was in no mood to be objective and it seemed a diplomatic moment to withdraw. No point in rubbing a newcomer up the wrong way on his first day ashore.

'Come on chaps. We'll just be in time for the five o'clock at Happy Valley.' He put his empty glass on the bar and smiled at Hamilton. 'That's the local racecourse,' he explained. 'You'll find most of the Navy there during the season. Why not join us tomorrow?'

'Thanks, but I've asked for an appointment with the Governor tomorrow. I expect I'll see you in here again once I've sorted things out.'

Like hell I will, he promised himself as the three officers went out. I'm used to fighting seamen - not bloody cocktail commanders. He stared broodingly at the bottles glittering against the mirror behind the bar counter. Perhaps if he got roaring drunk he'd feel better. He called Bennett over and ordered another double.

The ex-chief petty officer filled his glass, dropped in the regulation two ice cubes, and placed the drink down on the bar top.

'I know what you're thinking, sir,' he said quietly. 'But you've got it all wrong. They have to put up a show to hide their feelings. They hate the Jap's guts just as much as you do. But the Navy's under strict orders out here. They're merely doing what they're told.'

'It's a convenient excuse, chief. But it won't wash with me. This war has taught me how to look after myself- and my boat.'

'I know it isn't my place to go talking behind their backs, sir...' Bennett lowered his voice. 'But those three gentlemen 'ave all seen plenty of action in their time. Take the Lieutenant Commander. He was at Narvik in *Lapwing* - 'ad it sunk under his feet in a runnin' fight with three Jerry destroyers. And not before he'd taken one of 'em to the bottom with 'im. He might tell you about it one day, but I doubt as 'e will. And old Jock McVeigh won his first DSO in 1919 against the Bolsheviks in the Baltic. Then he ups and gets a bar at Dunkirk. They sent 'im out here for a rest and what 'appens? A Jap sentry puts two bullets in his arm when he tries to tow one of the Jardine & Mathieson steamers out of trouble up the Yangtse earlier this year.'

Hamilton drained his glass. 'Thanks, Chief. You've probably saved me from making a bloody fool of myself. It's my own fault for judging by appearances. But with that sort of service behind them, why the hell do they let the Japanese walk all over them?'

Alf Bennett picked up an empty glass and started polishing it. 'You'll find out, sir,' he said dismally. 'You'll find out soon enough.'

It was almost dark when Hamilton finally left the club, and the short tropical twilight had already deepened into a velvet blackness by the time he reached the quayside. *Rapier* was berthed between two destroyers and a precari- ously long gangplank stretched out across the murky water to the nearest ship, *Thracian*. Hamilton considered it care- fully for several moments and then launched himself on to it a trifle unsteadily. The swaying of the gangway did not help his equilibrium but, squaring his shoulders and staring straight ahead, he managed to stay on the narrow planking.

A marine sentry was guarding the far end and saluted smartly as he saw the officer approaching.

'Your pass, sir.'

Hamilton grabbed at a stanchion to maintain his balance and blinked at the burly figure blocking the step on to the destroyer's deck. He was not drunk, but the whisky, after an enforced abstinence of almost a fortnight, was making his head swim.

'Lieutenant Hamilton - *Rapier.*'

'Sorry, sir. Must see your pass. Captain's orders.'

'I *am* the captain, man. Let me through.'

Somehow the Marine corporal contrived to expand, so that his already large body completely blocked the shipboard exit from the gangway. He shone his night-lamp on Hamilton's face.

'No, you ain't, sir - with respect. Never seen you before.' He moved his head slightly and spoke to someone standing in the shadow of the starboard cutter. 'Nobby, go and fetch the OOW- this 'ere bloke says he's the Captain.'

'Not of *this* boat, Corporal,' Hamilton snapped impatiently, as the unseen Nobby vanished in the direction of the quarter-deck in search of the officer of the watch. 'I'm in command of *Rapier,* the submarine berthed alongside.'

'Let's see your pass then, sir,' Isaacs said stolidly. He was a man of somewhat limited conversational power.

The cool night air had cleared Hamilton's head, although it had done little to assuage his temper. He was about to give the corporal the full benefit of his impatience when he heard the sharp footsteps of the destroyer's OOW approaching.

'What's going on, Corporal?' The question was asked in

the high-pitched voice that Hamilton detested, and he squinted through the darkness at the OOW's uniform to see if he could pull rank. He was disappointed by the two gold rings on Jessop's epaulettes. Despite his growing irritation, he bottled his temper. After all, he reminded himself, the marine corporal was only carrying out his orders.

'Gentleman trying to come aboard without a pass, sir,' Isaacs explained portentously. 'Says he's the Captain.'

Lieutenant Jessop epitomized everything Hamilton hated about the Royal Navy. He was immaculately dressed in his tropical whites, with shorts just that trifle too long and the tops of his white stockings adjusted with almost mathematical exactitude an inch below his knees. Hamilton suppressed a snort of derision as he saw the telescope tucked under his arm in the approved Dartmouth fashion. Unaware of the impression he had made, Jessop stepped forward and examined the visitor carefully with his shaded lamp.

'He's not the Captain,' he confirmed to the corporal, in a tone suggesting an important discovery.

Hamilton clenched his hands. He had an enormous desire to push the pompous little duty officer into the sea, but he restrained the impulse. 'I am Lieutenant Hamilton - Commanding Officer of the *Rapier*. My boat is berthed to seaward and my only means of access is via your gangway. Now if you have completed this little farce, perhaps you'll let me go aboard my own boat!'

'He don't have a pass, sir,' Isaacs pointed out impassively.

'Of *course*, I don't have a pass. We only arrived today and I was immediately called ashore to see Captain Snark. I know nothing of your security system, but no doubt I can come to some amicable arrangement with your Captain in the morning. Right now I just want to get aboard my own boat.'

'We have to make sure the Chinese don't get into the ship,' Jessop explained earnestly. 'That's why we have passes.'

'Good God, man! Do I look like a bloody Chinaman?' Hamilton exploded.

Jessop agreed that he didn't. But without the magical pass, there appeared to be no way of crossing the threshold on to *Thracian's* deck. Hamilton fumed in the darkness and weighed up his chances of bursting past the gangway guard. He concluded, however, that Corporal Isaacs was a trifle too solid to be swept aside.

'Look, Lieutenant,' he gritted. 'I know I don't have a pass. But perhaps if my Number One was called over to identify me that would suffice until the morning?'

Jessop visibly brightened. 'Sounds a good idea, old man. Styles! Go across to the submarine, give the Executive Officer my compliments, and ask him to come to the gangway.' Nobby merged back into the shadows again on his latest errand, while Jessop endeavored to fill the interval with his own brand of light conversation.

'Sorry about all this, old man. Have to take all these precautions, you know. Can't have any of these damned Chinese on board - never know what they'll get up to.'

'I would have thought it more important to worry about the Japanese,' Hamilton said sourly. 'I was under the impression that the Hong Kong Chinese were on our side.'

The sarcasm was lost on Jessop. His high-pitched laugh reminded Hamilton of a donkey braying. 'To be frank, old boy, I can't tell the difference. Both look the same to me. But I take a jaundiced view.' He sniggered at his own tasteless pun.

'This should be Mannon,' Hamilton interrupted, as he heard the footsteps echoing across the deck planking. The tall familiar figure of the *Rapier's* executive officer ducked under the blast screen of the for'ard gun, and grinned cheerfully as he recognized the skipper.

'Thank the Lord you've arrived, sir,' he said without ceremony. 'We're having a spot of trouble on board - your girlfriend refuses to leave. Keeps on telling us you're her master. The other two are just as bad - gibbering away like a wagonload of monkeys.'

Jessop's jaw dropped incredulously. He'd heard that submarines were a piratical undisciplined bunch - but to have their own women aboard! He looked at Hamilton and gulped.

'Okay, Number One,' Hamilton said cheerfully. 'I'll come and sort them out.' He nodded towards Jessop. 'Our friend here wants you to identify me. Seems I don't have the right visiting card.'

Jessop was feeling slightly demoralized. He stepped back from the gangway as if Hamilton's licentiousness would contaminate him. Women aboard one of His Majesty's ships! *What* next? He forced his mouth into a ghastly smile.

'We can waive the formalities, Lieutenant Hamilton. I'm sure there is a great deal to be attended to on your boat - please proceed.'

'You'll have a word with your skipper in the morning and arrange about the passes? I don't want my men going through this charade every time they come aboard.' Hamilton made his way to the port side and paused as he reached the narrow gangplank leading down on to the *Rapier's* fore casing. 'By the way, old boy,' he said casually. 'Can we borrow one of your boats? Got to get rid of the evidence, you know.'

Jessop's shudder was mercifully hidden from view by the darkness. Surely they didn't intend to dump the women overboard. He recovered his composure. They probably wanted to ferry them ashore without being seen.

'There's a dinghy and a jolly boat tied up to the portside boom.

Hamilton guessed what was going through his mind. He started down the gangway to the submarine, grinning to himself. Jessop seemed such a bloody fool he couldn't resist a parting shot.

'Thanks, old boy. And don't worry if you hear a splash. It'll only be my Number One disposing of the bodies.' He winked broadly at Mannon. 'That'll give the pompous little prick something to think about,' he said in an undertone. 'Now let's go down and get our guests sorted out.'

The two Chinese seamen and the girl were squeezed into the control room, with what appeared to be at least half of *Rapier's* ship's company. The three survivors were stren-uously resisting the combined efforts of the submariners to drag them out on deck, and jabbering wildly to anyone who would listen. The arrival of the captain brought the fight to an abrupt stop and the men straightened up respectfully as Hamilton ducked through the forward hatch and entered the brightly fit compartment.

'Sorry about the commotion, sir,' Blood apologized anxiously. 'But we can't get these bloody Chinks to leave the boat. And I can't make head nor tail of what they're yelling about.'

Hamilton turned to the three Chinese, who immedi-ately threw themselves on to their knees and began kowtowing to him.

'Mister Captain,' Chen Yu began. 'We no go. We belong you. British sailors no understand.'

Hamilton hid his smile and looked sternly at his unwanted guests. Having made his speech, Chen Yu was again bowing with frantic urgency, while his companion kept his face pressed against the deck. The girl, however, sat back on her haunches and looked the lieutenant straight in the eye.

'You know ancient customs, sir. I am yours. You no want?'

At that precise moment Hamilton decided he wanted her very much. Now that she had recovered from her ducking, she looked delicately pretty with a soft mouth and dark, inviting eyes. And, despite the unflattering shapelessness of the submariner's sweater someone had lent her, he could see the promise of her slender body. He motioned them to get up off their knees.

'I did a tour out here in 1937,' he told Mannon, as the two men and the girl got up from the deck. 'It's a custom amongst the river people. If a Chinaman is saved from drowning, he becomes the property of his rescuer for the rest of his life.'

'I bet you're glad you were the one who saved the girl, sir,' Mannon grinned. 'I don't fancy Morgan's chances with that brute on the left.'

The gunner's mate apparently shared Mannon's apprehension. He had already been involved in the struggle to get the Chinese on deck and looked as if he had received the worst of the argument.

'You're pulling my leg, sir. What the hell can I do with him when I go back to Cardiff after the war? And what's my missus going to say about it?'

Hamilton rubbed his chin thoughtfully. 'Fortunately, I

think I know a way to solve the problem. It was a few years ago now, but I can still remember how one of our gunboat skippers got around the difficulty.'

'What did he do, sir?' Morgan asked eagerly, with a side-ways look of vengeance at Wan Fu. 'Threw 'em back in again?' The Chinaman, unable to understand what was being said, glowered back at the Welshman and bared his teeth ferociously.

'Not quite, Chief. We just take them inshore where the water's shallow and leave them to paddle the last few yards. That way we observe the ancient custom and *they* don't lose face. And 'face' is very important in the East.' He turned to Mannon. 'Take a couple of men with you, Number One, and bring *Thracian's* dinghy alongside.' The two Chinamen had not understood Hamilton's explanation and, expecting to be thrown over the side and drowned, renewed their struggle with Morgan and the other submariners as they were dragged out of the control room towards the fore hatch. The girl, however, seemed unperturbed. She stepped in front of *Rapier's* captain, looked up at him with her large dark eyes, and smiled. Apart from a slight difficulty with grammatical construction, her English was good, although Hamilton detected traces of an American accent.

'I am naturally disappointed, Lieutenant,' she told him with a wicked dimple, 'but perhaps you are a man of wisdom. I will explain to the others.'

'Thank you,' Hamilton paused awkwardly. 'What will you do about the boat? I hope it was insured.'

'The boat is of no consequence,' the girl said easily. 'My father has others. I will see that he rewards you for what you have done.'

'There's no call for that,' Hamilton said quickly. He didn't want some poor Chinese fisherman giving up his life's savings although, somehow, the girl didn't quite fit into that picture - and the Chris Craft cruiser must have been worth all of £20,000. 'It's just part of the Royal Navy's service.' He paused and searched for something else to say. 'You speak excellent English,' he added a trifle lamely.

'I ought to, Lieutenant,' the girl laughed. 'I graduated from Harvard two years ago. You mustn't think that all Chinese people are peasants. And, in any case, I am half-Portuguese.'

Pandemonium suddenly erupted above their heads, as the submariners dragged the two protesting Chinamen up onto the fore casing and struggled to put them into the waiting dinghy. The din was indescribable and it sounded as if Wan Fu and his companion were fighting a battle to the death with the British sailors. Hamilton was about to start up the fore hatch ladder to try and sort matters out when he felt the girl catch hold of his arm.

'No, Lieutenant. They are my people. I will go. They will listen to me.'

She kissed him lightly on the cheek and disappeared up the ladder before he could think of anything adequate to say....

Wan Fu's protestations quickly faded away as Chai Chen appeared on deck. She addressed the two men sharply in Cantonese and they exchanged sheepish looks with each other. Then, with expressive shrugs, they climbed down into the dinghy without further argument.

By the time Hamilton had reached the bridge, the little boat was already threading its way past the anchored destroyers towards the shore. And as it was finally swallowed up in the evening mist the small figure, still wearing the white regulation issue submariner's sweater, raised an arm and waved. As Hamilton waved back, he suddenly realized that he didn't even know her name....

COMMANDER ARITSU UNHOOKED his sword and laid it carefully on top of the low bamboo table against the wall. Then, dismissing the two army guards, he settled back in a comfortable armchair and gestured Hamilton to join him.

'Now that we have concluded the formalities, Lieutenant, I see no reason why we should not be friends. May I offer you a drink?'

Hamilton could think of several reasons for rejecting Aritsu's olive-branch. The public apology delivered at the end of the funeral of the two dead aviators had been an unnerving and humiliating experience and it had taken iron discipline to go through with it. The text of the apology had been drafted by the Foreign Office representative in Hong Kong, and the hypocritical and demeaning words had stuck in his throat. Hamilton personally entertained no regrets for what he had done, and he was still seething with fury at the British authorities for imposing such an unnecessary indignity on the Royal Navy. But when Commander Aritsu invited him back to his office after the ceremony, curiosity had got the better of his feelings. The gesture of friendship, abhorrent though he found it, only served to whet his curiosity even further.

'Thank you, Commander. A Scotch if you have one, please.'

Aritsu went across to the drink's cabinet and busied himself with the bottles.

There was something intriguingly different about this particular Englishman and he was anxious to learn more about him. It was never possible to know too much about a potential enemy.

'You understand, Lieutenant, that there is no enmity between your Navy and my own,' he observed blandly as he poured a large measure of Vat 69 into Hamilton's glass. 'The Japanese Navy does not enjoy this sort of thing. But, just as you have to obey your masters in Whitehall, we too must carry out the instructions of our leaders in Tokyo.' He handed the glass to *Rapier*'s captain and then resumed his seat.

'In the East, as you are probably aware, it is important to maintain "face",' he continued. 'Japan must prove to the Chinese that she is the dominant power. We have no quarrel with Britain or America. But, if an unfortunate incident occurs, it is important that we demonstrate our equality with the Western powers by demanding, and receiving, an appropriate apology.'

'Even when Japan is in the wrong, Commander?' Hamilton asked sharply.

Aritsu shrugged. 'Who is to say what is right or wrong, Lieutenant? I have no doubt that yesterday's incident was an unfortunate error of judgment by our pilots. They were, perhaps, unlucky to have picked someone who was prepared to hit back.'

'I may have been ordered to apologize, Commander,' Hamilton said coldly. 'But let there be no misunderstandings. If your aircraft or ships attack my boat again, I shall defend myself and my men in precisely the same manner.'

'Of course you will,' Aritsu smiled. 'Of course. But as I have said, these incidents unhappily happen. The Japanese Army is anxious to go to war with the British Empire and the United States. Our Navy wishes friendship. We do our best to control these wild men in Tokyo but...' he shrugged and left the sentence unfinished.

'But why create incidents?' Hamilton asked.

'Because to survive as a first-class power we must control all the resources of South-East Asia. To do this we must demonstrate our superiority, so that people fear us more than they fear you.' Aritsu leaned forward confidentially.

'There are many colonial races, the Indians for example, who wish to be free from English domination. Such people look to Japan for their freedom. It is understandable. If the English and the Americans stopped interfering with our actions, there would be no need for these unfortunate incidents.' The Commander sipped his drink thoughtfully.

'Believe me, Lieutenant, there is absolutely no possibility of war between our two countries. We in the Navy are realists. We know that Japan cannot win such a conflict. We do not have the raw materials or the industrial capacity to wage war against the British Empire or the United States. Even Admiral Yamamoto agrees - and he is in the best position to understand these matters.'

'So you are telling me that we should let the Japanese walk all over us?'

'Only in the cause of peace, Lieutenant. We are sitting on a powder keg - it only needs the smallest spark to start the fuse. And once the fuse has been lit, nothing can save the British Empire.'

Hamilton contemplated Aritsu's remarks as he finished his Scotch. Despite his antipathy to the Japanese, he sensed genuine sincerity behind the commander's words. 'But if you think Japan must ultimately lose a war with the Western Powers why bother to start one in the first place?' Aritsu shook his head sorrowfully. 'In Japan we have a proverb - a man who lights fire does not expect to burn his hands. The war party in Tokyo and the Army generals do not accept the possibility of defeat. It is only the Navy that understands the risks involved. But one fact is crystal clear, Lieutenant. If war comes, it does not matter whether Japan wins or loses - British influence and power in Asia will be finished for ever!'

Hamilton drained his glass and stood up. 'I beg to disagree, Commander, but I appreciate your frankness. I am sure our two navies can live in peace. But I repeat,' and the submariner's eyes hardened as he stared into Aritsu's impassive face, 'if anyone picks a fight with my boat again, they'll receive exactly the same treatment your bombers did yesterday - even if it means I have to crawl on bended knees and apologize to the Emperor himself.'

'I am sure it will not come to that, Lieutenant,' Aritsu smiled. He held out his hand. 'Remember, if I can be of any assistance please do not hesitate to contact me. And let us hope there will be no further incidents.'

Hamilton grasped the Commander's hand. He realized that Aritsu was only trying to give him a friendly warning and he appreciated the gesture. But he could not help wondering whether their next meeting would be so cordial. Replacing his cap, he saluted the Japanese officer, and hurried down the steps to the waiting staff car.

Despite Aritsu's reassurances, Hamilton was now firmly convinced that a major conflict was about to erupt in the Far East. And if the attack took place before reinforcements arrived from home waters, Hamilton could not see how the Navy would be able to defend the isolated colony with the pitifully inadequate resources at its disposal - a couple of antiquated destroyers dating back to the 1914-18 war, a few short-range MTBs and a handful of shallow-draught gunboats which, although valuable for policing duties on China's great river highways, were totally unsuited for the task that might soon face them.

Having mentally reviewed the full extent of the British naval presence in China, Hamilton realized with something of a shock that there was only one ship in Hong Kong capable of facing the Japanese Navy on equal terms. And that ship was *Rapier!*

So *that* was the reason the Admiralty had sent him to Hong Kong. All the talk about resting and enjoying a holiday at public expense had been so much eye-wash. If his premonition was correct, *Rapier* would soon be fighting for survival. And all the odds would be against her....

Mannon was surprised by the skipper's sudden change of mood. He had gone ashore that morning in the blackest of tempers and the executive officer had fully expected him to return in a similar state of mind. But, as he stepped off the gangway, Hamilton looked completely relaxed and at ease. Had Mannon known him better, he would have realized that it meant that the lieutenant was at his most dangerous.

'Number One - I want the bunkers and water tanks topped up and every single bit of gear checked. Muster all hands in the fore-ends at six bells. I want to put them in the picture. And from now on I want this boat maintained in a condition of readiness for war. Forget about polishing the brass work and cleaning the paintwork. And another thing. We've only been off operational service for a few weeks, but the men are already slowing down and losing their alertness. See to it that things are tightened up.'

Mannon recovered his breath and saluted obediently. As the submarine's executive officer, it was his job to see that the skipper's orders were carried out down to the smallest detail. And while it was not part of his duties to reason why, he had a natural curiosity.

'What's happened, sir?'

'Nothing's happened, Number One. Just put it down to instinct. I'll explain what it's about when I address the men.'

It was hardly a satisfactory explanation, but Mannon knew it would be useless to press Hamilton further in his present mood. He nodded and started to make his way towards the for'ard hatch, stopping suddenly as he remembered the message.

'By the way sir, there was a telephone call for you from a Senor Alburra just after you left this morning. He said he wanted to see you tonight. He gave an address in Macao.'

'Must be a mistake, Number One. Who the hell do I know in Macao - we only arrived yesterday?'

'I think he may be the owner of the Chris Craft cruiser, sir. He was very insistent. He said he thought he could be of service to you.'

'I doubt it,' Hamilton said shortly. 'Probably wants to reward me for saving the crew. What's his number - I'll give him a ring and tell him to send a donation to the Royal Navy Benevolent Fund.'

Mannon fished a piece of paper from his trousers pocket and looked at it. 'Sorry, sir, he didn't give his phone number - only his address, the De Gama Oil & Wharfage Company, Isabella Strado. He asked to see you in his office at eight o'clock tonight.'

Hamilton looked thoughtful. He had no idea what Alburra wanted to see him about, but if he was in the oil business they could well share certain mutual interests. He gave Mannon no indication of what was passing through his mind.

'On second thoughts, Number One, perhaps I *will* call

on him this evening. But if anyone asks where I am, just tell them I've taken the ferry to Macao to sample the gambling tables.'

Mannon raised an eyebrow and grinned. 'Not the women, sir?'

'All right, Number One. If you want the truth - the women as well.'

THREE

'I've no objection to taking part in a one-man war, sir. But I think we ought to be practical about it,' Mannon told Hamilton as the officers gathered in the wardroom after *Rapier's* skipper had finished addressing the crew. 'As you're often fond of reminding me - I was an accountant in civvy street, and that makes me very conscious of hard facts and figures. I daresay we would run amok in the China Sea for a couple of weeks - but that's all.'

'Roger's got a good point there, sir,' O'Brien agreed. 'We can only carry ninety-one tons of oil in the bunkers. So even at *Rapier's* most economical cruising speed, our maximum patrol range will be limited to around six thousand miles.'

'And it's one thousand six hundred and ninety miles back to Singapore,' Scott pointed out, after a quick reference to *Reed's Table of Distances*. 'According to my arithmetic, that leaves an effective operational endurance of less than four thousand five hundred miles - let's say three weeks at the most.'

Hamilton looked down at his erstwhile council-of-war. 'You're a lot of bloody dismal Jimmies,' he told them coldly.

'As for making for Singapore - forget it. If the balloon goes up we stay close to the China coast. We're the only submarine this side of Aden. It's our job to keep the Japs busy until the Navy can send a fleet out East. And the current staff evaluation for doing this is ninety days.'

'Well, short of stepping masts and fitting our own sails, I don't see how we're going to survive that long,' O'Brien said pessimistically. 'We'll have burned up all our oil inside twenty-five days. What do we use for fuel after that?'

Hamilton shrugged. 'I suppose we could hide amongst the islands and extend our operational duration that way. The important thing to remember is this: until they succeed in sinking *Rapier,* the Japs have got to divert valuable anti-submarine units into the area to hunt us down. Every single extra day we can remain afloat will make their attack schedule that much more difficult to maintain.'

'I still think we should be realistic, sir,' Mannon said patiently. 'I agree that Hong Kong will probably fall within a fortnight. And I agree that we shall then have nowhere to replenish our oil stocks. But don't forget we'll also need to replace torpedoes. *Rapier* carries six Mk VIIs in her tubes and a further six reloads. That means we will be limited to a maximum of twelve attacks. After that we cease to be an effective fighting unit. Once a submarine has exploded its torpedoes, it becomes a liability rather than an asset.' Hamilton looked at them in silence for a few minutes. He knew it was a crazy plan, but once embarked on an enterprise he did not believe in looking back. He turned to Scott.

'Start going through your charts with a fine toothcomb, Alistair. I want you to find me a small uninhabited island inside a five hundred mile radius of Hong Kong. Von Spee hid his squadron amongst the Pacific Islands in 1914 — and it took us four months to find him. So let's take a lesson from the enemy.'

As Scott began sorting through the charts, Hamilton turned his attention to Mannon. 'I shall want you to call on the Dockyard Superintendent tomorrow, Number One. Tell him we came out here without torpedoes and need a complete outfit. If he asks questions, you can always say we had to off-load ours at Alexandria because the Mediterranean flotillas were short of weapons.'

'But he'll want to examine our forms S304 and 319. And they'll show we had a full kit on board when we left Alex, sir.'

'You've got a twisted mind, Number One. You ought to have been a bloody civil servant not an accountant. Bring the forms to me and I'll write them up so that they back up our story. I used to be good at forging the Commander's signature for leave passes when I was serving in the Lower Deck.'

'Aren't you taking a bit of a chance, sir?' O'Brien asked quietly. 'Supposing the Japs don't attack. How the hell are you going to wriggle out of falsifying records and getting hold of a dozen torpedoes which you weren't authorized to draw?'

'That's my problem,' Hamilton told him crisply. 'I've been sent out here to defend Hong Kong. And I'm not going to let a load of bureaucratic bullshit stop me.' Mannon gave up his efforts to dissuade the skipper from hanging himself. In fact, he was beginning to understand what Hamilton had in mind. A lonely and uninhabited island. A private stock of ammunition and supplies. And every man's hand against you. It reminded him of the old Percy F. Westerman stories he used to read at school.

'Supposing Scott *finds* an island, sir. What then?'

Hamilton looked at the young RN VR Executive Officer. He could see the gleam of excitement in Mannon's eyes. Perhaps he'd misjudged him. Perhaps all chartered accountants were pirates at heart. He gave him a grin of encouragement.

'The first thing is to lay out an anchorage and make sure we have adequate cover from air search.' He glanced at Scott. 'That means deep water close inshore, Pilot, and plenty of trees and vegetation.'

'Shouldn't be too much of a problem, sir. There aren't any desert islands in this part of the world - the coral area is further to the south and east.'

'Good. Once we've found a suitable island, we'll transport as many supplies and as much fresh water as we can find and start building up a store's reserve. Then we offload our torpedo outfit and come back to draw replacement weapons from the RNAD depot. With luck we should end up with twenty-four torpedoes.'

The others nodded. It sounded plausible enough. O'Brien, *Rapier's* engineering officer, was the only one with any doubts.

'That's fine for stores and ammunition, sir. But you can't stockpile oil willy-nilly. It will still have to be kept in tanks or, at least, barrels. And how the hell do we smuggle barrels of oil out of the depot without being spotted?'

Hamilton smiled enigmatically. 'I've already thought of that one, Chief. And I think I've got the answer.' He looked around the table. 'Any more questions?'

The officers shook their heads.

'Right,' Hamilton told them. 'We start loading tomorrow. And remember - if you can't wangle it out of the depot, I shall expect you to buy the necessary supplies from the Chinese burn boats with your own money.'

The last weeks of October 1941 passed without undue incident. *Rapier* sailed on self-imposed exercises every four days, vanishing from sight for forty-eight hours, returning to Hong Kong noticeably lighter in draught than when she departed. Scott's island - a small tree-covered paradise off the north-east coast of Hai-Nan- provided just the privacy Hamilton required to carry out his plan and it was soon amply stocked with reserve stores. A convenient cave close to the water's edge provided an ideal torpedo store, although the task of manhandling the cumbersome mark VII tin fish, each weighing 4,106 pounds, was no picnic in the heat of the sun.

Hamilton, with Scott's expert assistance, carefully surveyed the coastline around Hong Kong in search of suitable hiding places, and by the end of the month he felt confident that he could exploit the sea area to his advantage, if the necessity arose.

Stores had been a problem at first. The depot superintendent had put up a stout fight but, surrendering to O'Brien's blarney, had finally supplied most of the items on Hamilton's apparently inexhaustible list. The gunboat skippers, too, having been taken into Hamilton's confidence, chipped in with useful extras and Charlotte Island rapidly developed into a miniature arsenal, as crate after crate was painstakingly hauled up the beach and hidden in the thick undergrowth. But despite the willing assistance of the other commanders, Hamilton took care not to reveal the identity of his secret base to anyone outside the circle of *Rapier*'s officers - the fewer who knew about it the better. And although he suspected that the C-in-C and his staff had guessed what was going on, they maintained a discreet silence and asked no awkward questions.

In spite of the hectic activity at Charlotte Island, *Rapi-*

er's skipper still found time to make regular visits to his newfound Portuguese friends in Macao. And, typically, he gave no reasons for his weekly jaunts across the estuary, although it was apparent from the expression on his face when he returned that Hamilton was well-satisfied with what had happened while he was there....

October passed into November without incident. The Japanese military forces in China seemed intent on maintaining a low profile and Hamilton was beginning to wonder whether he had misjudged the situation. The big Jardine & Mathieson steamers continued their normal trading routine and, despite the boom guarding the entrance to the Pearl River, the regular boats had been allowed upstream to Canton and Whampoa without hindrance from the Japanese Navy. Reports filtering through to the Colony indicated that Japanese control over the river traffic on the Yangtse Kiang further to the north had tightened; but no one in Hong Kong read any significance into the stories they received from Shanghai. The peace mission which Tokyo had dispatched to the United States suggested that their bluff had been called, and there was a general feeling amongst the Europeans that the situation would soon ease.

Ernie Blood was supervising a deck washing party on the foredeck casing at the beginning of the afternoon watch, when a grey painted staff car hooted its way through the dockyard and screeched to a halt at the head of the mooring gangway. Hamilton and the other officers were below in the wardroom finishing their lunch, and the rest of the submarine's crew were busy stacking the latest consignment of illicit stores, ready for the next shuttle run to Charlotte Island.

As a result of Hamilton's orders, *Rapier* was on war

routine and peacetime regulations had been relaxed in order to get the work done. The customary welcoming deck parties and correctly bedecked officer-of-the-watch pacing aimlessly up and down the narrow bridge, were conspicuously absent. But if discipline and ceremonial were not immediately apparent, Hamilton's security precautions certainly were. Two members of the submarine's crew armed with rifles and fixed bayonets stood guard over the dockyard end of the gangway while a third, perched high up the conning tower, kept an eagle-eyed watch over the quayside - the Lewis gun at his side ready to give instant support to the sentries if required.

The door of the Hillman staff car swung open and Captain Snark emerged. His white tropical uniform had lost its usual crisp freshness. Large sweat stains marked his shirt and he looked tired and haggard.

The two sentries snapped to attention and presented arms as he hurried across the burning concrete. There was no red tape about Hamilton's security system. The men were quite familiar with Snark's identity and he was passed through onto the gangway without question. Ernie Blood straightened up as he saw the captain approaching. Throwing a half-smoked cigarette into the dock, he hurried to the base of the conning tower and shouted to the Leading seaman standing beside the Lewis gun.

'Bladon! Tell the skipper Alice is coming aboard.' Snark's nickname had obvious connotations. 'At the double!'

Bladon's head disappeared behind the bridge screen as he reported Snark's unexpected arrival to the control room and, seconds later, Bell, the duty runner, delivered the news to the wardroom.

Hamilton put his coffee down and wiped his mouth.

'Thank you, Bell. Tell the gunner's mate to report to me immediately.' He seemed unperturbed by the visitation despite his companions' apparent alarm.

'Shouldn't we try and do something to hide those extra stores, sir?' Mannon asked anxiously.

'No time,' Hamilton told him with a shake of his head. 'Snark knows very little about submarine routine. I doubt if he'll notice anything untoward. And if he does, I'll just have to blind him with science.' He looked up as Morgan, *Rapier's* gunner's mate, appeared through the wardroom curtains. 'Ah, there you are, Chief. Captain Snark is coming up the gangway. Assemble the tidiest looking men you can find in the control room, and tell the rest to make themselves scarce in the fore and aft ends.'

'Aye, aye, sir.'

Hamilton finished his coffee with unhurried pleasure. 'There's no call for panic, gentlemen,' he told the other officers quietly. 'Probably just a routine visit. I'll get rid of him as soon as I can.'

Able Seaman Bell reappeared. Thrusting his head through the wardroom curtains like a spirit at a seance he announced sepulchrally: 'Captain coming down the control room ladder, sir. The Gunner says the men are fallen in as ordered.' Having imparted his news in a voice of doom, he entered the wardroom and saluted smartly.

Hamilton acknowledged the courtesy and nodded to Mannon. 'Come on, Number One. And try not to look so bloody guilty. Let's find out what the old bastard wants. Perhaps he just needs me to make up a four for bridge this evening.'

Snark was waiting by the diving panel as Hamilton and his executive officer came through the for'ard bulkhead hatch. He eyed *Rapier's* skipper belligerently.

'Boat's like a bloody pigsty, Lieutenant,' he grumbled. 'Lucky for you this isn't an inspection. I like to see a ship clean and tidy. Shows efficiency.'

'*Rapier* is fully armed and stored and ready to sail at thirty minutes' notice, sir,' Hamilton pointed out quietly. 'That's the sort of efficiency I look for.'

Snark snorted. His mission was too urgent to bandy words with a mere two-striper. 'Dismiss the men, Mister Gunner,' he growled at Morgan.

The gunner's mate came to attention and saluted. Snark smiled sardonically. *That* was the way he liked to see things done. When he said jump - they jumped! Morgan completed his salute and turned to Hamilton.

'Permission to fall out the men, sir?'

'Granted, Chief. Tell them to wait in the fore-ends mess space.'

Snark swallowed his anger. There was no mistaking Morgan's studied insolence. But the post captain had been in the service long enough to know there was nothing he could do about it. Hamilton was *Rapier's* captain and, on his own ship, his word was law despite his inferior rank. As soon as the control room was empty, Snark delivered his bombshell.

'The Japanese have taken *Firefly!*'

Hamilton accepted the news without any sign of surprise. He thought the Japs had been too quiet recently. But he could not help wondering whether Harry Ottershaw was all right, and he reflected bitterly on the uselessness of the Station's Standing Orders not to provoke the Japanese. It hadn't done Ottershaw much good by the sound of it. 'How did it happen, sir?' he asked.

'We've been shadowing the Japanese troop convoys passing down the coast,' Snark explained briefly and, as

Hamilton raised his eyebrows, he added: 'Just because Higher Authority imposes restrictors upon our behavior, does not mean that the Navy is content to take an inactive role in the defense of our Far Eastern dependencies, Lieutenant, although I realize that this is *your* impression of the Hong Kong Station. We have been keeping Japanese warships under surveillance for several months. *And* we've learned a thing or two.' He paused for a moment. '*Firefly* was sent out to investigate a large troop convoy coming out from Shanghai. The ships were outside the three-mile limit, so Ottershaw had every right to be there. We don't know precisely what happened, but *Firefly* was forced into Hai-An Bay and the Japanese have boxed her in.'

'For what reason, sir?'

Snark shrugged. 'We've no idea. They haven't communicated with us yet and it's all a bit of a mystery. No doubt they've got something up their sleeve.'

'Can't we send out a destroyer, sir?' Hamilton suggested.

'Unfortunately not,' Snark said shaking his head. 'For two reasons. Firstly we have no ships. *Thanet* and *Thracian* are cruising off Amoy Island on exercises and *Scout* is in dry-dock for rudder repairs and bottom scraping. And, secondly, even if they *were* available they would be unable to assist. The Japs have thrown a temporary boom across the entrance to the bay to make sure *Firefly* can't escape.'

'Are we in radio contact with the gunboat?' Hamilton asked. 'Surely we could tell Ottershaw to ram the boom and break out. The other gunboats could be sent in to give him support.'

'It's not as easy as that,' Snark told him gloomily. 'If *Firefly* tries to escape, Ottershaw will be left behind. Apparently he's been taken aboard the Japanese destroyer for what they diplomatically called discussions.' The captain paused for a moment and then looked Hamilton in the eye. 'That's where *Rapier* comes into the picture.'

'If it means a chance of having a crack at the Japs...' Hamilton began, but Snark cut him short.

'I know you have a reputation for disobeying orders, Lieutenant. But this time you will have to be careful. Otter-shaw's life will depend on your handling of what looks to be a very tricky situation.' Snark picked up a sheet of paper from the chart table and sketched an outline of Hai-An Bay. He marked two crosses inside the bay and drew a straight line across the entrance to represent the boom. His pencil tapped one of the crosses. 'This *is Firefly's* present mooring position. And the destroyer is anchored here. As you can see, the Japanese commander is able to cover both the gunboat and the entrance with his main armament. If he gets any sort of warning, he can sink the gunboat within seconds and *still* have time to deal with the rescue boat.'

Hamilton forgot his dislike of the captain as he concen-trated on the practicalities of the problem. At a time like this, they were all members of the same team and personal feelings could not be allowed to intervene.

'I take it that Ottershaw is aboard the destroyer?' he asked quietly.

Snark nodded. 'As far as we know - yes. And that's the crux of the problem. A consensus of Staff opinion is that a submarine could get under the boom and alongside *Firefly* without the Japanese being alerted. After that, any further action would be on the initiative of the submarine commander.'

'You mean I'll be running the show?'

'Yes, Lieutenant. You'll be running the show. But your orders are to take no belligerent action against the destroyer.

Providing you can act quickly the Japanese commander will have no time to call up support, and on his own, I reckon a submarine and a gunboat will be sufficient odds to deter him from being foolish. Your task will be to obtain Otter-shaw's release and then bring *Firefly* safely back to Hong Kong.'

Snark somehow contrived to make it sound easy, but Hamilton noted that he made no effort to tell him how the impossible was to be achieved. But perhaps it was better that way. At least he could not be accused of disobeying orders. He looked down at the sketch map again.

'What's the depth of water inside the bay?' he asked. 'Ten fathoms - although it's probably only about eight over the bar. Unfortunately we have no accurate charts for this part of the coast.'

'Do the Japs have Asdic equipment?'

Snark shook his head. 'Not as far as we know. You'll only have to contend with hydrophones. And I doubt if they'll be maintaining a listening watch. I don't think they'll be expecting a submarine.'

Hamilton knew it was a gamble. Taking a submarine into an uncharted bay was tantamount to suicide. And what the hell was he going to do even if he succeeded in getting under the boom. But his reputation was at stake, and the challenge to show off in front of the Colony's top naval brass was too much to resist.

'Very well, sir. I'll try it. But I'll do it my way.'

Snark looked at him coldly. 'I'm sure you will, Lieu-tenant. Fortunately for you, this is how it must be. We cannot afford to antagonize the Japanese, even in a situation like this where they are entirely in the wrong. Your mission will be regarded as completely unofficial - if anything goes wrong, the authorities will make it clear that you were acting contrary to orders. Your reputation for disobedience, in fact, may prove very useful. And make no mistake about it, Lieutenant. Your head will be handed to the Japanese on a platter if the plan fails.'

And don't you hope it will, Hamilton thought to himself. He did not, however, demur. This was the way he preferred to do things. At least he could handle the situation as it developed without the constraint of superior orders.

'I have only one question, sir,' he said slowly. 'How much longer are we going to play second fiddle to the Japs?'

Snark allowed himself the luxury of a thin smile. 'Not much longer. The nucleus of a Far East Fleet is already on its way to Singapore. Two capital ships and a carrier. They should arrive next month. And there are more to follow. Take my word for it - Tokyo will be singing a very different tune once they see we mean business. But this is in the future. For the moment the situation remains unaltered. Now, how soon can you sail?'

'In thirty minutes, sir.' Hamilton would have liked to stress his combat readiness after Snark's complaints about *Rapier's* efficiency, but he felt the plain statement of fact was proof enough.

Snark appeared to take it as a matter of course. He had no intention of allowing Hamilton to enjoy his moral victory. The taciturn expression on his face did not soften even though he held out his hand.

'Good luck, Hamilton. And remember - you're on your own.'

Rapier left Hong Kong via the easterly channel. As Taikoo shipyard passed on the starboard side, Hamilton could see the destroyer *Scout* in dry-dock having her venerable old bottom scraped. The gunboat *Moth* was also ashore being refitted, and he wondered how the Navy would cope with a Japanese attack with one-third of the Station's largest ships out of commission. Dismissing the problem from his mind, he guided the submarine through the narrows at the eastern end of the channel and altered course to the south-east towards Lam Tong Island.

Two motor torpedo boats from the 2nd Flotilla swept up from the south as *Rapier* came level with Pottinger Peak and their ensigns dipped in salute as they thundered past at forty knots. Lieutenant Commander Gandy, the flotilla commander, waved a cheery farewell from the spray-soaked bridge of the leading MTB and Hamilton returned the greeting. *Rapier's* bows rose and fell sharply as the submarine pushed into the currents of the South China Sea and, having passed clear of Lam Tong, Hamilton altered course to the south - to mislead any shore watchers in the pay of the Japanese.

'Stand down Harbor Stations, Number One.'

Mannon leaned over the conning tower coaming. 'Sea Duty men below! Secure for'ard hatch.'

He waited for Morgan to dismiss the men on the fo'c'sle and then flipped the lid of the voice-pipe. 'Take over lower steering. Course 1-7-5.'

'Control Room, aye, aye, sir. On lower steering. Course 1-7-5.'

'On lower steering, sir.' He reported to Hamilton. 'Fore hatch shut and clipped. Hands fallen out to passage routine.'

Hamilton acknowledged Mannon's report with a nod and stared east as the peaks of Victoria Island shimmered in the heat haze. Despite the approach of winter the weather was unreasonably warm. Day temperatures should have dropped to a mean seventy degrees by now but when *Rapier* had left the Colony was still sweltering in a humid eighty-three. The latest Met report was forecasting an approaching cold front later in the day, but Hamilton had very little faith in the weather experts with their little charts and multi-colored inks. The China Seas were notoriously treacherous. Sudden squalls could appear from nowhere and vanish as quickly as they had come; and miniature storms of surprising ferocity could shut down visibility and lash a ship with gale-driven rain out of an almost clear blue sky. *Rapier* was lucky that the typhoon season was over.

'Stand by to dive, Number One. Diving in two minutes.' Mannon passed the preliminary order to the control room and waited while the duty signalman and the two look-outs swung into the upper hatch and clambered down the steel ladder.

'Bridge clear, sir. Ready to dive.'

'Thank you, Number One. Get below and stand by.' Diving on the klaxon was restricted to emergencies and the submarine service did not officially acknowledge the term 'crash dive'. Hamilton was in no hurry. The men had had more than their share of emergency dives during their last spell of duty in the Med. He had little doubt that diving on the klaxon would become part of their standard routine again in the very near future but, for the moment, he was content to let the crew take it easy. He moved to the voice pipe.

'Take her down to periscope depth, Number One.'

'Periscope depth aye aye, sir.'

Hamilton heard the metallic clang of the vents thrusting open as the hydraulic power came on, followed by the thundering roar of the sea flooding into the empty ballast tanks. Abaft, in the engine room, Chief ERA Bates acknowledged the order from the control room and passed the executive command to the motor room.

'Out clutches - secure for diving.'

'Clutches out, Chief.' Yarden confirmed. 'Engines stopped.'

'Switches on. Group up - half-ahead both.' The urgent throb of the diesels faded away and Bates felt the deck plating vibrate as the motors came on. He reached for the telephone link to the control room. 'Engines off, sir. Motors running. Clutches out and secured for diving.' Hamilton closed the upper hatch, fastened the clips, and slid down into the brightly-lit nerve center of the submarine. The monotonous chant of the reports, orders, and acknowledgements echoed quietly inside the crowded apartment.

'Upper hatch shut and clipped.'

'Permission to close lower hatch, sir?'

'Granted.' Hamilton glanced at the big dials of the depth gauges facing the two coxswains. The red pointer needles fingered towards the twenty-feet calibration. 'Level at thirty, Number One. Maintain course and speed.'

Petty Officer Arnold leaned back in his seat and watched the needle swing down. As it touched the thirty feet mark he reversed the big steel-rimmed diving wheel and brought the for'ard planes into the horizontal position. Rapier's bows levelled off as the submarine gently came out of the dive.

'Fore 'planes amidships, sir!'

As Arnold made his report, Ernie Blood eased the controls of the aft hydroplanes and deliberately balanced the submarine's buoyancy as he coaxed it to the required depth.

'Aft 'planes amidships, sir. Thirty feet. Trimmed and level.'

'Up periscope!'

Bush moved the telemotor pump controls of the

periscope mechanism and the bronze column sighed up from the womb with a soft hiss. Pulling down the steering handles, Hamilton pushed his face into the rubber cup of the binocular eye-pieces and waited for the water to clear from the upper lens. After the soft glare of the tungsten lamps in the control room, the strong sunlight made him blink, but it was only a slight discomfort and it quickly passed. Swinging the 'scope through a full circle, he carried out a preliminary routine sweep of the surface to ensure that there was no shipping in the immediate vicinity of the submerged submarine and then, flicking the sky-search lever with his thumb, he tilted the big search lens upwards to scan the sky.

A few wisps of cirrus cloud hung over the southern horizon but the remainder of the sky was clear; although Hamilton noticed a strange bronze sheen to seaward that contrasted with the brilliant blue over Hong Kong itself. A small float-plane, probably a Fair Sea Fox, droned slowly towards the peaks of Victoria Island trailing a large drogue, and he watched a speckle of tiny brown splashes of smoke bursting around it as the Colony's anti-aircraft defenses put in some much needed live ammunition practice.

Moving the lens a few degrees to port, he stared in the direction of the Ninepin Islands group and watched a large trading junk tacking northwards to round the eastern coast of the New Territories towards the Chinese mainland. Suddenly, and without warning, he snapped the steering handles upwards and stepped back.

'Down periscope! Flood Q! Sixty feet. Attack team close up.'

The bronze column sank softly into the heavily greased well in the deck with a sigh of hydraulic power and

Venables, the 'outside' ERA, quickly spun the valve wheel to open the vents to the quick-diving tank in the bows.

'Planes to dive!'

Despite the unexpectedness of the commands, there was no panic. Arnold angled the bow planes into a steep dive and watched the depth gauge like a hawk, as Ernie Blood juggled with the aft hydroplane controls.

'Faster!' Hamilton snapped.

'Full ahead both!' Although Mannon was in the process of moving from his diving station alongside the skipper to his attack team position at the venting panel, he found time to pass the order back to the motor room and wait for the acknowledgement from the chief ERA. *Rapier* needed the extra thrust from her propellers to get her down to the required depth more quickly.

'What's the depth of water, Pilot?' Hamilton asked Scott. The navigator left the torpedo director and glanced at the opened chart on the table.

'Twenty fathoms, sir. Plenty of diving room.'

Hamilton nodded his head and waited.

'Sixty feet, sir. Trimmed and level.'

Having made his report, Ernie Blood eased his large bottom into a more comfortable position on the narrow unpadded seat. As a veteran submariner, he was accustomed to emergencies and he sat phlegmatically behind the diving wheel, sucking his teeth thoughtfully, ready for the next order. Despite his outward calm, however, he could not help wondering about the reason for the skipper's sudden decision to take the *Rapier* deeper. Probably something he had spotted on the surface. Well, he knew best. The coxswain's confidence in Hamilton's skill was completely unshakable. But, like every other member of the submarine's crew, he had no idea what might be happening in the bright sunlit world above the surface of the sea. Only the captain was privy to the secrets of the periscope's lens. And in an emergency he was too busy to explain his actions to a group of curious matelots.

Hamilton looked at his stopwatch and checked that the attack team was closed up in the correct stations - Mannon behind the 'outside' ERA watching the trim and indicator lights of the blowing panel. O'Brien ready to mark up the plot, Scott at the 'fruit machine' and the two electrical artificers, Blake and Sutton, ranged alongside the periscope, ready to read off the angles and make the slide-rule calculations for the navigator to feed into the torpedo director.

The expressions on the faces of the attack team reflected the tension of the sudden emergency, but they stood at their stations with the easy casualness of men who knew what they were doing. Hamilton said nothing and reached for the telephone to the fore-ends compartment.

'Bow tubes?'

'Fore-ends, aye aye, sir.'

'Action stations. Blow up tubes one, two, three and four.'

The chief torpedo gunner's mate had served with Hamilton since the first day of the *Rapier's* commissioning. He knew his skipper and he knew exactly what was expected of him. Moving the lever of the telemotor controls from left to right, Newton waited for the needle of the pressure gauge to swing across the dial before glancing up at the mechanical indicators. The warning lights glowed as the tubes flooded up and Bruce, the sub lieutenant and fourth hand in charge of the bow compartment, nodded to Langton to check the test cocks. A trickle of water emerged from each end and the torpedo man passed a thumb's-up signal back to the officer.

'Bow caps open.'

Newton moved the lever on each tube and the sub lieutenant saw the markers of the mechanical indicators swing to the 'open' position. He put his mouth to the telephone.

'Tubes flooded up, sir. Bow caps open. Standing by.' 'All received, Number Four. Standing by for firing.' 'Fore-ends aye aye, sir.'

'Losing trim, sir! Bows dropping!'

Ernie Blood's warning report was almost casual in its delivery. His voice gave no hint of alarm and Mannon, alerted by the warning, glanced at the inclometer for confirmation.

'Blow One and Two compensating tanks.'

Venables reached forward across the panel and twisted the control valves of the bow compensating tanks. There was a sudden whine of compressed air as the water was transferred to the main ballast tanks under pressure, and Mannon saw the artificial horizon of the inclometer tilt back to equilibrium.

'Trimmed and level, sir.'

Hamilton frowned. *Rapier* shouldn't have lost trim so easily. And the fact that the heaviness in the bow coincided with the flooding of the torpedo tubes suggested something amiss with the first officer's trim calculations. Alternatively, the by-pass valves used to transfer water ballast to balance the extra weight of the flooded tubes were malfunctioning. Either way *something* was wrong, and he made a mental note to check as soon as time permitted.

'Any Asdic contacts, Glover?'

'No, sir.'

'HE?'

'Negative.'

'Take her up to periscope depth, Number One.'

'Planes to rise - level at thirty. Blow Q!'

'Thirty and level, sir.'

'Up periscope!'

The big search 'scope rose up from the deck and Hamilton swung the column onto a north-east bearing. He focused the lens on the trading junk he had seen before their emergency dive and then, with pointedly unhurried calm, he swept the horizon through a full circle.

'Down periscope. Attack team fall out.' He reached for the telephone. 'Bow ends - secure from Action Stations. Close bow caps and blow tubes.' Putting the telephone back on its cradle, he lifted the microphone of the internal tannoy system. 'This is the Captain. All hands stand down to Watch Diving routine.'

Mannon carried out a final check on the glowing warning lights of the main venting panel before turning to Hamilton. The tension of the unexpected emergency still showed in his face, but he managed to conjure up a grin.

'Panic over, sir?' he enquired cheerfully.

'Just a drill, Number One. I wanted to make sure we hadn't got stale after a few weeks enjoying the flesh-pots of Hong Kong.' Hamilton glanced at the stopwatch hanging from a cord around his neck. 'I suppose you didn't do too badly - all things considered,' he admitted grudgingly. Walking to the gyro-repeater, he stared at it in silence for a few moments. 'Reduce to half speed. Steer zero-four-five.' Finnegan brought the submarine on to its new course and centered the wheel as the gyro-repeater came on. 'Half-ahead, sir. Course zero-four-five.'

Mannon knew that the alteration of the helm had pointed the submarine's bows towards the Chinese main-land, and he could not help wondering what sort of plan Hamilton had in mind. Snark's scheme had seemed wild enough when he first put it forward but, looked at afresh in the cold light of reality, it now seemed totally impossible. Boarding a destroyer - a submarine's arch enemy - in its lair was an invitation to suicide. And Mannon did not feel very enthusiastic about dying young.

'Bring your trim calculations to the wardroom, Number One,' Hamilton told him sharply. 'The bows shouldn't have gone heavy when we flooded the tubes. There must be an error somewhere and I'd like to check your figures.' Mannon was quite certain his calculations were correct, but Hamilton was probably wise to check, and he harbored no resentment. The answer probably lay in a malfunction of the ballast by-pass valves and, fortunately, that wasn't *his* responsibility. Pulling down the file containing *Rapier's,* trim figures, he ducked through the for'ard bulkhead hatch to wait for the skipper in the wardroom.

Hamilton, meanwhile, had joined Scott at the chart table. He located Hai-An Bay without too much difficulty and circled it with his pencil.

'What time is high water?' he asked.

Scott checked the tables printed on the right-hand side of the chart and scribbled some figures on a scrap of paper.

'About six o'clock, sir. It's difficult to be precise. It's not marked on the chart and these islands to the north could affect the tidal flow.'

'Will we have enough water under the keel?'

'Inside the bay - yes. But I'd reckon only six to seven fathoms over the bar at this time of the year at high water - and that's a pretty risky gamble.'

Hamilton shrugged. 'It's my gamble, Pilot, not yours. But I can't see an alternative. We've *got* to get inside the bay.' He stared down at the various symbols printed on the chart and tried to picture what the scene would look like in reality. There were times when he wished he'd been blessed with a more vivid imagination. 'I want to be half a mile off the bar at high water. *Rapier* will remain submerged through the approach - no point in revealing our presence before we have to. Let me have a course and speed.'

Scott picked up his dividers and made some quick calculations. The submarine was only twenty-five miles from the bay and it was not a difficult task to plot a suitable course. He only wished he could be more certain about the tide.

'Course zero-three-nine, sir. Speed five knots, reducing to four for the last hour's running.'

'So be it, Pilot. Take over the watch while I check the trim figures with Roger. And call me when the plot shows we're five minutes before high water.'

FOUR

'Captain to the control room!'

Hamilton pushed the slide rule to one side and considered the results of his revised calculations. Despite his lack
of experience Mannon's trim figures were mathematically
correct- which meant the drain valve to the bow tubes was
malfunctioning. And that was a dockyard matter.

'You'll have to shift the ballast in the for'ard section,
Number One,' he told Mannon as he put his pencil away.
'It's only a temporary expedient, but I can't have the bows
sinking every time we flood up the tubes. And if we find
ourselves in an emergency situation there won't be time to
start balancing the trim.' He pushed the wardroom curtain
aside and made his way aft.

Scott was waiting in the control room. He looked
pleased with himself. Underwater navigation could be a
damned unreliable game of chance but, on this particular
occasion, luck had been on his side.

'We're directly off the bay, sir. Three minutes to
high water.'

'Well done, Pilot.' Hamilton turned to Baker, who was

sitting at the hydro-phone equipment in his miniscule cabinet at the rear of the control room. 'Any HE, Baker?'

'Nothing, sir. Apart from the surf under the cliffs.'

'And the Asdic?'

Baker leaned across and twisted a large red knob. The steady pulse revealed no answering echo. 'No contacts, sir.'

'Up periscope.'

Hamilton set the upper lens on to the bearing indicated by Scott and examined the narrow entrance to the bay. Steep tree-clad cliffs descended down to the sea on either side, and the bobbing orange colored floats of the boom were clearly visible on the surface. Not even the faintest breath of wind ruffled the waters of the bay, and the leaden sheen of the sky confirmed the storm warning he had received from the Fleet Met Officer on leaving Hong Kong. Hamilton was unable to decide whether bad weather was likely to be an advantage or a disadvantage. But one factor worried him. The forecast had shown the center of the storm as approaching from seaward and, like all experienced sailors, he had no desire to find himself trapped on a lee shore. Too many good ships had been lost that way.

'Steer two points to starboard.'

The slight alteration of course brought *Rapier* into a position where he could see right inside the land-locked bay. The Japanese destroyer, purposeful and menacing in her dark grey war paint, was anchored close inshore on the right-hand side while, almost half a mile away to the left lay the white hulled gunboat - a wisp of smoke rising vertically from her buff colored funnel, her white ensign hanging limp and dejected in the still air. Nothing was happening. There was no sign of activity on either ship, no signals were passing and there was none of the usual small- boat traffic. Hamilton noted with relief, however, that the destroyer's

guns were safely pointing fore and aft and that was a reas-
suring sign.

'Down periscope.'

Walking across to the chart table, Hamilton motioned
Mannon and Scott to join him and, taking a clean sheet of
paper, he drew a rough sketch of the bay and the position of
the two warships. 'I think our best place is inside the bay
and alongside *Firefly*,' he told them. 'But we'll have to
gamble on passing through the entrance without being spotted. If it's an anti-submarine defense boom, we won't stand
a chance. But the floats look too light to support a steel net
so I think we'll be okay. Any questions?'

'What do you intend doing once we're inside, sir?'
Mannon asked.

'Wait and see,' Hamilton said flatly. It sounded off-hand
and impressive. But it was an empty promise. In reality
Hamilton had no idea how he was going to handle the task
that lay ahead. He was a man who disliked planning and
following a set pattern. He preferred to exploit a situation as
he found it, relying on his reactions under stress and his
intuition. Once inside the bay *something* was bound to
happen. And when it, did he hoped he would be able to
turn it to their advantage.

'We'll go under the boom submerged,' he told Mannon.

'Apart from luck we'll need two things - sufficient depth
of water and inefficient look-outs on the Jap destroyer.'

'I would think the latter requirement highly unlikely,
sir,' Mannon said primly.

'And so do I, Number One. But my guess is they'll be
watching the surface. No one but a fool would try to take a
submerged submarine into a landlocked bay with its only
exit guarded by a destroyer. The Japanese are a logical race.
They'll have considered the possibility - and dismissed it.'

Scott looked up from the chart table where he had been studying a large-scale map of the mainland coast. It was not an official Admiralty chart, but a crudely drawn native map used by local fishermen. He had purchased it in a Hong Kong shop behind the harbor a few days earlier.

'I reckon we'll have fifty feet of water over the bar, sir. This map shows fish in the area that wouldn't normally live in shallow water.'

Hamilton nodded approvingly. Scott was the type of officer he appreciated - a man who was anxious to use his brain and his initiative. He wondered how many other navigators would have thought of estimating the depth of the water by studying the type of fish inhabiting the sea. It reminded him of the time he had used the feeding habits of seagulls to steer *Rapier* through the shallows of the North Sea in pursuit of a U-boat.

'We'll have to go through blind,' he explained. 'If the Japs are watching the surface they'd spot a periscope immediately. And we'll have to proceed at our slowest speed to avoid causing too much disturbance on the surface.' He looked around the control room. 'Is everyone ready?'

There was a murmur of assent and Hamilton clicked his fingers sharply. 'Up periscope... *down* periscope!'

The lens had poked inquisitively up through the waves for no more than ten seconds. But it was sufficient for his skilled eye to estimate the bearings and distance involved. He decided to keep to the westerly side of the entrance so that *Rapier* was as far away from the destroyer as possible. Then, outwardly relaxed, he walked across to the gyro-repeater and checked the reading. He projected a mental picture of the entrance to the bay in his mind as he made his final calculation.

'Steer three-zero-zero, Helmsman. Slow ahead both motors. Take her to forty feet.'

'Three-zero-zero, sir.'

'Down planes, level at forty feet.'

'Forty feet, sir.'

'Thank you, Cox'n. Hold her steady.'

There was nothing more to do but wait. Hamilton had already started his stopwatch and he followed the sweep of the second hand as *Rapier* crawled towards the boom. 'Stop all fans and motors. Rig for silent running.' Mannon tried to hide the tension gnawing in his belly by carefully studying the warning lights of the venting panel over Venables' shoulder. As he did so, he mentally rehearsed which levers would have to be pulled to blow the appropriate ballast tanks - Numbers Six and Nine if the bows grounded. Numbers Twenty-two and Twenty-five if the stern touched bottom. He wiped the perspiration from the palms of his hands and stretched his fingers like a concert pianist preparing to play.

Scott seemed unconcerned. Unlike the executive officer, he was a regular Navy man and he'd been in submarines since 1938. Picking up a pencil, he began sketching a series of directional arrows on the chart, to indicate the probable flow of the tidal currents inside the bay. Although he had not voiced his opinions aloud, he was certain that Hamilton had made a grave error by choosing to go through at high water. If *Rapier* had been taken in on the flood tide, the strength of the current could have added at least two knots to their speed. But now, battling against the ebb, the motors could dissipate fifty per cent of their power in just fighting the tide.

Hamilton smiled to himself as he watched the navigator drawing his little barbed arrows. It wasn't difficult to guess what was passing through Scott's mind. But Hamilton had already considered the point when issuing his original orders. The changing of the tide, especially in the confined waters of the narrow entrance, would create a considerable disturbance on the surface as the ingoing and outgoing currents clashed. It would only last for two or three minutes, but the tumbling waters would help to conceal the presence of the submarine creeping stealthily beneath the surface. He thought about explaining his reasons to Scott but, on an impulse, changed his mind. He glanced down at the stopwatch.

'Three minutes,' he said quietly. 'We should be approaching the boom at any moment.'

The success or failure of the mission was now beyond the control of human hands. *Rapier* was committed to her course, depth and speed. And, as if he could still play some part in the submarine's destiny, each man inside the control room stared at his instruments and concentrated on the task in hand. The tense silence was broken only by the faint vibration of the motors, the soft whisper of the sea against the outer plating, and the familiar sound of Ernie Blood sucking his teeth.

'Let's hope Alistair's fish know what they're doing,' Hamilton said lightly, in an effort to ease the tension. The men in the control room grinned, but no one felt in the mood for joking and the oppressive silence descended once again, as each man shut himself away in his own private thoughts....

A sudden jolt shuddered through the submarine, followed by a soft slithering rasp from under the keel. Scott's fish had obviously let him down - his estimate of the depth of water over the bar had been too optimistic. Hamilton reacted without hesitation.

'Full ahead both!'

The hum of the motors rose to a shrill whine as the power came on. *Rapier* lurched like a prehistoric sea monster rising from its muddy nest on the sea bottom, and then slid smoothly forward as the propellers kicked her clear of the underwater obstruction.

'Slow ahead both.'

The high-pitched whine faded away to the familiar soft hum and the ammeter needles flicked back as the drain on the batteries eased. The dials showed the submarine riding level and the depth gauges indicated forty feet.

'Any HE, Baker?'

'No, sir.'

'Do you want an Asdic sweep, sir?' Mannon asked.

Hamilton shook his head. 'Negative. They might detect the pulses. As it is, I've got to gamble that they didn't spot the disturbance on the surface when we switched to full power.'

He glanced down at his stopwatch to calculate how far they had penetrated inside the bay. He felt like a blind man feeling his way down an unfamiliar street by counting his footsteps. In a few moments he would have to cross the road. If he had counted correctly, he would have reached the safety of the other side. If not, he was likely to be struck down by a large truck. The minute hand of the watch clicked into the third segment of the dial. He looked up.

'Steer one point to port, Helmsman.'

'One point to port, sir.'

The overwhelming temptation to raise the periscope and check their position was almost irresistible and only Hamilton's long experience and iron nerve enabled him to fight off the urge. *Rapier* was by now well into the bay and moving invisibly towards the anchored gunboat. The stretch of clear water ahead would be under close observation by the Japanese look-outs, and the faintest wisp of spray from the tip of the questing periscope would be sighted and reported as soon as it broke surface. And once trapped inside the bay, *Rapier* would stand no chance of escaping from the inevitable depth charge attack.

Hamilton seemed unconcerned by the strain of the blind approach, and he stole a quick glance at Mannon to see how he was reacting. He could recall his own nervous tension when the skipper of *Surge* had crept unseen into Kiel Bay before the war. And he had not forgotten the tragedy that followed. But despite his lack of experience, Mannon was standing up to it well. Leaning forward over the 'outside' ERA's shoulders, he kept watch on the glowing warning lights of the venting panel like the alert hawk he in many ways resembled. Hamilton decided it was time he took the young RNVR officer into his confidence.

Taking a rough sketch map of the bay from his pocket, he called Mannon over to join him and spread the paper out on the chart table so that he could see it.

'This is our estimated track,' he explained drawing a line with his pencil. 'And this...' he marked a cross on the map, 'is where we altered course a few minutes ago.

The idea is to get around behind *Firefly* so that the destroyer's look-outs won't see us when we surface.'

'A bit like Blind Man's Bluff, sir,' Mannon observed.

'I suppose it is,' Hamilton agreed. 'A great deal will depend on the strength of the tidal currents inside the bay. The pilot reckons a two knot surge on the ebb.' He paused to draw a directional arrow. 'If he's right, that would make us just about - here. We don't seem to have been spotted so far, so I'll maintain course to here...' Hamilton marked another small cross behind and astern of the gunboat. 'Then

I'll have to raise the periscope to check we're in position before we surface.'

Mannon nodded. He was beginning to understand the skipper's strategy. 'I think I follow it so far, sir. We come up on the blind side of the gunboat so that the Japs can't observe what's happening.'

'That's part of the plan, Number One. But there's more to it than that. If we do have the misfortune to be spotted, the gunboat will act as a shield. And if the Japs open fire they'll have to sink *her* before they can get at us. Needless to say, by that time we'd be well under the surface again and out of harm's way.'

It sounded a trifle cold-blooded to Mannon. He wondered what the men onboard *Firefly* would say if they knew of Hamilton's scheme. He had not served with *Rapier's* skipper long enough to have seen the ruthless streak in his character before - and he was not sure that he liked it. But, being objective, he could appreciate the careful thinking behind the plan. Hamilton was protecting his boat and his men. And if anyone got hurt, he was making sure it would not be one of *Rapier's* crew. In the circumstances Mannon supposed he should be grateful.

The second hand of the stopwatch circled the dial twice more and, in an uncharacteristically nervous gesture, Hamilton passed the tip of his tongue over his dry lips. His outward air of calm detachment hid the maelstrom of inner tension. His crotch was wet with sweat and he felt slightly sick as a violent spasm knotted his stomach muscles.

'Up periscope!'

The column glided upwards and he stopped its ascent as soon as the tip broke surface. He had already brought the lens onto an estimated bearing to save time and it took him only a few seconds to fix the submarine's position.

'Down periscope. Steer one point to starboard. Stop motors. Stand by to surface.'

'One point to starboard, sir.'

'Switches off - motors stopped, sir.'

Hamilton concentrated on the stopwatch. 'We'll be going straight up, Number One,' he warned Mannon. 'Stand by to blow the tanks. I intend to rely on positive buoyancy so we won't need to use the 'planes.'

Mannon wiped his hands down the sides of his trousers to get rid of the sweat and leaned forward over the venting panel, ready to give Venables his support when the order came.

'Blow main ballast! Surface!'

'Close main vents - blow all tanks.'

As Venables moved the hydraulic levers to close the vents, Mannon reached forward to turn the valve wheels of the compressed air reservoirs and a shrill scream of high pressure air echoed the length of the submarine.

'Duty watch on deck!'

Hamilton pulled the clips of the lower hatch as the yeoman and look-outs lined up behind him at the bottom of the ladder.

'Gun crew stand by! Morgan - bring your men topside at the double if I give the word.'

'Aye aye, sir.'

'Fifteen feet, sir.'

Hamilton reached up and pushed back the hatch cover. Swinging his body sideways with the agility of a monkey, he avoided the worst of the water streaming down into the control room from the conning tower compartment, and he heard the yeoman swear as he caught it full in the face. Then, hoisting himself up through the narrow opening, he started climbing the ladder leading to the upper hatch....

. . .

LIEUTENANT FORSYTH, *Firefly's* executive officer, raised his binoculars with a weary sigh and trained them on the destroyer again. He wondered how much longer Ottershaw was going to be. The Japanese commander had been studiously polite, and the skipper had offered no objections when the destroyer's motor boat had come alongside to take him across to the *Suma*. But that had been more than eight hours ago.

'Have they replied to my last signal, Yeoman?'

'No, sir. They acknowledged receipt - but nothing else.'

'How many damned signals have we sent now?'

Bartlett consulted the signal log. 'Seven, sir.'

'And no replies to a single one of them?'

'No, sir.'

Forsyth looked towards the narrow entrance to the bay. It was difficult to resist the temptation. His background and training, to say nothing of the age-old traditions of the Royal Navy, urged him to make a break for it and take *Firefly* through the boom and out into the open sea. And to hell with the Japs if they tried to stop him. But his loyalty to Ottershaw overcame his natural instincts. It wouldn't be right to abandon the skipper to his fate, and he reluctantly decided to hang on a little longer.

'They'd blow us out of the water before we were halfway across the bay, sir,' Bartlett observed flatly, as if reading the officer's thoughts. Forsyth nodded. The yeoman was right. But they couldn't sit around waiting much longer. And why the hell didn't Hong Kong send some assistance?

'What d'you make of that, sir? Starboard side of the entrance.'

Forsyth welcomed the diversion. At least it took his

mind off their present predicament. Putting his binoculars to his eyes he stared seawards towards the entrance. The orange floats of the boom were still bobbing gently on the surface and he could see nothing untoward.

'Looks normal to me, Jones. What was it?'

'Couldn't say for sure, sir. It happened too quickly. There was some sort of disturbance just below the surface. Those bloody floats were bobbing up and down like a Maltese whore on piece-work.'

Forsyth lowered his glasses and shrugged. 'Probably the tide on the turn - it's just about due, or perhaps a large fish swimming into the bay looking for food. It all seems quiet enough to me.' He paused for a moment and then made his way across the voice pipe. 'Send Sub-Lieutenant Peters to the bridge.'

Peters, an RNVR officer and a former Hong Kong shipping agent, bustled up the companionway to the bridge and saluted cheerfully. He'd been involved in similar incidents before as a civilian, and he did not seen unduly worried by the skipper's enforced absence. While Japan and Britain remained at peace Ottershaw would be quite safe. The Japs might bluff and bluster, but they would take great care not to overstep the mark.

'Any news, Number One?'

'Not a damned thing, Sub. What the hell do you think they're doing to him?'

'Probably filling him full of booze and trying to make him so drunk he won't know what's going on. Then they'll talk him into a signing a public apology for shadowing the convoy.'

Forsyth did not feel so optimistic. While Peters was probably correct in this particular instance, the gunboat's executive officer had judged the Japanese character more accurately and he knew they were quite capable of torturing Ottershaw into signing a confession if it suited their purposes. If, and God forbid, war should break out, he hoped and prayed he would never fall into their hands as a prisoner.

'The bottom's dropping out of the glass,' Peters added by way of conversation. 'And I don't like the way the clouds are building up to the south-west.'

Forsyth glanced towards the entrance of the bay. The breeze had died away and the air was unnaturally still. And, as Peters had remarked, the sullen coppery sheen of the sky looked distinctly unpromising. He shrugged. 'Certainly seems like a storm brewing. Perhaps we'd better lay out an extra anchor. I don't want to get caught on a lee shore.'

'Looks more like a typhoon than a storm,' Peters told him.

'Don't be ridiculous, Sub. The typhoon season ended a couple of months ago. There's no point in being alarmist.'

'Suit yourself,' the sub-lieutenant shrugged. 'Don't tell me you've never been in England when it's snowed on Midsummer's Day. Seasons are all very well in their way - don't rely on them. All the signs point to a typhoon and I ought to know. I've lived out here for fifteen years.' Forsyth looked thoughtful and then, without saying a word, he went into the wheelhouse to check the barograph. The jagged purple trace left by the pen showed the isometric pressure falling rapidly - more rapidly than he had ever seen in the whole of his career. He moved across to the synoptic weather chart and studied it carefully. The center of the depression lay to seaward and was clearly approaching at unusual speed. Although he was no meteorological expert, Forsyth could see they were in for a hell of a storm within the next hour or so. He opened the door and went back to the bridge.

'Weigh out a storm anchor, Chief, and pass the word below to secure all scuttles. Then bring up a deck party and lash down all loose equipment.'

'Aye aye, sir.' Johnson glanced up at the threatening sky. 'Looks like we're in for a packet.' He seemed to derive a certain enjoyment from his pessimism.

'The boilers are still on two hour's notice, sir,' Peters reminded the first officer. 'We'll need a good head of steam if we're hit by a typhoon - the anchors won't hold unless we can take the strain on the engines.'

'I daren't take the risk, Sub. If the Japs see us raising steam they'll think we're going to make a dash for it. Let's hope we can work up enough pressure when the storm breaks.'

'Officer of the Watch to the starboard side!'

The look-out's shout brought the discussion to an abrupt end as the two officers hurried to the starboard side of the bridge to investigate. Forsyth peered down at the water. There certainly *was* something happening. The surface of the sea was heaving violently and streams of air bubbles were rising up from the depths like an evil brew simmering in a witch's cauldron.

'Cor!' breathed the look-out. 'Looks like a bloody under-water volcano - I've 'eard about them sort of things in these parts.'

The sub-lieutenant's explanation of the unexpected phenomena was more prosaic, but no less dramatic in its implication.

'Good God, sir! It's a submarine!'

Forsyth hesitated indecisively as the top of the conning tower thrust out of the swirling water. What the hell were the Japs up to now? He wondered whether *Firefly*'s bosun would know the pipe for 'Stand by to repel boarders' and decided it was highly unlikely.

'Action Stations! Submarine on starboard beam!'

It was the only order he could think of in the circumstances. But even as he gave it, he knew that the submarine was too close for the guns to bear. The rush of water fell back to a frothing tumult from which emerged the glistening steel plating of *Rapier*'s conning tower. Viewed from such close quarters, it was almost impossible to identify and it bore little resemblance to the neat silhouettes issued for recognition purposes.

'It's okay, sir, she's one of ours.'

Forsyth did not know how Peters could be so certain, but he was willing to accept his judgement. And, as he ordered *Firefly*'s crew to fall out from Action Stations, he saw the upper hatch of the submarine swing back and an officer emerge onto the bridge...

Hamilton seemed unaware of the furor he was causing aboard the gunboat. At that moment he was too busy with his own problems. And as the yeoman and look-outs scrambled out onto the bridge he moved to the voice pipe. 'Start motors and send up the deck party.'

Petty Officer Blake led the sea-duty men up through the gun hatch and Hamilton ordered them on to the foredeck, with instructions to secure a line from the submarine's bows to the stern of the *Firefly*. There was a moment of confusion aboard the gunboat, but Forsyth quickly appreciated what was wanted and sent a party to the stem to grab the line and secure it around a bollard.

'Ease the line when I tell you,' Hamilton shouted across. 'I want to swing my stern ninety degrees so that I'm lying abaft your rear.'

'Understood, *Rapier*. Go ahead when you're ready.'

Hamilton moved to the voice pipe again. 'Half-ahead starboard. Full right rudder.' The submarine quivered as the motors increased speed, and a confused tumble of white water erupted from the fantail as the starboard propeller churned the sea to foam. The stern of the submarine began to swing outwards. 'Slacken off bow lines - port motor half-astern.' The swinging action increased as the counter movement of the port propeller tightened the angle of the turn. *Rapier's* bows drifted slowly away from the stem of the gunboat and Hamilton watched the maneuvers anxiously. 'Hold hard on the lines, *Firefly*. Keep them taut.' He leaned over the voice pipe. 'Stop port motor. Stop starboard. Half-ahead starboard... stop!' *Rapier* was now standing at right angles to the gunboat, with her bows just clear of *Firefly's* stern and her torpedo tubes pointing directly at the Japanese destroyer.

'Secure bow lines! Lay off a stern anchor to stop us swinging in the current, Chief. But use a hemp hawser and have a man standing by it with an axe in case we need to cut ourselves free in a hurry.' He returned to the voice pipe. 'Report to the bridge, Number One. And tell the gun crew to come topsides.'

Walking to the side of the conning tower nearest to the gunboat, Hamilton surveyed the mooring position with the expert eye of a seaman. Bearing in mind the difficulties, they hadn't done too badly. Then raising his glasses he examined the destroyer. There was some movement on her bridge but, as yet, the Japanese showed no signs of responding to *Rapier's* sudden appearance. He wondered how the destroyer commander would react when he realized his ship was lying broadside on to the submarine's torpedo tubes.

'Nicely executed, sir,' Forsyth called down from *Fire-fly's* bridge. 'Do you need any more help?'

'Yes - I don't like getting my feet wet. Drop a rope ladder over the stern so that I can come aboard.' Hamilton glanced round as Mannon joined him on top of the conning tower. 'I'm going over to *Firefly*, Number One. You'll be in charge while I'm away. As things stand at the moment, the next stage will be a visit to the Japanese commander to see if I can persuade him to release Otter-shaw.' He paused for a second. 'If anything goes wrong you have my authority to torpedo the enemy immediately he opens fire. But make bloody sure he fires the first shot. Is that understood?'

'Yes, sir,' Mannon hesitated. 'But supposing you're still on board?'

'Then it's too bad for me,' Hamilton told him flatly. 'My primary task is to protect *Rapier* and secure the release of *Firefly*. If it means putting two lives at risk, so be it. Any questions?'

Mannon knew what the skipper meant. He was beginning to understand the awesome responsibilities of command. He nodded. 'Understood, sir. If the destroyer opens fire I am to torpedo her and then escort *Firefly* clear.'

Hamilton grinned suddenly. 'Good man. But don't look so worried - it won't come to that. It's just that I like to cover all eventualities.' Swinging his leg over the conning tower rail, he started climbing down the rungs to the deck. Morgan, the gunner's mate, was standing in the bows holding the rope ladder and he grinned expectantly as the skipper came down the fore casing.

'Will you be needing some help, sir?' he asked hopefully.

Hamilton shook his head. 'Sorry, Chief. I think I'd best

play this one solo. But keep your chaps standing by... you never know your luck.'

He grabbed the precariously swaying rope ladder and quickly hauled himself up on to the stern of the gunboat, where Forsyth was waiting to receive him.

'Welcome aboard, sir.'

'We've no time for that sort of thing, Lieutenant,' Hamilton snapped impatiently. 'Give me a rundown on the situation since you arrived.'

Forsyth felt slightly abashed by the submarine commander's brusqueness. He noticed that Hamilton was only a two-striper like himself and wondered which of them was the senior. It was a pity he hadn't checked the Navy List beforehand. The clipped authority of the demand, however, seemed to assume his subordination and, almost without thinking, he accepted his junior status.

'The Japanese escorted us into the bay at dawn,' he explained briefly. 'They sent a boat at 0900 hours and Lieutenant Commander Ottershaw was invited back to the destroyer for discussions. I've tried signaling for information, but they just ignore everything we send.'

'Did Ottershaw leave any instructions?'

'He left *me* in command.' Forsyth saw that Hamilton appeared unimpressed by the information. 'He gave no precise instructions... just said he didn't expect to be long.'

'Why the hell didn't you make a break for it?' Hamilton asked curtly.

'I couldn't leave the Captain in the hands of the Japanese.'

'Why not? Good God man we're not at war with them, you know. They've got to release him eventually. If you'd made a run for it, at least it would have shown those squint-eyed bastards what we think of them.' Hamilton paused to regain his temper. 'Are you sure they haven't taken him ashore?'

'Definitely not, sir,' Peters broke in. The sub-lieutenant didn't like the way Hamilton was treating *Firefly's* executive officer but, instinctively, he sensed a firm decisiveness in the submariner's attitude which sharply contrasted with Forsyth's docile acceptance of the situation. Hamilton was clearly a man who did not believe in dancing to other people's tunes. 'The Japanese only occupy the coast around the major parts,' he explained. 'The rest of the shoreline is still in the hands of the Chinese. If the Japs tried to land, the local guerillas would wipe them out inside an hour.'

Hamilton turned his attention to the young RNVR officer. 'Are they likely to give us a hand if we need it?'

'I doubt it, sir. This part of the coast is controlled by Tien Shan - the local warlord. He might help if he was offered enough money, but it's unwise to trust a Chinaman.'

'But I thought we were on the same side,' Hamilton objected.

'In theory, perhaps,' Peters agreed. 'But you're thinking in terms of the Nationalist Government in Chungking. The trouble is that China is hardly a single united country as we understand the word. They're all fighting the Japs right enough, but most of them are busy fighting each other as well. Up in the north there's the Communists under Mao Tse Tung. At the moment he's supposed to be supporting the Government, but once they've settled with the Japanese he won't rest until he has control of the entire country. He and Chiang-kai-Shek are the big boys. But all the way down the line there are minor warlords fighting to maintain their local power, bandits and pirates who are only interested in loot, and the guerillas - usually Communists who have been infiltrated into Nationalist areas.'

'You make it all sound very jolly,' Hamilton smiled. 'Where the hell do *we* fit into this tangle?'

'If you want my honest opinion, sir, we *don't*. No one wants the British in Asia any longer - or the Americans, or the French, or the Dutch. That's why the Japanese are bound to succeed in the long run. And by continually talking about the overthrow of colonialism, they've got a substantial part of the native population behind them. Unfortunately, the poor devils don't realize that Tokyo's brand of imperialism will be even worse than ours.' Peters paused for a moment. He didn't mind giving Hamilton a lecture on the political situation in the Far East, in fact he rather enjoyed it, but there were other much more urgent dangers.

'Whatever you decide to do, sir, I suggest you do it quickly. We're going to be hit by a typhoon within the next two hours.'

An oppressive stillness hung over the mirror-smooth water inside the bay. Nothing stirred and even the shrill chatter of the birds was silent. Hamilton stared up at the molten copper sky and watched the black storm clouds gathering on the horizon.

'The Sub's exaggerating,' Forsyth said easily. 'We're in for a blow - and a nasty one by the look of it. But this isn't the typhoon season.'

'You seem to know a lot about local conditions,' Hamilton pointed out to the young RNVR officer.

'I ought to, sir. I've lived in Hong Kong for the last fifteen years. Whatever Lieutenant Forsyth may say, I'm certain there's a typhoon on the way. And I don't care whether it's the season or not.'

Hamilton stared down at his feet thoughtfully. For some reason the old proverb about an ill-wind kept running through his brain. A typhoon would certainly complicate the situation - yet it might just provide the key he needed to obtain Ottershaw's release.

'Bring your motor sampan alongside,' he told Forsyth. 'Give me a couple of minutes while I go back to *Rapier* and give my instructions. Then I'll take the sampan across to the destroyer and find out what's happening.' He glanced over the side. 'What's the depth of water here?' he asked unexpectedly.

'Ten fathoms according to the echo sounder,' Forsyth told him. 'But it's shifting ground and I doubt if the anchors will hold.'

'Well, that's *your* problem,' Hamilton said unsympathetically. 'But if I were you, I'd try to get her out to sea before the typhoon breaks. She'll be smashed to pieces if you stay inside the bay.'

Forsyth ignored the advice. He objected to Hamilton telling him how to handle his ship. And he resented the way in which the submarine commander was taking over and running the show. He vented his irritation on the chief petty officer, waiting respectfully for orders at the rear of the bridge.

'Well don't just stand there, Bosun! Clear away the sampan and bring it alongside. Lieutenant Hamilton will tell you what he wants you to do when he returns. I'll be in my cabin if I'm wanted.'

No one's likely to want *you*, mate, Phillips grumbled to himself as he saluted and made his way for'ard. There was little love lost between them and he had derived considerable satisfaction from the way Hamilton had trampled over the gunboat's executive officer. And serve the bugger right.

'Sampan alongside port quarter, sir,' *Firefly's* bosun

reported smartly as Hamilton came back on board. 'Ready when you are.'

'Thank you, Chief.' He turned to Forsyth who had emerged from his cabin to supervise the sampan's departure. 'Have you sent a signal to say I'm coming?'

'No.'

'Good - let's keep the buggers guessing. I don't see why they should have a monopoly on initiative.' He stepped down into the motor sampan. 'There's no need for you chaps to hang around once you've dropped me off,' he told the bosun. 'The Japs will be far more impressed if I go aboard and send you back. They have an odd way of looking at things. If they think I've deliberately got rid of my only means of escape they'll be much more likely to listen to what I have to say.'

'And how to you intend to get back?' Forsyth asked tartly. 'I suppose you're also an expert at walking on water!'

'There'll be no need for miracles,' Hamilton said easily. 'I'll arrange for the Jap skipper to bring Ottershaw and myself off in one of the destroyer's own boats. I'm a great believer in kicking a man when he's down.'

Forsyth hated Hamilton for his supreme self-confidence. He could not help wondering what made the submarine commander so certain he could succeed in obtaining Ottershaw's release.

He would have been surprised to discover that Hamilton was asking himself exactly the same question as he settled into the sternsheets of the sampan. In point of fact, *Rapier's* skipper hadn't the remotest idea what he was going to do when he arrived on board the destroyer. But he did not believe in worrying about things until they happened.

Having been commissioned from the lower deck, he had

never set foot inside the sacred portals of the Royal Naval College at Dartmouth but he had often heard of the motto painted up over one of the doors: *'There is nothing the Navy cannot do.'* Well, he decided, let's put the boast to the test and see if it works....

FIVE

'Welcome aboard, Lieutenant Hamilton.'

Rapier's captain looked up sharply as he recognized the voice and was surprised to see Aritsu leaning over the rails of the upper deck waiting to receive him. He might have guessed the dapper Little Commander was mixed up in the affair - he seemed to make a specialty of finding new ways to humiliate the Royal Navy. Perhaps that was the only way to obtain promotion in the Japanese Fleet. *Firefly's* motor sampan nudged her bows gently against the lower platform of the gangway, and the lieutenant jumped across the narrow strip of water separating the two vessels with the confident aplomb of long experience.

'Return to *Firefly*, Chief.' He pitched his voice so that it was loud enough for Aritsu to hear the instructions. 'I'll call you up when I'm ready to be taken off.'

The sampan went astern, swung its nose to starboard, and circled away from the destroyer. Hamilton watched it run clear and then started up the accommodation ladder to the deck. He saluted the Rising Sun ensign dangling lifelessly from its jack staff with punctilious regard to etiquette, as he came over the side and turned to Aritsu.

'Lieutenant Hamilton, Commanding Officer of His Majesty's submarine *Rapier.*' He saluted again. 'May I present my compliments to the Captain.'

Not to be outdone in the politeness of the occasion, Aritsu bowed and made a strange clicking sound with his mouth. 'It is an honor to have you aboard, Lieutenant Hamilton,' he acknowledged affably. 'May I offer you a drink in the wardroom?'

'Thank you, Commander. But I wish to see Lieutenant Commander Ottershaw first. After that I am sure we will both be pleased to enjoy your hospitality.'

Aritsu bowed. 'Lieutenant Commander Ottershaw is already waiting for you in the wardroom.' He smiled with satisfaction at scoring the first point. 'You seem to be under an unfortunate misapprehension. He is not a prisoner. Like yourself, he is an honored and welcome guest.'

Hamilton wasn't too sure how to take the commander's statement. There was an underlying sharpness in the words that suggested that *he* was also now a prisoner, and he began to rue his bravado in sending *Firefly's* sampan back to the gunboat. Swallowing his doubts, however, he smiled appreciatively and followed the Japanese officer down the narrow steel corridor to *Suma's* tiny wardroom. The armed sentry guarding the entrance gave the lie to Aritsu's assurance, but Hamilton ignored his presence and passed straight through the door without invitation.

'Good God, Nick! Where the hell did you spring from?' Harry Ottershaw certainly looked comfortable enough. The furnishings of the wardroom were sparse and austere, but he was ensconced in the only armchair with a large glass of Scotch standing on the table at his elbow.

'You must forgive me for being an inattentive host, gentlemen,' Aritsu smiled politely. 'But if you will excuse me, I must have a few words with the Officer-of-the-Watch. I will rejoin you in a few moments. In the meantime, Lieutenant, please help yourself to what you want.'

The door closed and Hamilton restrained an impulse to check the handle to see if they had been locked inside. He knew he must maintain his outward show of self-confidence and it would be fatal to give any hint of nervousness. Moving to the sideboard he picked up a likely looking bottle and poured himself a large glass of malt whisky.

'I managed to sneak *Rapier* into the bay without being spotted,' he explained to the gunboat captain. He glanced through the open scuttle and beckoned Ottershaw over.

Firefly was lying broad-side on the destroyer, just over a mile away on the western side of the bay and the bows of the submarine were just visible abaft her stern. Ottershaw nodded.

'Very neat,' he conceded. 'But I don't see what good it's going to do. You can't torpedo a Japanese destroyer in broad daylight and get away with it.'

Hamilton shrugged. 'Let's hope it won't come to that. But I most certainly intend to if the worse comes to the worse. *And* Aritsu knows I will.'

'You're forgetting one thing,' Ottershaw retorted sharply. 'I happen to be the Senior Naval Officer present. You therefore take your orders from me. And *I* have no intention of allowing you to cause a major diplomatic incident merely for the sake of maintaining appearances. We'll sort this matter out by negotiation. And if that fails we'll have to rely on the authorities in Hong Kong getting us off the hook.'

Hamilton said nothing. Ottershaw might be SNO but if

Rapier fired her torpedoes neither of them were likely to survive the resulting explosion. In which case seniority wouldn't matter a damn!

Ottershaw closed the glass scuttle and returned to his armchair. 'We've got to play for time. It looks as though there's a nasty storm brewing and Aritsu's bloody twitchy. Don't ask me why, but that's how it seems to me. In my opinion he'll bluff it out as long as he dares, but I'm certain he intends to up-anchor and steam clear of the bay before the storm hits us.'

The steel door behind Hamilton's back opened and before he could reply Aritsu returned to the wardroom. He looked completely at ease and was smiling to himself as if enjoying a secret joke.

'I meant to congratulate you on the way you handled the submarine, Lieutenant,' he said ingratiatingly. 'My lookouts had no idea you had passed under the boom until you surfaced behind the gunboat. They will be suitably punished, of course, for their inefficiency.'

'I hope they were not too inefficient to note the position in which *Rapier* has been moored,' Hamilton stressed pointedly.

Aritsu looked at him impassively. He was quite willing to acknowledge the lieutenant's skill in seamanship, but he was not prepared to accept that he had been outsmarted.

'A little unfriendly, I thought, Lieutenant. After all *Suma* has her guns trained fore and aft and is in no way menacing the gunboat.' He spread his hands. *Firefly* is free to leave whenever she wishes.'

'Without her Captain?'

'I see no reason why not, Lieutenant. He is, as you can see for yourself, an honored guest. He will come to no harm.' Aritsu smiled expansively to reveal his over-large teeth. 'We were in fact, just considering the terms of a suit-able apology when you arrived. The matter would have been concluded within a few more minutes.'

'Is this correct, sir?' Hamilton asked Ottershaw.

'Well, more or less, I suppose,' *Firefly's* captain agreed. 'Of course I don't accept that an apology is called for, but if Commander Aritsu insists and provided Hong Kong agrees, it would seem the simplest solution.'

'You will be pleased to know that Hong Kong has already authorized an apology,' Aritsu said smoothly. He took the folded signal clip from his pocket and handed it to Ottershaw. 'The signal was apparently received about fifteen minutes ago - my wireless operator passed it to me when I went up to the bridge.' He smiled. 'So there now seems no impediment to clearing the matter up.'

Hamilton who had been listening to the exchange, walked back to the scuttle, pulled it open, and sniffed the air.

'Except for the typhoon,' he said casually.

'What typhoon?' Aritsu asked with unexpected sharpness.

'It's probably nothing worth worrying about,' Hamilton shrugged. 'Our Met officer is always getting his facts mixed up. Everyone knows it's not the season for typhoons.' Aritsu was not so easily put off. He suddenly seemed ill at ease. Walking to the barometer hanging on the bulkhead he tapped it with his finger. The mercury dropped a full inch and Hamilton could see tiny beads of sweat glistening on the Commander's forehead. The expression on his face, however, remained as impassive as ever as he turned away from the glass.

'A bad storm perhaps, Lieutenant,' he agreed. 'But

surely not a typhoon? I have received no weather warnings from Combined Fleet HQ.'

'There was a freak wireless blackout a couple of hours ago,' Hamilton told him with seeming innocence. 'An electrical storm or something. My radio operator picked up a Japanese Navy transmission, but it was practically unreadable. Perhaps that is why you have heard nothing.' Aritsu strode to the opened scuttle and stared out at the glowering mauve-grey sky. He made no comment, but Hamilton could see him gnawing at the knuckle of his right hand with his splayed front teeth. So Ottershaw had been right. It was a situation that might prove to be worth exploiting and he decided to play on his fears.

'I've never been caught in a typhoon myself,' he continued conversationally. 'But I hear they can be damned frightening. Didn't your people lose a destroyer in one a few years ago, Commander?'

Aritsu was too busy with his own private problems to pay much attention to the question and he nodded absently. 'That is correct, Lieutenant. The *Tomodzuru* capsized off Sasebo in a typhoon during exercises in 1934. I was serving in the same flotilla when it happened.'

'Must have been an unpleasant experience,' Hamilton said sympathetically. 'Isn't this boat - *Suma* - one of the *Tomodzuru* class?'

Aritsu was slowly pacing up and down the wardroom. He nodded curtly but ignored the question and Ottershaw wondered what *Rapier's* skipper was leading up to. He was more than a little surprised at the depth of technical knowledge shown by Hamilton's next remark. Nick had obviously been doing his homework.

'That's odd then,' Hamilton continued. 'I thought they'd cut down top-weight and added bilges to increase stability. I don't recall seeing any additional bilges on *Suma*. And, if you'll forgive me for saying so, she looked bloody top-heavy when I came alongside in the sampan.'

Aritsu stopped pacing and turned to face the two British officers. 'You are very observant, Lieutenant. And, unfortunately you are quite correct. They modified *Chidori* and the other ships of the class, but for some reason, *Suma* was never taken in hand. Believe me, gentlemen, this boat is a death trap in bad weather. We have less than a two to one chance of surviving a-typhoon on the open sea. If we are trapped inside this bay we might just as well commit suicide here and now.'

Ottershaw suddenly grabbed the drift of Hamilton's carefully guided conversation and, taking his cue, he stood up. 'In that case, Commander, perhaps we should not detain you any further. You will obviously wish to get to sea as soon as possible.'

Aritsu gestured in agreement. 'Of course, Lieutenant Commander. I will have my motorboat take you and the Lieutenant back to your ships. As professional sailors, we are all aware that our greatest enemy is the sea itself. I am sure you will be equally anxious to get back to your own ships before the typhoon strikes. I suggest we tell our respective governments that the whole incident was due to a misunderstanding and that no apologies are called for.' Ottershaw picked up his cap from the table and started towards the door, but Hamilton reached out his hand and stopped him.

'Hold hard, Harry,' he whispered, 'we've got the bastard on the run. Let's rub his bloody face in it while we've got the chance.' He turned to Aritsu before the gunboat captain could object. 'It's too late to get out of the bay, now, Commander.' The cutting edge of authority in Hamilton's voice caused the Japanese officer to look up sharply. 'I reckon the typhoon will hit us inside the next thirty minutes - and that won't even give you time to flash up your second boiler. I suppose you could lay out extra anchors, but if you can't hold your bows into the wind I don't give much for your chances.'

Aritsu nodded with stoic resignation. 'I have no doubt you are right,' he agreed quietly. 'I would like to have a few minutes alone while I consider what to do. In the circumstances, gentlemen, I must ask you to return to your ships without delay.'

Hamilton could feel the deck of the destroyer moving beneath his feet as the sea took on the long swell that normally preceded the approach of a typhoon. Ottershaw fidgeted impatiently at the delay. What the hell was the fool playing at? Aritsu undoubtedly had problems, but *Firefly's* predicament was no less worrying. And even Hamilton would have more than his fair share of trouble when he tried to steer the submarine out of the storm- lashed bay. And yet, for some unaccountable reason, *Rapier's* skipper seemed in no great hurry.

The three men made their way along the narrow steel corridor leading out to the well deck just abaft the bridge companionway. *Suma's* officer-of-the-watch greeted the Commander with a copybook salute and acknowledged Aritsu's clipped instructions before scurrying away to carry them out. Taking advantage of the hiatus, Hamilton walked to the rails and surveyed the worsening weather conditions.

The sea was already rising and small white wave crests scattered the bay as the wind grew in strength and intensity. The entrance of the bay, flanked by tree-clad cliffs, seemed sealed by an impenetrable black curtain as the front moved towards the coast.

'What's your maximum speed with one boiler?' he asked Aritsu.

'Fifteen knots if we're lucky.'

Hamilton did not answer immediately. He stared at the ominously dark storm clouds gathering over the sea beyond the entrance to the bay. 'I suppose that's not much if you've got to fight your way out in the teeth of an eighty knots gale,' he commented. He turned away from the rail and glanced up at *Suma's* single funnel in time to see a billowing mass of black smoke spluttering from the stack, as the engineer switched on the sprays and flashed up the cold Number Two boiler. Then his eyes moved down to the heavy bridge hamper and he shook his head sadly.

'The Commander's right, Harry,' he said loudly enough for Aritsu to hear. 'The sooner we get off this floating bloody coffin the better. She'll be over in a couple of seconds if she breaches and the wind catches her.'

'I couldn't agree more,' Ottershaw said fervently. 'I don't know why you're hanging about.' He made his way across to where *Suma's* motorboat was waiting to take them off. Hamilton's gloomy comments were beginning to send cold shivers down his spine. And what they were going to do to Aritsu was anyone's guess!

But Hamilton continued to survey the situation with all the leisure of a man intent on solving an abstract technical problem from the quiet depth of a comfortable armchair. 'Of course,' he observed to Aritsu, 'it's unfortunate you chose to anchor with your stern facing the entrance. It means you'll have to swing completely round to get your bows to the wind. We do things differently in the Royal Navy. We always make sure we're pointing in the right direction to begin with.' He nodded towards *Firefly* and *Rapier* and swallowing his pride, the Japanese was forced to concede his point. Hamilton's cruelly objective analysis of the situation only served to increase his own unease over the impossibility of his position.

Even assuming he could perform the herculean task of turning the destroyer through a complete half circle of one hundred and eighty degrees without breaching, Aritsu was doubtful whether *Suma*'s engine would produce enough power to make headway against the ferocious strength of the hurricane-force winds.

'Not much use laying out extra anchors either,' Hamilton continued as if he could read Aritsu's mind. 'Bad holding ground - shifting sands according to our charts. You'll be hurled back onto the reefs.'

'Are you quite...' Ottershaw began, but Hamilton cut him off brusquely in mid-sentence.

'If you're willing to take part in a spot of unorthodox seamanship, however. I reckon I *might* be able to help,' he told *Suma*'s skipper with a sudden and totally unexpected smile.

'I am quite prepared to consider anything you suggest, Lieutenant.' Aritsu successfully hid the eagerness in his voice, but Hamilton knew the reaction was that of a drowning man clutching at a straw. And, in the circumstances, it was an apt analogy. He rubbed his chin thoughtfully as if considering his plan.

'I reckon we could use *Rapier* as a sort of sea anchor. If we pass a couple of six-inch hawsers around the conning tower and I submerge to say, thirty feet, I could drag your bows around in half the time it would take you using your engines and rudder. Then, having got you pointing into the wind, *Rapier* could act as an anchor. What's your weight?'

'535 tons standard - probably less at the moment as our bunkers are half-empty.'

'Excellent! *Rapier* displaces just under a thousand tons in diving trim. If I poke my motors up to full power, I reckon I could just about hold you until the typhoon blows itself out.'

'It'll never work,' Ottershaw interjected before Aritsu could answer. He had learned his seamanship at Dartmouth and he did not believe in unorthodox solutions. Hamilton's ideas were all very well in theory, but practice would be another matter. It was just the sort of foolhardy scheme he would have expected from this crazy submariner.

'Perhaps it won't,' Aritsu agreed. 'But it's worth trying. And I can see no alternative.'

Hamilton grinned, patted the Commander on the shoulder reassuringly, and swung himself over the rail. Ottershaw followed and moments later they were huddled in the sternsheets of the open motorboat, as it throttled to full power and eased away from the destroyer's beam.

The epicenter of the storm was still some thirty minutes away, but the waters of the bay were already being whipped to a frenzy of flying spray by the rising wind. The two British officers were quickly soaked to the skin as the coxswain of the motorboat swung the bows towards the distant *Rapier*. Once out of the protective lee of the *Suma,* the mounting strength of the sea swept the cockleshell boat to starboard and it pitched violently as Shinikani fought the controls to maintain course.

'You must be bloody mad, Nick,' Ottershaw grumbled as a wave broke against the side of the boat and threw several gallons of unpleasantly cold water into his lap. 'After all the things you've said about the Japanese, I'm surprised you're prepared to help them. If I had my way they could bloody well drown.'

Hamilton ducked as another wave struck the motor boat

squarely on the beam and kicked it to port. He wiped the water from his face and grinned. 'You've got to admit one thing, Harry. I succeeded in getting you away from Aritsu. *And* saved you from making that apology.'

'We'd have got away in any case,' Ottershaw objected. He clung to the gunwales as the motor boat pitched and yawed. It was worse than riding on a giant roller-coaster, and, for once in his life, he felt the insidious pangs of seasickness. Exposed to the full blast of the gale now roaring through the entrance to the bay, the motorboat wallowed unsteadily and then dug its bows into the foam- flecked seas. The well-deck was several inches deep in water, and Heichiro started operating the manual bailer as the mechanical pumps failed to cope with the inrush. 'If you'd have left when Aritsu first suggested it we might have had a more comfortable ride home. But *no* - you have to hang around until the weather conditions made things virtually impossible.' He paused for a moment. 'And why the hell did you say this was bad holding ground?'

Shinikani spun the wheel sharply to avoid being pooped by a towering wall of water coming up from astern, threw the motorboat into the trough that followed and then allowed it to climb the next wave. There was a loud crash and a shuddering jolt as the little boat fell into the trough beyond but, apparently undeterred by the punishment he was inflicting on the vessel, the Japanese coxswain kept the throttles wide open and continued steering towards the submarine.

'I'm quite friendly with a Portuguese merchant in Macao,' Hamilton explained as the boat corkscrewed from wave top to wave top. 'He's taught me a lot of things about the East that I didn't know before. The worst thing that can happen to an Oriental is to lose "face", and that's precisely what I'm planning for our friend Aritsu. I had to hold on to the last moment in order to convince him that nothing could save his ship. And by then he was so shit- scared he never thought of checking the facts on his own charts. As it is, I reckon we *can* save him. And, if I do, the Japanese Navy is going to lose "face" to us in a big way-enough, probably, to make up for all those damned apologies we've been forced to make recently.'

By some unexplained miracle, Shinikani brought the motorboat alongside *Rapier* without mishap although, for one horrifying moment, Hamilton thought the wind would sweep them hard against the submarine's sharp steel bows. But, with a deft touch of the helm, the Japanese coxswain swung the motorboat under the sheltering lee of the hull. The deck party quickly threw a line to Heichiro, who grabbed it and wound it tightly around the fo'c'sle mooring cleat. Hamilton and Ottershaw struggled up the sloping, wave-swept ballast tank like mountaineers scaling the Matterhorn in a blizzard. The smooth steel plating offered no footholds and their leather shoes slipped and slithered on the weed covered surface. Morgan and one of the deckhands came to the rescue and moments later both officers had been hauled up to the foredeck.

Having delivered his passengers, Shinikani ordered Heichiro to let go of the rope, opened the throttle and circled away from the submarine. The strength of the wind had rapidly increased in the past few minutes and spray spuming from the tumultuous waves cut visibility to little more than a hundred yards. If the motorboat was not equipped with a compass, Hamilton did not give much for its chances of completing its return trip. He turned away. There was no time to worry about Shinikani and his companion - they were expendable. He was after bigger fish!

'You've no chance of getting back to *Firefly*,' he shouted to Ottershaw. 'Best if you stay aboard *Rapier* until the typhoon's blown itself out.'

Hamilton was clearly in no mood to be trifled with and, despite his senior rank, the gunboat's skipper acquiesced without argument.

'Morgan! Cut the anchor cable! Jackson! Go for'ard and release the bow lines. Then all of you get below at the double!' Hamilton cupped his hands as he shouted up to Mannon on the bridge. 'Full ahead both engines, Number One! Steer towards the destroyer.'

Mannon's acknowledgement was lost in the shriek of the wind, but Hamilton felt the deck plating vibrating under his feet as the diesels roared into life. Giving Ottershaw a helping hand to climb the rungs of the conning tower, he checked that Morgan and the deck party were safely below and then followed the lieutenant commander to the bridge.

'There's a small cove on the north-west side of the bay,' he told him as he swung himself over the screen. 'The wind has veered to the south-east and the promontory will act as a wind-shield. If *Firefly* can get to the cove and under the lee of the hills she should be able to ride out the storm fairly comfortably.'

'Sounds OK to me, Nick. The old girl certainly hasn't got enough power to head into the wind and reach open sea. Can you pass a signal to my Number One?'

Hamilton nodded and called the yeoman of signals over, dictated a brief message and, a few seconds later, the submarine's Aldis lamp was flashing instructions to the gunboat.

As *Rapier* came out from under the lee of *Firefly's* high superstructure the typhoon struck her with savage fury. The sea, lashed by the rising wind, had steepened into ugly, white-crested waves that rolled across the bay like serried ranks of soldier ants, destroying everything that lay in their path. A spume of spray hung like a mist over the angry waves and, peering ahead, Hamilton was relieved to find that Aritsu had switched on *Suma's* riding lights.

A gigantic wave struck the submarine's bows and burst with the roar of an exploding shell. *Rapier's* stem lifted under the initial impact and then fell back with a sickening jolt. The following crest, meeting with no resistance, swept across the foredeck, crashed against the base of the conning tower and threw a solid wall of cold, black water over the men on the bridge.

Hamilton clung to the rails. The salt water stung his eyes and, half-blinded, he reached out his hands to make sure Ottershaw was still there. A third wave tossed the submarine to starboard with contemptuous ease and he suddenly found himself sliding helplessly across the flooded deck, until the steel bridge screen brought him to a bruising stop. Something cannoned against him with a force that knocked the breath from his body and, disentangling himself, he found Ottershaw sprawled like a drowned rat at his side. Hauling himself upwards, he leaned forward and helped the gunboat skipper to his feet.

Hamilton wiped the water from his eyes and searched into the darkness ahead for the destroyer. *Rapier's* bows lifted to meet another breaker and, as the deck tilted at a crazy angle, a large black object slid towards the rear of the bridge with the ungainly grace of an elephant seal slithering over the rocks towards the sea.

'It's the Yeoman, Harry!' he shouted to Ottershaw. 'Grab hold of him. I'll give you a hand as soon as I can.'

Rapier executed a weird war dance, as the combined ferocity of the wind and waves hurled her from side to side like a pea in a rattle. Even the thrusting power of her Admiralty Standard Range diesel engines seemed pitifully inadequate when matched against the terrifying strength of the typhoon. She wallowed drunkenly, pushed her bows upwards with sluggish reluctance and then wearily buried her nose beneath the surface like an exhausted and drowning swimmer. Hamilton peered through the murk and managed to pick out the green navigation light from *Suma*'s bridge. Grasping the rail with one hand, he flipped open the watertight cover of the control room voice pipe.

'Steer one point to port!'

'One point to port, sir,' Mannon acknowledged. 'How are we doing?'

'Fine,' Hamilton told him laconically, as another cascade of freezing water swept over the bridge. 'How are things below?'

'Mustn't grumble, sir. At least we're not getting wet.'

Hamilton knew that the first officer was lying. Submarines were not designed to ride on the surface in severe storms and he knew only too well what conditions would be like below deck. The interior of a submarine was no place for a queasy stomach, with the hatches secured and the cramped atmosphere reeking of diesel oil, human sweat and stale vegetables. And, in bad weather, the sour smell of vomit added a new dimension of horror to the already revolting stench.

Hamilton's hands were bleeding, his face was raw from salt burns and he was drenched to the skin. But the hardships that he was enduring on the exposed bridge was nothing when compared to the misery of the men cooped up in the *Rapier's* iron hull. They were the real heroes of the submarine service.

'Can you lend a hand, Nick?' Ottershaw yelled from the other end of the bridge.

Fighting against the motion of the boat, Hamilton half slid, half-stumbled, across the flooded deck and knelt down, beside the gunboat skipper. Jack Drury, *Rapier's* signal's yeoman, was barely conscious and blood was trickling from an ugly gash in his forehead, where he had struck the compass binnacle.

'We'll have to get him below,' Ottershaw shouted above the shriek of the wind. 'His leg's broken.'

Hamilton felt Drury jerk with pain as he reached forward to confirm Ottershaw's diagnosis. He glanced up and shook his head.

'He'll have to stay here, Harry,' he said flatly. 'I'm not opening the top hatch until I have to. An agile man could be through the hatchway in ten seconds and we could probably get it open and shut again before the next sea broke over the bridge. But Drury's a dead weight. And he's a big man into the bargain. It would take all of thirty seconds, perhaps even a minute, to get him inside. And I can't afford to take the risk of flooding the Control Room. Try to make the poor sod comfortable and then lash him on to the periscope standard. We don't want him washed overboard.'

Leaving Ottershaw to cope with the injured yeoman, Hamilton groped his way towards the for'ard section of the bridge to check the bearing of the destroyer. *Suma* was now barely two hundred yards away and he could see her anchor chains straining against the mounting pressures of the wind and sea. He moved to the voice pipe.

'Number One - send Morgan up with a deck party. And

tell them to rig life lines. It's sheer bloody murder up here and I don't want any more accidents.' He paused as *Rapier* plunged into a trough and rose clear. 'We'll be passing inside the lee of the destroyer in exactly one minute. When I give the shout, I want Morgan's party topside at the double. Then stand by to receive Drury - his leg's busted and he's unconscious.'

'Understood, sir. Deck party closed up. Ready when you are.'

'Stand by to shut down engines. Stand by motors.'

Hamilton had waited as long as he dared before making the critical transfer of power and he knew that the decision could not be deferred any longer. The primitive gear-box of a submarine did not permit it to go astern on its diesel engines and *Rapier* would have to rely on her electric motors for the delicate maneuvering that lay ahead. It meant a heavy drain on the batteries, but in the circumstances, there was no alternative. The submarine steadied suddenly as she came under *Suma's* lee.

'*Now.*'

Hamilton saw the upper hatch swing open and, a moment later, Morgan's head thrust into view. Grasping the lipped rim of the hatchway, the gunner's mate heaved himself upwards, swung his legs onto the deck, and immediately turned to help the next man through the narrow opening. Within thirty seconds, all four members of the deck party were on the bridge and two of them hurried aft to help Ottershaw lift the unconscious yeoman into the hatchway.

'Stop engines! Clutches out - switches on! Half astern both motors. Stop! Slow ahead together... stop!'

Rapier hung inside the protective lee of *Suma's* starboard beam just long enough for Drury to be carried below.

'Hatch shut, sir!' Morgan shouted.

'Full astern both motors... steady as she goes. Full starboard rudders.' Hamilton reached for the loud hailer and watched the bows swing in a semi-circle to bring the submarine's stern in line with *Suma's* bows. Ottershaw, now freed from the burden of looking after the signaler, came for'ard to join him.

'I must be imagining things, Nick. But I'd swear the wind is moderating - and veering to the south.'

'You're quite right, Harry. That's why I was in such a bloody hurry to get across the bay. Let's hope Aritsu is too damned scared to notice.' He put the microphone of the loud hailer to his mouth and pushed down the thumb switch, 'Ahoy, *Suma I* Do you hear me! Can you get a line to my stern?'

A fo'c'sle party, wearing black oilskins that flopped like gigantic bats in the wind, appeared in the destroyer's bows and Hamilton stared astern through the driving rain and flying spray as he passed steering instructions to the helmsman in the control room below. Aritsu was standing on the starboard wing of the destroyer's bridge with an old fashioned megaphone in his hand. He seemed too intent on the submarine's careful approach to notice the almost imperceptible improvement in the weather conditions.

A line snaked down from *Suma's* bows, struck the fantail of the submarine with a loud clatter, and slid back into the sea before Morgan's men could grab it and haul it aboard.

'Try again, *Suma.'*

This time, the line landed close to the deck party huddled in the stern of the submarine and two of the men seized it and began dragging it back towards the conning tower. Miller and Davidson came to their assistance, while Morgan encouraged them to haul away like a regatta tug- of-war team. The after deck was almost continuously under water as the sea pounded against the ballast tanks and threw white swirling foam over the hull. A heavy six-inch twin towing wire was attached to the line and Morgan's men heaved and swore as they drew it around the front of the conning tower and then began dragging it back towards the small auxiliary capstan above the engine room hatch.

A large wave smashed against the windward beam of the submarine and *Rapier* rolled to starboard. Luckily, the deck party managed to hang on to their life lines as they vanished beneath a roaring wall of ice-cold water. And, as *Rapier* swung back again, they emerged from behind the conning tower and quickly shackled the hawser in position.

'All secure, sir!'

Hamilton pushed the microphone to his mouth. 'Ahoy, *Sumal* Stand by to take the strain. Make five knots when I tell you - and let go your anchors!'

'Aritsu won't be very popular if he loses his anchors,' Ottershaw grinned at Hamilton.

'Probably not- but I daresay he'd rather lose his anchors than his ship.'

Holding the microphone against his chest to shield it from the rain, Hamilton moved to the voice pipe. 'Slow ahead together, Number One.'

'Slow ahead aye aye, sir.'

He watched the towing wire lift slowly out of the water as *Rapier* began to creep forward.

'*Suma*.'

'Standing by, *Rapier*.'

'Make five knots. Let go anchors. Port your helm!' Hamilton waited for the acknowledgements from the destroyer's bridge and then bent over the voice pipe. 'Steer six degrees to port, Number One. Increase to half-speed.'

Ottershaw's mouth went dry as he watched the hawser strain taut. This was the critical moment of the entire exercise. Either the towline would part under the terrible stress to which it was being subjected - or Hamilton's delicate equalization of speed would ease the strain sufficiently to balance the two opposing forces. Once the line was taut and both ships were moving at identical speeds the worst of the danger would have passed.

'I think we're going to make it, Nick.'

Hamilton said nothing. Leaning his arms on the after bridge screen he watched the towing hawser tighten with the concentration of a gambler playing his last chip.

'Well done, *Rapier*.'

Aritsu's voice sounded strangely hollow through the megaphone and it was only just audible above the shriek of the winds. But Hamilton heard it all right and he waved his arm in acknowledgement. The darkness and the driving rain hid the grin on his face.

The violent rolling action of the submarine suddenly eased, as *Rapier's* bows came into wind. He bent over the voice pipe again. 'Midship's helm, Number One.' He pressed the switch of the loudhailer. 'Ahoy, *Sumal* Helm amidships!'

A faint glimmer of light on the south-eastern horizon drew Ottershaw's attention and he pointed it out to *Rapier's* skipper. Hamilton glanced at it and nodded disinterestedly.

'We only just had time for the big rescue act,' he commented enigmatically.

'Odd sort of typhoon,' Ottershaw said doubtfully. 'If anyone asked me, I'd say the epicenter passed over a good ten minutes ago.'

'What typhoon?' Hamilton enquired innocently.

'The one you warned Aritsu about.'

Hamilton turned away from the bridge screen, stared towards the growing patch of blue sky over the bows, and smiled.

'I must have made a mistake, Harry,' he admitted cheerfully. 'Just a rather nasty tropical squall I'd reckon.'

'But you told Aritsu there'd been a weather warning of a typhoon,' Ottershaw persisted. 'He would never have agreed to a tow if he'd known it was only a squall.'

'Don't blame me,' Hamilton said with a shrug. 'It was your damned sub, Peters, who told me it was a typhoon.' He contrived to look innocent. 'I've only just arrived in Hong Kong - how on earth was I supposed to know?'

Ottershaw was not so easily fooled. Although the sea was subsiding, the waves were still breaking angrily, and he could feel *Suma* pitching unpleasantly astern of the submarine.

'You bloody well *knew!*' he said accusingly.

'I didn't when young Peters first told me. But I *was* aware that the typhoon season was over. So when I went back to *Rapier* I put a radio call through to the FMO in Hong Kong to double check.' Hamilton paused and smiled at the memory. 'Hawkins confirmed the approach of a rather deep low, but he was a trifle sarcastic about typhoons in November. Nevertheless, it struck me as a good idea. All I had to do was to sell it to Aritsu. After that it was easy.'

'So it was all a bloody great bluff,' Ottershaw said bluntly.

'I suppose you could say it was,' Hamilton agreed equably. 'But I *had* to persuade Aritsu to let me take *Suma* in tow. It was the only thing I could do to make him lose face - and the fact that he accepted the assistance of a British warship when his own vessel was in no real danger merely makes it all the worse. I don't think Tokyo is going to be very pleased with him after this little affair.' Ottershaw digested the explanation in silence for a few moments. Then he grinned.

'Next time we meet in the club, Nick, just promise me one thing. Promise me you'll never invite me to join you in a poker game.'

SIX

The two capital ships swinging gently at their moorings in the center of the anchorage dominated the dockyard, and dwarfed the slim destroyers grouped astern. They were the largest warships Singapore had seen for more than a decade and their massive presence fulfilled the solemn promise of successive British Governments, that the Royal Navy would throw its protective shield around the Malayan Peninsula if war ever threatened to engulf the Far East.

When the news first reached the city on 2 December, excited crowds had thronged the shore to witness their arrival. Even now, five days later, these great grey symbols of Britain's sea power continued to attract attention.

Captain Gerald Edwards, Deputy Assistant Chief of Staff to Vice Admiral Sir Geoffrey Layton, C-in-C China, stared down at the two ships from the window of his office overlooking the harbor and considered the future. The arrival of Admiral Phillip's Force Z was going to put him out of a job. The admiral had already been appointed to succeed Layton as C-in-C Eastern Fleet and, naturally, he would put his own men into the key staff positions. And in a few day's time Edwards would be returning home. He wondered whether he would have time to see his younger brother, who was serving as a junior gunnery lieutenant on *Repulse,* but decided it was an unlikely possibility. As soon as Phillips returned from his conference with the US Fleet commander in Manilla, it seemed probable that the battle cruiser and her consort, *Prince of Wales,* would sail immediately. Edwards had already seen a copy of Churchill's telegram ordering Phillips to sea to 'disconcert the Japanese and at the same time increase the security of the force' and he knew that the new C-in-C would be anxious to carry out the Prime Minister's command.

It was hardly surprising that Churchill was concerned for the security of Force Z. No doubt Admiral Phillips entertained similar fears. And if he did, who could blame him? Without an aircraft carrier, Force Z was as helpless as a rabbit in a tank of piranha fish - and the end was likely to be equally bloody. Only a politician could be guilty of such gross stupidity. Admittedly the armored carrier *Indomitable* had originally been assigned to Phillips' command. But she had run aground in the West Indies and the admiral's two capital ships had been told to sail east without her. If the politicians had not been running the show there was little doubt in Edwards' mind that the task force would have been recalled until adequate air cover could be provided. But Churchill refused. *Prince of Wales* and *Repulse* were to be the great deterrent to Japan's grandiose plan to seize Malaya and to conquer the whole of SouthEast Asia. There would be no need to fight - their mere presence in the Far East would be sufficient....

A sharp knock on the door broke the captain's train of

thought. Turning away from the window he walked to his desk as the flag lieutenant entered.

'Message from the AOC, sir. Most immediate.'

Edwards took the slip, put on his horn-rimmed glasses and read the brief text of Pulford's signal. He nodded. 'This confirms the intelligence reports we received earlier,' he told Jameson. 'I'd been wondering why Palliser recalled *Repulse* from her Australian trip. Looks as though the balloon's about to go up.'

The flag lieutenant glanced down at the signal to refresh his memory. 'It doesn't follow that the Japs are heading for Malaya, sir,' he pointed out. 'The air reconnaissance reports only confirm two convoys steaming west - they could be making for Siam.'

'They could be - but I very much doubt it,' Edwards paused and looked out of the window at the two great warships in the harbor. He wondered what use such antediluvian monsters would be against Rear Admiral Matsunaga's 22nd Air Flotilla. And he suddenly remembered his brother telling him that *Prince of Wales* had never fired her AA armament in anger since she had been commissioned. He shrugged. They were likely to get plenty of practice shortly.

'Is Layton still C-in-C?' he asked.

'Yes, sir. I understand that Admiral Phillips takes over tomorrow morning when he returns from Manila.'

'Any alterations to the dispositions since yesterday's conference?'

'Nothing immediately affecting Singapore, sir. But the destroyers *Thanet* and *Scout* are to be ordered to leave Hong Kong and return here. And I believe *Rapier* has also been recalled.'

Captain Edwards chuckled. 'I can see the C-in-C's hand in *that* one, Flags. He's an old submariner himself. We've only one submarine operating in the whole of the Far East and he obviously intends to keep an eye on it. Mind you he's probably right. *Rapier* will be a darn sight more use patrolling the Gulf of Siam than she will be defending Hong Kong.'

Captain Snark made no effort to hide his satisfaction when he read Layton's recall signal. Hamilton had been a thorn in his side from the day of his arrival in Hong Kong and, since the incident in Hai-An Bay, their mutual antagonism had been paraded quite openly. Snark was one of the old school - a disciplinarian who believed in complete obedience to orders no matter how unpalatable they might be. Like most officers of his generation he was a born fighter. And the strain of suppressing his natural instincts and being forced to *kow-tow* to the Japanese for the past three years had warped his judgement and soured his brain.

Blessed with very little tact and absolutely no imagination he was unable to understand the subtlety of Hamilton's reasons for saving the Japanese destroyer. Had *Rapier's* skipper been under orders to rescue *Suma,* Snark would have endorsed every action he had taken. But to undertake the salvage of a Japanese warship when he was under no obligation - and when his orders only required him to obtain Ottershaw's release - was, in Snark's eyes, little short of treason.

That his antagonism towards the submarine captain was due to his own subconscious resentment of their two different roles never entered his head. Snark wanted to be in the fight as well - most of his contemporaries were commanding Escort Groups in the North Atlantic - but, instead, he was desk-bound in China and charged with the humiliating task of pacifying the Japanese no matter what the provocation. And yet Hamilton, a man promoted from the lower deck and who lacked the background and training of the traditional officer-class, had been in combat operations since the beginning of the war. And, in Snark's view, it just wasn't fair.

Hamilton knocked on the cabin door, entered, and saluted respectfully. Despite his outward self-confidence he wondered what the hell Snark wanted *this* time. The old fool had never forgiven him for the *Suma* episode. The psychological game of 'face' was a conception beyond the limits of the narrow world in which he lived. He could not grasp that the Royal Navy had secured a normal victory over the Japanese that more than compensated for its recent humiliations.

Snark looked up at *Rapier's* commander but said nothing. Let the bugger sweat, he thought to himself. His finger's toyed with Layton's signal for a few moments and then he put it down on the desk.

'If I remember correctly, Lieutenant,' he said finally, 'you expressed a wish to leave Hong Kong on the very day you arrived.'

'Yes, sir,' Hamilton agreed. 'I believe I did at the time.'

'Do you still want to go?'

'No, sir. I have a feeling something is going to blow up this weekend. I've heard reports of Japanese convoys moving into the gulf of Siam, and Macao is full of rumors. I reckon there's something in the wind and I'd hate to miss it.'

'I'm sorry to disappoint you, Lieutenant.' Snark's tone of voice belied the spoke sentiment. 'The C-in-C has ordered your immediate recall to Singapore.'

Hamilton had no intention of giving Snark the satisfaction of seeing that he was in any way upset by the decision. He nodded and smiled. 'So my guess seems to have been correct, sir. The Admiral obviously thinks the convoys are heading for Malaya and he needs a submarine across the enemy's lines of communication.' He carefully picked on Snark's weak point and twisted the knife. 'It looks as if the war has passed you by again, sir. I'll probably be in action again in a few days while you'll still be....'

Snark beat him to it.... sitting on my arse in a bloody office! 'Well don't be so damned sure about that, Lieutenant. If the Japanese attack Malaya you don't expect them to ignore Hong Kong do you? And when they come I'll show you young whipper-snappers how to fight.' The mere thought of the coming battle was sufficient to bring a flush to his pallid cheeks and, for the first time since they had met, Hamilton actually saw him smile.

Despite their deep-seated antagonism Hamilton felt suddenly sorry for the lonely, passed-over staff officer, even though he was not yet prepared to express his sympathy openly.

'If *Rapier* is being withdrawn and two of the destroyers recalled to Singapore it doesn't look as though they intend to leave you anything to fight *with*, sir.'

Snark snorted. 'That's the trouble with your generation, Lieutenant - always concerned with materials. Well, I shall do *my* bit even if it means sitting in a sampan holding a Lee Enfield!'

Hamilton could not restrain a small smile at the thought of Snark sitting alone in a small boat with a rifle across his knees and defying the entire Japanese Navy to cross the straits. And yet, somehow, he knew it was no idle boast. The old Navy man had been brought up the hard way and it was just the sort of thing Snark *would* do.

'The C-in-C wants you back urgently,' Snark pointed out as he reluctantly dragged himself away from his vision of glory. 'How soon can you leave?'

'Within two hours, sir. *Rapier* has already shipped a full outfit of torpedos and we topped up our bunkers this morning. I've kept her at maximum combat readiness all the time we've been here.'

'You've certainly been taking on enough stores to last two ships for about six months,' Snark observed drily. He held up his hand as Hamilton prepared to launch into his excuses. 'No - don't say anything. It would be improper to lie to your superior officer.' He smiled conspiratorially. 'I'm quite sure you are not engaged in smuggling or similar nefarious activities - we leave that sort of thing to the local police. But I share your view - if Hong Kong falls to the Japanese it would indeed be prudent to have some stores hidden elsewhere for you to fall back on if necessary.'

You crafty old bastard, thought Hamilton. All this time I've been taking you for a fool and yet you *knew* what I was up to. He could not help wondering just how much the captain *did* know.

Snark stood up. He looked at Hamilton with steady eyes. 'Don't worry, Lieutenant. I'd prefer *not* to know your secrets.' He thrust out his hand and Hamilton grasped it firmly. 'Well, good luck. I wonder which of us will get the first Jap?'

Hamilton grinned. 'You'll have to get your skates on, sir. If my arithmetic is correct I'm already leading you five to nothing!'

The roar of the Hurricane fighter, taking off from Kai Tak across the Straits in the New Territories, echoed back from the hills. Hamilton looked up as it skimmed low across the Peak towards Deep Water Bay to begin the first leg of its patrol. As he crossed the road to the waiting staff car he glanced back at *Tamar*. The old hulk, now flying the broad pendant of Commodore Collison, the SNO Hong Kong, had been moored against the stone wall of the dockyard since 1895 - a symbol of the British Empire's steadfast immovability. He wondered how many more days she would remain there to enjoy her fading glory.

'Get back to *Rapier*,' he told Hardacre briefly as the driver thrust his head through the open window. 'Tell Lieutenant Mannon we sail at 1900 hours. I'll be back on board in about an hour - I've got a couple of matters to attend to ashore!'

I bet you have, Hardacre grinned to himself as he acknowledged the instructions. Like that little Chinese popsy. Despite Hamilton's attempts at discretion, most of *Rapier's* crew knew about the ferry trips to Macao. Trust the skipper to find a snug berth. He put the old Austin into gear, let in the clutch, and swung out into the traffic stream. Hamilton watched the seaman drive off in the direction of the dockyard and then started walking towards the Officer's Club.

He was not altogether pleased to encounter Ottershaw in the entrance hall. There were a number of urgent matters to attend to before *Rapier* sailed and he had no time to spare for social chit-chat. However, the gunboat skipper insisted on stopping him as he tried to hurry past.

'I hear you're another of the rats leaving the sinking ship.' Ottershaw's broad grin removed any possibility of offence in his choice of phrase and he clearly regarded it as a good joke.

'Word seems to get around quickly,' Hamilton said shortly, taking care to neither confirm nor deny the rumor.

'You can't be stationed in Hong Kong for eighteen months without learning a few things.' Ottershaw explained. 'Come on into the bar for a farewell snifter.'

Hamilton shook his head. 'Sorry, Harry, but I want to keep a clear head over the next couple of hours. Next time, perhaps.'

'I doubt if there'll be a next time, Nick,' Ottershaw's expression was suddenly serious. 'They're stripping the Colony bare. The only reason they haven't recalled Pears is because his boat's in dry dock at Taiko. Once they've finished cleaning her bottom she'll be on her way to Singapore like the rest. Then all we're left with are five gunboats and the MTB flotilla. It would be laughable if it wasn't so damned serious.'

'I suppose they think it's the Army's responsibility,' Hamilton suggested. 'The Navy can't stop the Japs coming over the border and seizing the New Territories.'

'OK, then, it's an Army job. So why do we only have six battalions of troops available when we all know the Japs have deployed three full divisions along the border?'

'I really couldn't say, Harry. I'm not one of the top brass. Perhaps they intend to send *Repulse* and *Prince of Wales* up in support. Or maybe the US Fleet at Manilla.' He patted Ottershaw on the shoulder. 'Look, old man, it hasn't happened yet. Now that Tom Phillips has taken over he's bound to start reorganizing things the way he wants them- that's what has triggered off the rumors.' Hamilton did not mention that his own recall orders had come from Layton and not Phillips. He did not believe in giving gratuitous information to anyone- not even a fellow officer. 'So stop worrying about it. And now I'm sorry to rush away, Harry, but I must make some phone calls before I go-'

The telephone booth at the end of the corridor was

empty and, picking up the instrument, Hamilton asked the operator for a Macao number. He waited impatiently for the connection. A girl answered.

'Put me through to Senor Alburra, please.'

'Sorry, sir, Mister Alburra not here. You speak Miss Chen?'

Hamilton swore to himself. Alburra would have understood the meaning behind his cryptic call and asked no questions. But Chen had a more personal - one could say intimate - interest in him. Evasive answers would only make her suspicious. He waited for her to come on the line.

'Hello, darling. This is Nick. I'm afraid there's a bit of a flap on. I can't say too much on the phone. Will you tell your father that although he may have heard about me leaving Hong Kong for a while I want our arrangements to stand.'

'Are you going away, Nicky?'

'Perhaps - I don't know. I have to do as I'm told. But I promise I'll be back. So don't go worrying your head about it. Now, can you remember the message for your father- it's extremely important.'

'I will tell him this evening. My father and I have no secrets. I know all about your arrangements with him.' She paused for a moment. 'But if you do not want the plans altered you will not be far away?'

'It all depends on what happens,' Hamilton told her enigmatically. 'But I promise to get in touch as soon as I can. 'Bye for now, darling.'

He replaced the receiver before Chai Chen could reply. It was an unfortunate complication. Hamilton preferred to keep his women entirely separate from service affairs. But, if Alburra had chosen to tell his daughter, there was nothing he could do about it. He could only pray that she would know when to keep her mouth shut.

'Hands are at Harbor Stations, sir,' Mannon reported as Hamilton joined him on the bridge. 'Motors ready and grouped down.'

The first lights were already beginning to twinkle from the windows of the hotels nestling under the shadow of Victoria Peak and Hamilton could see the sailors on board the other warships anchored in the harbor assembling on deck for the time-honored ceremony of hauling down the colors at sunset. On the opposite side of the Straits, the reflections from the lights of Kowloon shimmered on the water like glittering diamonds scattered on a black velvet cloak. He paused to watch a train steaming slowly northwards towards Shatin and the mainland border. He glanced at his watch. It was exactly 7 p.m. He leaned over the voice pipe.

'Obey telegraphs.' He waited for the acknowledgement and then nodded his head to Mannon. 'Let go the springs, Number One.'

'Let go for'ard! Let go after spring!'

Hamilton heard the wires being hauled inboard by the sea duty men. 'Let go after-breast - let go for'ard!'

Mannon peered over the side of the conning tower. 'All gone aft, sir. All gone for'ard.'

'Half astern port. Helm starboard thirty.' The telegraph repeater bell tinkled in the motor room and Hamilton waited as *Rapier* backed cautiously away from the weed-encrusted stonework of the dockyard jetty. 'Stop port! Half ahead starboard. Port thirty, Cox'n. Half astern port.'

A yellow froth boiled from under the submarine's stern, as the propellers disturbed the mud on the harbor bottom and *Rapier* swung in a tight half-circle. Hamilton kept his eyes firmly fixed on the two beacons marking the dockyard's narrow exit.

'Stop port - stop starboard! Half ahead both. Midships helm. Steady as she goes, Mister Blood.'

The darkened submarine glided past *Scout* and *Thanet* at their mooring buoys, but the men on board the destroyers were too busy preparing for their own departure to take notice of *Rapier*. Leaning his elbows on the coaming, Hamilton carefully noted every detail of the familiar Hong Kong scene as the submarine swept out to sea: *Circala* tied up against the north wall of the dockyard, the diminutive *Robin* guarding the boom across the Tathong Channel at the eastern end of the harbor and, in the distance, silhouetted against the looming shadow of Victoria Island, the gunboat *Moth* marooned high and dry on blocks in the graving dock. He remained where he was, staring at the assembled warships, until they were safely in mid-channel and then moved back to the voice pipe.

'Stop both motors. Stand by to start engines.'

'Switches off! Engaged port and starboard clutches!' Black oil smoke blasted from the exhaust trunks abaft the conning tower, as the diesel engines rumbled to life.

'Both clutches engaged, sir. Engines ready and standing by.'

'Half-ahead together. Course two-six-zero, Cox'n.' Hamilton stepped back from the voice pipe and glanced quickly around the horizon to check for other shipping. He turned to Mannon. 'You can fall the men out from Harbor Stations, Number One.'

'Fall out Harbor Stations! Control Room - stand by to take over lower steering. Duty Watch to passage routine.' Hamilton leaned against the periscope standard and lit a cigarette as he watched the fo'c'sle party make their way below through the gun hatch. 'I'll finish the first Dog Watch, Number One,' he told Mannon. 'You take the second and I'll give Alistair the middle. I'll work out a proper routine in the meantime.' He threw the cigarette over the side. 'Once we're clear of Lantau Island I intend to hold south on the surface at ten knots. That should bring us about halfway to Helen Shoals by dawn.'

'Are we making for Charlotte Island, sir?'

Hamilton shook his head. 'I wish we were, Number One. But it's beginning to look as if we've been wasting our time. We've been recalled to Singapore.'

'What the hell for?'

'Your guess is as good as mine. But I know one thing,' Hamilton added bitterly. 'This was the first time I've ever tried my hand at forward planning - and it'll be the last. Next time I play it by ear.'

Mannon nodded sympathetically. They had all, from the skipper down to the most junior rating, worked like galley slaves to set up the secret base on the island and now, on the whim of an admiral thousands of miles away, all their efforts had been reduced to nothing. Not that Mannon had ever been completely happy about the scheme. The lack of oil storage facilities on the island had worried him. But whenever he queried the matter of fuel reserves with Hamilton his questions were never answered, although the skipper's smile suggested he had something up his sleeve. That was at least one problem they would not have to face if they were operating out of Singapore. But, even so, he could understand Hamilton's disappointment.

'I suppose I ought to be getting below, sir. I'll see if I can get Monty to rustle up some food before I start my watch.'

'Good idea, Number One. Ask him to have something

ready for me when I come down. And tell Alistair I want to see him in the wardroom at four bells.'

He looked up at the sky. Night descended quickly in the tropics and the stars were already twinkling brightly in the black vaults of the heavens. A single searchlight, probably from the *Tern* patrolling off Castle Peak Bay, swept the northern horizon with monotonous regularity and, to the north-east, the gaudy lights of Hong Kong glowed red against the dark backcloth of the New Territories.

He could not help wondering how much longer the Colony had to enjoy its peaceful tranquility.

Hamilton stirred restlessly on the narrow bunk. After the cool chill of the air on deck, the interior of the submarine was unpleasantly stuffy and he was finding it difficult to sleep. The deck head fan made little impression on the turgid atmosphere and the wardroom reeked with the smell of stale human sweat.

Mannon was sitting on the settee looking at an old magazine and the dim glow of the reading-lamp was an irritating distraction which Hamilton could have well done without.

Damn the bloody C-in-C! Why the hell did he have to recall *Rapier* just when things were beginning to look interesting? And, he reminded himself, it wasn't just pique at being deprived of his private hideaway and the cache of stores he had so carefully laid up in readiness for just such an emergency. He was quite prepared to admit that the secret base had been a crazy idea from the start - the sort of thing the hero did in a kid's story book.

He rolled over and tried to sleep, but his brain refused to switch off and, to add to the agonies of insomnia, tiny drops of condensation from the deck head over the bunk dripped on his face with the relentless regularity of a primitive Chinese torture....

'Sir! Wake up, sir!'

Hamilton couldn't believe that he'd really been asleep, but apparently he had. His eyes opened and he was fully awake in an instant.

'Murray's picked up a broadcast from Singapore radio, sir,' Mannon said excitedly. 'The Japs are landing at Kota Bharu.'

Hamilton swung his legs out of the bunk and pushed his feet into the pair of plimsolls Monty had left in readiness. 'Where the hell's Kota Bharu, Number One!' he grumbled irritably.

'East coast of Malaya, sir - up near the Siam border.'

'Is it, by God! It looks as though my hunch was right after all. Perhaps Layton knew what he was doing when he recalled us.'

He made his way through the bulkhead hatch into the control room. He had no doubts that the entire ship's company had heard the news by now, but the men on duty gave no hint of excitement or curiosity when he appeared. They knew the skipper would tell them what he intended to do in his own good time. And, in the meantime, discipline demanded that they carried out their duties without question.

The radio compartment was situated aft of the control room and Hamilton glanced up at the clock as he entered. It was 3.55 a.m.

'What's this report you say you've picked up?' he asked the operator brusquely.

Murray slipped off his headset and put it down on the bench alongside the radio. 'I was searching around the medium band about five minutes ago, sir.' He looked a little sheepish. 'To be honest I was trying to find some late night dance music. And someone suddenly broke into the programme to say the Japs were landing.'

'Where was this - Singapore?'

'No, sir,' Murray picked up a small book and pointed his finger to the top of the opened page. 'According to the station call-sign it was Kuala Lumpur.'

'Tune into Singapore and see what you get.'

Murray obediently twiddled the knobs and through the crackle Hamilton could hear the measured tones of the station announcer repeating instructions to the civilian population regarding blackout regulations and air raid precautions. After a few minutes, he repeated the initial news reports of the Japanese landings in the north.

Hamilton glanced at Mannon. 'Sounds genuine enough and if Murray's already heard similar reports from KL I'd say we'd got all the confirmation we need.'

'Shall I call up Singapore base, sir?' Murray asked.

'No! Maintain strict radio silence until we know what the situation is. Keep tuned to the Admiralty transmitting station and send me a resume of the signals every fifteen minutes. But call me if you hear something urgent.' He turned to Mannon. 'Alistair is due off watch in a couple of minutes, Number One. Get up on the bridge and take over. I want to discuss our course with him. I'll be up to relieve you as soon as we've worked something out. Then you get some shut-eye. We could have a busy day on our hands tomorrow.'

Back in the control room, Hamilton opened the small scale map of the South-East Asia area and stared down at it. Kota Bharu was approximately fourteen hundred miles away and Singapore seemed even further. Running at ten knots to conserve fuel, *Rapier* could not possibly arrive off the Malayan coast for at least five days and, even if he gambled on the oil supplies and steamed at maximum speed, it would take all of seventy-two hours to cover the distance. If only Layton had recalled them earlier. The presence of the two Japanese invasion convoys must have been known to the Singapore staff for some time. Surely *someone* could have made an intelligent guess!

He looked round as Scott came down from the bridge to join him and he moved to one side so that *Rapier's* navigator could see the chart.

'Shall I lay off a course for the Malayan coast, sir?' Scott asked. 'Or should we move up into the Gulf of Siam so that we're across their lines of communication?'

Hamilton stared at the map thoughtfully. Scott's suggestion of turning north into the Gulf of Siam was good - but until they had cleared the Indo-China coast they would have to continue westward. If they tried to reduce the distance by closing the coast and cutting towards the Mekong delta, they stood a good chance of being hunted by Vichy French patrols operating out of Saigon. No - far better to hold well to the south of Indo-China. The decision to move north could be made when the battle situation was clearer. And that could be another seventy-two hours.

'I'll decide our patrol area later, Pilot. Meanwhile, I want you to give me a course for the invasion area following a line about two hundred miles to the south of the Mekong.' Leaving Scott to carry out his instructions, Hamilton made his way back to the bridge to tell Mannon what he had decided. The night was still fine and the sea smooth. A phosphorescent glow from the bows was a silent reminder that *Rapier* was in the tropics.

'Is it Malaya, sir?' Mannon asked.

'At the moment, yes. But it's my guess the Japs will

move into Hong Kong fairly soon. It would be the logical thing to do now that they've shown their hand.

'And if they do?'

'I'd be inclined to turn back.'

Mannon raised his glasses and surveyed the horizon in silence for a few moments. It wasn't his place to remind the skipper that they were under the C-in-C's personal orders to return to Singapore. But Hamilton was right in one respect - if they returned to Hong Kong immediately they would be in time to strike the enemy during the critical initial stages of the attack. It made more sense that arriving at Kota Bharu several days too late.

'It's a pity we can't call on the Yanks to help us out - their Pacific Fleet would make mincemeat of the Japs.'

'I wouldn't underestimate the enemy, Number One. Even the Americans could have a fight on their hands. But, to be honest, I can't see Japan taking on the United States at this juncture. Once they've disposed of us, and perhaps the Dutch, and secured their oil supplies from the East Indies, they *might* attack the Philippines. But I doubt it. Tokyo *knows* it can't defeat America so why invite a hiding for nothing?'

As Hamilton picked up his binoculars and examined the dark rim of the starboard horizon, he was unaware that five thousand miles away, Admiral Nagumo's carrier strike force was treacherously closing in on its unsuspecting-target.

In less than four hours, a sequence of tragic events were to prove the fallacy of his misplaced optimism....

As eight bells signaled the end of the morning watch, *Rapier's* officers assembled in the overcrowded wardroom for Hamilton's council-of-war. Only Villiers, the new fourth hand, who had joined the boat at the last minute after Bruce had gone down with malaria, was missing. And at that precise moment, he was standing nervously on the bridge discovering the awesome responsibilities of watch- keeping under the benevolently paternal eye of Coxswain Blood.

Despite his natural misgivings about the new sub-lieutenant's lack of experience, Hamilton had been forced to throw the young reservist in at the deep end so that all of the submarine's regular officers could attend the meeting. Not that he was seeking their approval of his proposed course of action. But if he was going to disobey orders, he at least wanted them to understand his reasons.

'We have received no further reports of any significance during the morning,' he told them briefly. 'The Japanese are apparently well ashore in the Kota Bharu area and are enlarging their bridgehead. From the signals we've picked up they appear to have seized a number of advanced airfields.' He turned to a large chart of South-East Asia which was hanging by a piece of string from a convenient deck head pipe. 'It's only guesswork, but it seems the Japs are using French Indo-China as their staging post for the invasion. With Vichy approval no doubt,' he added bitterly.

Mannon stared at the map. 'It seems a bit odd they're only attacking Malaya, sir,' he said voicing his doubts. 'The RAF reconnaissance reports indicated only a small escort force with the troop convoys - where's the rest of the Japanese Navy?'

'A good question, Number One. I've been asking myself the same thing.'

'Well, we've got plenty of options,' Scott broke in cheerfully. 'They could be going for the Dutch Indies or even Australia. If you want my opinion, sir, we ought to head for Singapore - then we can move in whichever direction is needed. If we go north to Kota Bharu, we'll be too far away to be of any use to anyone. After all, the Malayan landings could be purely diversionary.'

A similar thought had crossed Hamilton's mind. He looked at O'Brien, the submarine's engineering officer. 'Any ideas, Sean?'

'Well, so long as they're not heading for Belfast I'm not especially bothered. But whatever they're doing I'd be after thinking they're up to no good.'

Hamilton grinned. He was about to say something when the wardroom curtain was suddenly pushed aside and Jamieson, the wireless room runner, entered breathlessly and snapped to attention.

'What is it, Jamieson?'

'Message from the Leading telegraphist, Murray, sir. The Japs have started bombing Hong Kong, sir. And some other places. He says all hell's been let loose, sir.'

'Thank you, Jamieson. Tell Murray I'll be along to the Radio Room in a few moments.' Despite the atmosphere of electric excitement which the news had created in the wardroom, Hamilton seemed totally unflustered. 'I think we should adjourn our meeting until I have clarified the situation, gentlemen,' he told the others calmly. 'You'd better go up and keep an eye on young Villiers, Alistair. He's probably hiding in a corner being sick.'

'Very good, sir.'

'And remember - any vessel flying the Japanese flag is to be regarded as hostile. However, no attacks are to be carried out until we receive confirmation from Singapore.'

'Will you be needing me, sir?' O'Brien asked.

'Not for the moment, but we're short-handed so I'll probably have to rope you in for some watch keeping. You'd best get some sleep while you can. I shall want you in the

Radio Room with me, Number One. I may need a second opinion.'

Murray was busy with his receiving equipment as Mannon and the skipper squeezed into the tiny cupboard that did duty as *Rapier's* radio room. He turned in his chair, but kept one pad of the headset pressed against his ear.

'What's the scare, Sparks,' Hamilton asked.

'Japanese aircraft are bombing Hong Kong, sir. And there's been a raid on Singapore,' Murray leaned forward, took a pink signal slip from the pad alongside the main transmitter, and handed it to the captain. 'This came through about two minutes ago, sir.'

Hamilton glanced down at the message. It was brief and to the point: *'From C-in-C Eastern Fleet to all ships. Commence hostilities against Japan'.*

He passed it to Mannon without comment. 'Have you verified the source?' he asked Murray.

'Yes, sir. It's definitely genuine.'

'And those other reports - where did you get them from?'

'I picked up the Singapore raid from general traffic, sir. There was a hell of a flap on. Mostly plain language transmissions. I got the second on the other set - news announcements on Hong Kong Radio.' Murray paused for a moment. 'Every station in the Far East seems to be transmitting, sir. It's bloody chaos. I've been picking up several reports about an attack on a place called Pearl Harbor- but there's so much going on it's difficult to sort out the facts.'

Hamilton looked up sharply. The name obviously meant nothing to Murray, but Pearl Harbor was the main base of the US Pacific Fleet in Hawaii. No wonder everyone was in a panic.

'Can you pick up any of the Australian stations?'

'I doubt it, sir. The Aussies mostly use low-power local transmitters. I think I could get Saigon radio - but they'll be broadcasting in French.'

'I can speak French,' Mannon said quietly.

Hamilton nodded. 'See if you can find Saigon, Sparks.' He thrust his head out of the compartment as Murray began turning the dials. 'Jamieson! Tell Kingham to report here at the double!'

'Aye aye, sir.'

Hamilton turned back into the compartment. The second operator would be able to listen out on the main communications channel for instructions, while Murray was busy making his way around the dial searching for news from the civil stations. A crackle of atmospherics spat from the loudspeaker above the main receiver and the voice of a French newscaster was gradually distilled from the noise, as Murray twiddled the fine tuner. Mannon listened intently, while Hamilton idly leafed through the wireless signals received during the morning. He could pick out odd words like 'Washington' and 'Roosevelt' but the rest meant nothing and he waited a trifle impatiently.

'Got enough yet, Number One?'

'I think so, sir. Japanese carrier aircraft and midget submarines hit Pearl Harbor at dawn. They caught the Yanks by surprise. According to Saigon - and their reports are based on American news agency wires - the entire US Pacific Fleet has been destroyed!'

'Bloody Hell!'

'There'll be bloody hell for you, Murray, if you don't concentrate on your job,' Hamilton snapped curtly. 'You are not to repeat what you have just heard to anyone - understand? I will tell the ship's company in my own good time.

tioningly to the left in search of another prominent feature. 'Castle Peak - zero-zero-five. Down periscope!'

Stepping back from the column, he joined Scott at the table and waited while *Rapier's* navigator ruled the lines of the cross bearings onto the chart and neatly calculated the fix.

'I'll check Castle Peak Bay as far as Brother's Point first,' Hamilton explained. 'If there's no sign of enemy activity we'll double back around Lantau and run up the eastern side of the island so that we can approach Hong Kong from the south-west.'

'What then?' Mannon asked.

Hamilton shrugged. 'I don't know until I've established the situation, Number One. If I can contact one of the gunboats and get a report, well and good. If not, we'll have to fight our own private war. Tell Morgan and his cut throats to close up in the gun-tower. I doubt if we'll find any targets worth wasting a torpedo on.' He snapped his fingers at Bushby and waited for the periscope to slide upwards.

Patches of early morning mist were still rolling gently over the surface of the sea as Hamilton peered through the eye-piece, but the sun was already glinting on the rock outcrops of Castle Peak as it rose clear of the shimmering haze covering the New Territories to the east. Everything looked deceptively peaceful and, as far as he could judge, the invaders had failed to penetrate the western sector of the mainland during the night. Glimpsing something moving in the direction of Lung Kwu Chan he switched to the high magnification lens.

Circala, her white hull gleaming in the morning sun, was steaming slowly south-east in the direction of Castle Peak. Her battle flags were flying and a plume of spray whispered like silver from her bows. Hamilton could see the urgent flash of the signal lamp on her bridge and swung his lens to starboard in search of her companion. He found *Firefly* close inshore two miles to the eastward. Ottershaw's ship was moving fast and the anti-aircraft gun in front of the bridge was firing at an invisible target high up in the sky. Moments later, two enormous geysers of water erupted astern of the little white gunboat and he glimpsed a Japanese dive-bomber as it flashed across *Firefly's* quarter-deck and climbed for height at the end of its attack run.

Hamilton knew there was nothing he could do to help. Submarines did not usually engage aircraft unless they happened to be caught unawares on the surface and, with a fine sense of personal preservation, he decided to remain discreetly out of sight beneath the waves. The Japanese pilots would be too intent on the gunboat to spot the periscope of a submerged submarine.

'I've found *Firefly* and *Circala*,' he told Mannon. 'Both ships bearing one point off the starboard bows at a range of four miles. They're under attack from enemy bombers, but so far they seem to be getting the best of it.'

'Can't we do anything to help, sir?'

'I'm afraid not, Number One. We wouldn't last five minutes on the surface. We'll just have to sit it out and see what happens. If you want to do something you could always try praying!'

It was almost an hour before the last of the Japanese bombers swung away from their targets and vanished north-wards towards their airfields inside the Chinese border. During that time, Hamilton had seen them drop no fewer than fifty bombs and yet, by a miracle, neither gunboat had been hit. He could not help wondering whether Mannon had taken him at his word. Perhaps that's what came from having a father who was a clergyman.

He waited for five minutes to make sure the attack would not be renewed and having assured himself that there was no immediate danger, he told Mannon to take *Rapier* up....

Firefly's guns swung to port as the look-out reported a submarine surfacing to seaward and Ottershaw raised his binoculars anxiously in anticipation of a fresh hazard.

'Range 1000- bearing Green-two-five! Hold your fire.' He turned to Forsyth. 'Any idea what a Jap submarine looks like, Number One?'

'They all look the same to me, sir. I suggest we open fire before he has a chance to hit back.'

Ottershaw shook his head and kept his glasses focused on the patch of white foam bubbling on the surface half a mile off the gunboat's port bow. He knew he was taking a dangerous risk, but something warned him not to be too hasty. No enemy submarine commander would be fool enough to surface under the guns of two warships and yet, so far as he knew, there was no possibility of there being any British boats in the area. *Rover* was dry-docked and refitting in Singapore and *Rapier* was by now several hundred miles to the south *en route* to Malaya. It might just be an American boat, or a Dutchman. And while the doubt lingered in his mind he was not prepared to take chances.

The bows of the submarine thrust from the cauldron of foam, followed, moments later, by the periscope standards and conning tower. Ottershaw thought that there was something vaguely familiar about the shape of the surfacing boat and he was still trying to identify it when the bosun shouted excitedly, 'It's the *Rapier,* sir! It's bloody *Rapier* come back to give us a hand!'

'Check the guns, Number One. Two points to port, helmsman. Half-ahead together.'

Hamilton scrambled out of the upper hatch and leaned over the conning tower rails as *Firefly* drew alongside. The look-outs followed him out on deck and quickly stationed themselves on either side of the bridge - their eyes already scanning the empty blue skies as they raised their binoculars. Hamilton had warned them to get below at the first sign of aircraft. It was no time to take risks and he knew he could rely on *Rapier's* highly trained crew to get the submarine safely beneath the surface within thirty seconds of the diving alarm.

'What's the score, Harry?' he yelled as soon as the gunboat was within hailing distance.

'The Army's falling back on Kowloon. The Japs will probably be there in another two days - we're completely outnumbered.' He turned to pass an instruction to the helmsman as the two boats began drifting apart and then continued his report. 'Kai Tak airfield has been knocked out and we've nothing left to stop the bombers. It's sheer bloody murder. We were under attack all day yesterday.'

Rapier rolled suddenly as the gunboat's rubbing strake rode up over the bulge of the starboard ballast tank and forced it under the surface. Ottershaw yelled something to the coxswain and *Firefly* backed off gently. Hamilton peered down over the side, but fortunately the collision had caused no damage.

'If you touch me there again I'll scream,' he grinned across at the gunboat commander, who rewarded his humor with a two-fingered gesture. He waited for the two vessels to drift together again. 'Where do you suggest we go - and no cracks, Harry!'

'Anywhere in the Straits once the Japs succeed in taking Kowloon. They'll have to use boats to get their troops across to Hong Kong.'

'What about the gunboats?'

'We won't survive that long if the air attacks continue. But we'll do our best to support you while we can. If you run to the south and he on the bottom for forty-eight hours you should be just in time for the big show.' Ottershaw paused for a moment as Forsyth joined him at the bridge rail and handed him a message. He nodded. The submarine and the gunboat were drifting apart again and he cupped his hands to his mouth so that his voice would carry across the water. 'If you're after bigger game, Nick, try the south-west approaches. *Thanet* has reported seeing a cruiser and destroyer in the offing. Collinson has nothing he can send out against them. And if they find any of our gunboats it'll be a massacre.'

'Three aircraft astern, sir!' *Rapier's* starboard look-out reported urgently. 'Five thousand feet and approaching!' Hamilton pressed the diving alarm. He made no effort to confirm the report. If Jacobs said aircraft were approaching that was enough for him. Geysers of water erupted along the side of the submarine as the main vents swung open and, almost before the two look-outs had slid into the hatch-way, *Rapier* was dipping beneath the surface. Hamilton waved a hasty farewell to Ottershaw as he made for the open hatch.

'See you around, Harry! And don't get your feet wet.' The hatch cover shut with a bang and within seconds the submarine's conning tower had vanished into the bubbling cauldron of foam.

'Action Stations! Bandits astern - range 2000 - height 4000. Full ahead both!' Ottershaw watched the three Mitsubishi dive bombers coming out of the sun. 'Starboard helm! Pass air attack signal to *Circala,* Number One!'

Forsyth raised his head above the level of the bridge

screen in time to see the other gunboat open fire and circle to the west with bombs exploding on all sides. *Firefly* shuddered from stern to sternport from the effects of a near-miss and, as he crouched on the deck, he could hear the shrill shriek of more bombs. He gritted his teeth and waited. Damn that bastard Hamilton! It was bloody unfair. Why should he be able to escape the bombs? Why couldn't *Rapier* stay on the surface and fight it out alongside the gunboats? Damn it all - they were all in the same bloody Navy....

'Thirty feet and diving, sir,' Mannon reported quietly as Hamilton slid down the ladder into the hushed brightness of the control room.

'Take her to sixty feet, Number One. Fortunately for us it's only an air attack. If the japs had sent in destroyers it wouldn't have been so funny.'

'Planes to dive. Group up - full ahead together. Level at sixty feet, Coxswain.'

Mannon felt pleased with the smooth efficiency with which he had taken *Rapier* out of danger, but he looked for no compliments. Hamilton did not regard efficiency as meriting commendation. He expected nothing less.

'What now, sir?'

Hamilton was leaning over the chart table in conference with Scott. The navigator was making some calculations on a note-pad and he passed the results to the skipper for approval.

'We're going cruiser hunting, Number One,' Hamilton said casually. 'If Harry Ottershaw is right, it will take the Japs two or three days to reach Kowloon, so there's nothing much we can do until they try crossing the Straits to Hong Kong. According to the Staff Appraisal Snark showed me, they reckon the island can hold out for fourteen days - so we've plenty of time.' He glanced up at the calendar hanging down from one of the deck head high-pressure air pipes. 'It's the 9th today. That means we've got a fortnight to send Tokyo our Christmas cards!'

O'Brien came through the bulkhead door. He was sweating heavily and wiping his glistening face with a piece of the engineer's traditional cotton waste. 'I've been checking the fuel stocks, sir. The bunkers are down to sixty tons.'

Hamilton did a quick calculation. They'd used up a quarter of their stocks already and that meant about twelve day's supply left at economical cruising speed. It was his own fault for making that high-speed dash back to Hong Kong.

'Thanks, Chief. I'll take her back to the dockyard to top up once we've run down this cruiser.'

'How long's that likely to be, sir?' O'Brien enquired. 'And when do we get topside for a breath of air - it's like a damned furnace in the motor room.'

Hamilton nodded sympathetically. His own clothes were wet with sweat and his underpants were sticking to his body. 'I'm afraid it's something we must learn to live with,' he said unhelpfully. 'I've no intention of showing myself on the surface in daylight. Unfortunately these S-class boats weren't built for the tropics so we'll have to lump it and like it.'

Mannon glanced at the control room thermometer. It was standing at 110°F.

But it wasn't just the heat. The humidity was worse. Everything was wet to the touch and beads of water continuously dripped from the deck head as the condensation built up. Reacting to an irresistible impulse, he pushed his hand up inside the waistband of his shorts and scratched violently.

'When you've finished doing your monkey act, Number One, I want you to go for'ard and check the tubes and the mouldies. If we meet up with that cruiser tonight I don't want any slip-ups. Young Villiers is doing his best but he's no expert, so go along and see if he needs any help.'

'Aye aye, sir.'

Ernie Blood was busy scratching his ample stomach and, as the skipper looked in his direction, he withdrew his hand guiltily like a child caught stealing sweets from a tin. He tried the old sailor's trick of sucking his teeth but it did nothing to ameliorate the persistent irritation of the heat rash. Hamilton moved across to the chart table. He kept his voice low so that the men could not overhear what he was saying.

'I reckon that Jap cruiser force must be to the southwest, Alistair. The trouble is we don't know where it's heading. Could be a bombardment support squadron to back up the invasion of Hong Kong - or a covering force for another troop convoy heading for a fresh landing somewhere to the south.' He looked down at the chart as he weighed up the alternatives. 'We'll carry out a two-hundred-mile box search centered on Gap Rock.' He pointed his finger at a small black dot some forty miles to the southwest of Hong Kong and Scott nodded. 'Fifty miles due south from the rock - then fifty miles east and so on. It's only a small area, but it will take us across the main shipping channel into the Pearl River.'

Scott circled the pin-point denoting Gap Rock on the chart and picked up his ruler and protractor. 'Any particular time-table, sir?' he asked.

'I intend to remain submerged until sunset. Then, if

conditions are favorable, we'll stay on the surface throughout the night. We can cover the search area more quickly that way - and it will give O'Brien a chance to re-charge his batteries.'

Jamieson hurried into the control room in his usual state of breathlessness. 'Urgent radio signal coming through, sir,' he reported. 'Murray says he thinks you ought to listen.'

Hamilton glanced at the clock above the chart-table. It was nearly 2 p.m. It hardly seemed possible that they'd been running six hours since *Firefly* had been attacked. He wondered when he was going to get some rest.

The radio compartment was immediately aft of the control room and Murray glanced around as he heard the partition curtains swish open. He kept one earphone clasped firmly against his head as he passed on the gist of what he had heard.

'The Japs have got Force Z, sir. I've just picked up signals from Singapore. Both ships sunk.'

Hamilton felt the blood drain from his face. 'Are you quite certain?' he asked.

Murray nodded. 'Absolutely, sir. I've been picking up signals from both *Express* and *Electra*. They're bringing the survivors back to Singapore. *Repulse* went down at 12:30 and *Prince of Wales* about an hour later. One message said that the Admiral was missing.'

Hamilton tried to think, but the enormity of the tragedy seemed to paralyze his brain. 'Have you received any battle reports, Sparks? If I decide to take *Rapier* up into the Gulf I'll need to know the size and composition of the Jap fleet.'

'There were no surface ships involved, sir. It was an air attack.'

Hamilton had always been a submarine man. In his opinion a well-handled submarine was a match for any battleship. And, although he had a certain respect for aircraft - his experience in the North Sea had taught him to treat them with caution - he had never subscribed to the theory that airplanes had made the capital ship obsolete. But if Murray's information was correct, and there seemed no reason why it should not be, today's action had witnessed the opening of a new chapter in the history of naval warfare.

Two battleships, with plenty of sea-room in which to maneuver and equipped with modern anti-aircraft guns backed by radar and the latest fire control instruments, had been attacked and sunk by aircraft. The prophets of air power had been proved right in their predictions. From now on, the mighty battle wagons that had ruled the seas for more than a century must yield pride of place to the aircraft carrier.

'Keep listening out, Murray. And let me know if you get further details. I'll make an announcement to the ship's company later on. They might as well know the worst.'

'There *is* one other thing, sir.'

'Yes?'

'The Japanese have landed in the Philippines. And I gather that things aren't going too well for the Americans.'

Hamilton thought of the *Repulse* and *Prince of Wales* lying on the bottom of the Gulf of Siam. Things were not exactly going too well for the British either....

'*Captain to the Control Room!*'

Hamilton's eyes opened and he was wide awake in an instant. Swinging his legs off the bunk, he thrust his feet into the waiting slippers, and padded quietly through the hatchway into the dim red glow of the control room. It was *Rapier's* fourth night on patrol in the search area and he knew it was probably another false alarm. All they'd seen so far were trading junks and a solitary Dutch coaster *en route* from Canton to Java.

The draught of cool night air sweeping down through the open conning tower hatches, showed that *Rapier* was still running on the surface and the low rumble of the diesels provided further confirmation that they had not submerged. He wondered what the cause of the panic was - if they'd spotted a possible target Mannon should have taken the submarine under the surface immediately. But he hadn't.

Villiers, *Rapier's* fourth hand, was waiting to make his report as the skipper entered the control room.

'Asdic contact, sir.'

'Why the hell haven't we submerged?' Hamilton demanded.

'Not reported to the bridge yet, sir,' Villiers explained. 'I was waiting for further information from the Asdic operator. Contact not yet positive.'

'Good God, man! Don't you realize you've put the entire boat at risk?' He almost pushed the young sub-lieutenant aside as he reached for the intercom.

'Diving stations! All hands to diving stations! Stand by to dive.' As he pulled the cover from the bridge voice pipe, the dimly lit control room was suddenly filled with silent men moving to their positions. 'Clear the bridge, Number One. Emergency dive!' Reaching down he pressed the klaxon button. He had given Mannon and the look-outs the routine warning. It was up to them to get below before *Rapier* vanished beneath the waves.

AHOOA... AHOOA... AHOOA.

O'Brien arrived in the engine room as the first squawk of the klaxon blasted through the hull. He had been peacefully dozing in the wardroom when the skipper was called to the control room, but he was wide awake and at his post before the third and last raucous squawk of the alarm had faded.

'Shut off for diving! Out clutches - switches on. Group up. Full ahead both motors.' The Irishman peered across the narrow compartment to check that Miller had closed down from the diesels. 'Shut exhaust valve!' He reached for the intercom. 'Shut off for diving, sir. Motors grouped up. Standing by.'

Hamilton acknowledged the report and made a mental note to commend O'Brien for the efficiency of his instantaneous reaction.

'Take her down, Cox'n. Level at thirty feet.'

'Open main vents. 'Planes hard a'dive!'

'Stand by to close lower hatch.'

Rapier was diving fast - faster than even her usual emergency routine. If Mannon and the look-outs did not move quickly enough, the conning tower would be under the surface before the upper hatch was secured. And that would mean closing the lower hatch and marooning them on deck.

The first of the look-outs slid down the ladder and landed at the bottom with a thud. Mannon's voice echoed hollowly from inside the empty cavern of the conning tower.

'Upper hatch shut and clipped!'

The second look-out came down the ladder followed, moments later, by Mannon himself. He had made it with only seconds to spare and his face bore an expression of faint surprise tinged with excitement as if, bearing in mind his civilian profession- he had just found a significant error in a company's balance sheet.

'What's up, sir?'

'Asdic contact,' Hamilton told him briefly. In fact, at that precise moment, he knew no more himself. 'Villiers didn't pass on the message to the bridge. I'll deal with him later.'

'Don't be too hard on him, sir. He's not in the Trade like the rest of us. Don't forget, we only shipped him as a passenger.'

Hamilton had difficulty in repressing a smile. Mannon seemed to have forgotten that less than eighteen months ago he was working as an accountant in a City office under the shadow of St Paul's and had never seen the inside of a submarine, except on the cinema screen. And yet now he regarded himself as a fully-fledged professional.

Like most regular officers, Hamilton took a conceited pride in his skill and knowledge. It needed years of training and dedication to produce a naval officer - and even more to produce a submariner. Yet in a few brief months, as Mannon had so correctly implied, the young lieutenant was already on equal terms with the regulars. Perhaps it was in the blood. Perhaps that's what made the true submariner. Not years of training, although that was important, nor hours of dedicated study, although that, too, had its place, but the primitive instinct of the hunter - of a man who was prepared to gamble his personal survival against the overwhelming odds against him in the deadly arts of underwater warfare.

'Positive contact, sir,' Glover reported from the Asdic scanner. 'Range three miles, bearing three-zero-zero, course south-west, speed 20 knots.'

'Attack team stand by. See what you can make of the HE, Glover.'

Although the Asdic echoes gave a more accurate range and bearing than the primitive mechanical ears of the hydro-phones, the electronic gadgetry could not analyze the nature of the contact it indicated. And Hamilton needed more than mere range and direction at this stage of the game. No point in hunting a freighter.

Glover moved the sensitive microphone onto the bearing of the Asdic echoes and turned the amplification up to maximum power. Three miles was stretching his equip-ment to the limit of its range and he had to strain his ears to interpret the vague sounds in his headphones.

'I'm getting turbines, sir. I'd say a cruiser and perhaps a couple of destroyers. That's the best I can do until they get closer.'

'Up periscope!'

It was a routine Hamilton had carried out many times before and yet, despite his achievements on special missions, success had always eluded him when operating under ordinary patrol conditions. Perhaps this time his luck would turn.

The periscope lens was already set to the Asdic bearing. As it emerged above the surface Hamilton's trained eyes found the fleeting dark shadows of the ships almost immedi-ately - three black masses moving at speed against the night horizon, with bow waves that glistened in the moonlight. By sheer chance *Rapier* was on the perfect interception course and the range was decreasing to his advantage with every passing minute.

'Down periscope! Attack Team close up. Bow ends stand by!' The men who made up the attack team moved obediently to their stations - Mannon to the diving panel where he could watch the trim and keep an eye on the two planes men, Alistair Scott at the torpedo director, and O'Brien, hurrying in from the engine room to the chart table to enter up the plot. It was a skilled and experienced team and Hamilton knew they would not let him down. If the attack failed, the only person to blame would be himself.

'Up periscope.'

He guided the lens a fraction to the left to allow for the movement of the target and brought the leading ship into sharp focus. 'Start the attack! Range- *that* Bearing- *that* Blake, the senior electrical artificer, read the figures from the scale engraved into the brass ring encircling the periscope column and passed them back to Sutton who was standing behind him with a slide rule.

'Green - one - zero, sir. Range thirty-five hundred.'

'Course three-two-five, sir. Speed four knots.'

Scott's torpedo director - the fruit machine as it was irreverently known to submariners - clicked busily as he fed in the data.

'Down periscope! Group up main motors. Steer three-zero-zero.' Hamilton picked up the intercom. 'Bow ends - blow up one, two, three, and four tubes.'

'Bow ends, aye aye, sir.'

'Up periscope!' Despite the quiet calm of the control room Hamilton could feel his heart pounding with excitement as the cruiser came into his sights. Take it easy - no hurry. Remember, they don't know you're there. Plenty of time for a double check. No point in making silly mistakes. He carefully centered on the cruiser's pagoda-like bridge structure and moved the handle-bar grip so that the two images of the rangefinder element came together. 'Range *that*!' Blake noted the angle and relayed it to Sutton. 'Bearing *that* Hamilton paused for the electrical artificer to read the scale. 'Down periscope!' He stepped back as the periscope slid down into its well. 'Looks like a *Mogami* class heavy cruiser plus a couple of destroyers. The moon's out and visibility is good.' He didn't add that all they needed was a modicum of luck, but the men in the control room knew his unspoken thoughts. 'What's the DA, Alistair?' he enquired with the casualness of a man asking the bus fare to Aldgate.

'Twenty-seven Red, sir.'

Hamilton rubbed his nose thoughtfully. No problems there. His slight alteration of course at the beginning of the attack had shown sound judgement.

'Up periscope.'

Hamilton's knuckles suddenly whitened as the lens mockingly reflected an empty sea. He scanned to the left but the dark shadows had vanished. Swearing softly to himself he swung the 'scope to the right. *Shit!*

'Target moving to starboard - *away* from us. Speed increasing.' He peered intently through the lens. 'Now twenty degrees to starboard of old course. What does that make it, Alistair?'

'Two-nine-five, sir.'

Of all the bloody luck! The enemy ships were now steering an almost identical course to *Rapier* and, with their superior speed, the range was rapidly lengthening.

'Director angle for three-degree track angle?'

'One degree Red, sir.'

'Down periscope. Open bow caps.' Hamilton realized the hopelessness of the situation, but he was loath to pass up even an outside chance of sinking a Japanese cruiser. He moved to the monocular attack 'scope at the rear of the control room.

'Up periscope - put me on director angle.' Blake placed his hands on top of the skipper's and guided the column onto the critical bearing.

'On director angle, sir.*

The targets were now moving steadily towards the horizon. Only the cruiser was still in range - and then only just. 'Stand by 1-2-3-4. Prepare to fire....'

He waited until the stern of the cruiser centered in the graticule sights of the attack scope. 'Fire One... Two... Three... Four! Down periscope. Flood Q. Eighty feet!'

Rapier nosed deeper. Now they could only wait. Perhaps the skipper would be lucky this time, although the expression on his face did not encourage optimism.

'Torpedoes running, sir,' Glover reported from the hydro-phones.

No one spoke a word and all eyes went to the sweeping second hand of the control room clock and a dozen brains wrestled with the same arithmetical problem - two miles at forty-five knots equals three minutes. If there was no explosion in the next one hundred and. eighty seconds they knew the torpedoes had missed. And sitting quietly at their stations, leaning against the bulkheads, or standing motionless in the center of the tiny claustrophobic compartment, they waited....

It was Hamilton who finally broke the tension. 'Secure from diving stations.'

'I suppose we ought to look on the bright side, sir,' Mannon forced a smile. 'At least we haven't had to put up with a depth charge attack. They didn't even know we were there.'

'That's what makes it all the more damnable, Number One,' Hamilton retorted bitterly. 'Perfect conditions, a sitting target, and everything in our favor. They say the devil looks after his own and I'm beginning to believe it.' He straightened up. The attack may have been abortive but it wasn't the end of the world. 'Maintain depth and course. Reduce to half speed.'

Mannon walked over to join Hamilton and the navigator at the plotting table. 'Do you think we should hang about and see if they turn up again, sir?' he asked.

Hamilton shook his head. 'No - we can't even be sure they *will* come back. And we can't afford to waste time. According to the last radio report the military situation is deteriorating in Hong Kong. We haven't had much success against the Japanese Navy - let's see if we have more luck with their bloody army!' He looked up at Scott. 'Well, what are you waiting for, Pilot? Lay off a course for Hong Kong.'

EIGHT

'Stand by for gun action!'

Hamilton moved back as the periscope sank down into its well under the deck plating and waited while Morgan and the gun crew scrambled into the cramped tunnel of the gun tower.

'Gun crew closed up and standing by, sir.'

'Stand by to surface! Blow main ballast. Full ahead both motors.' There was a hiss of compressed air as Venables opened the valves and, restored to positive buoyancy, *Rapier* lurched upwards like a cork. Only the skill of the two coxswains controlling the fore and aft hydroplanes kept her safely below the surface, and Hamilton could see the sweat beading Blood's face as he jockeyed the big diving wheel with the delicate care of a *chef de cuisine* mixing a *soufflé*.

'Main ballast clear, sir.'

'Surface!'

'Up helm 'planes... blow Q! Watch the trim... blow stern compensating tank.'

'Ten feet, sir.'

'Reverse 'planes. Open gun hatch.'

Hamilton was already climbing into the empty steel vault of the conning tower. The damp salt air tasted good after the sour atmosphere inside the submarine and he drew it deep into his lungs as he pulled back the clips of the hatch. A blast of foul-smelling vapor, forced upwards by the pressure inside the boat belched through the open hatchway and, with the wisdom of experience, Hamilton held his breath until it had blown clear. Then, gripping the edges of the narrow hatchway, he heaved himself up on to the bridge.

Butterfield and Swire's shipyard at Taikoo lay to port and, so far as Hamilton could make out, it seemed to be deserted - no doubt the Chinese workforce had fled at the first sign of trouble. A heavy pall of smoke hung over the mainland and fierce fires were burning in Kwun Tong and amongst the shattered remains of the Kai Tak airfield. Further to the west, the glow of more fires reddened the sky above Kowloon and the stabbing flames of Japanese field guns ranged along the waterfront showed that the enemy was now in occupation of the entire mainland area of the New Territories.

Hamilton put his mouth to the voice pipe. 'Obey telegraphs. Transfer helm to upper steering position.' A small nagging doubt made him wonder whether he was being wise. A fast dive would be impossible with so many men on deck. However, on the other hand, *Rapier* would be three times more effective as a surface warship in the event of the enemy attempting to launch an attack across the waters of the Strait. Torpedoes would have little value against small landing craft. 'Stop motors. Engage both engine clutches. Half-ahead together.'

There was a momentary pause. Then the diesels

rumbled into life and a blast of oil smoke erupted from the exhaust trunks.

'Send both Lewis guns to the bridge.'

Hamilton raised his glasses and searched the darkness ahead of the bows. He wondered how many ships of the original Hong Kong defense force were still left. He had passed *Circala* patrolling to the south of the island during the final approach past Cape El'Aguilar, so at least *one* of the gunboats was still afloat. The destroyer *Thracian* had not been so lucky. Mannon had reported her as aground and beached on the eastern side of the island an hour or so earlier. Hopefully *Tern* and *Firefly* were still in the fight although, so far, he had seen no sign of them.

As the two machine gunners emerged onto the bridge and clamped their weapons to the support brackets on the port and starboard wings, Hamilton lowered his binoculars and bent over the voice pipe again.

'Hand over to Alistair, Number One, and then come topside. Things are likely to get nasty if the Japs try and attempt a landing. I'll need a back-up on the bridge in case something happens.'

'Aye aye, sir.'

Hamilton raised his glasses and continued his careful search of the darkened shoreline as *Rapier* circled northwards and then eastwards around Quarry Bay. In the far distance, he could just make out the dockyard with *Moth* canted over and abandoned in dry-dock after being scuttled by her crew. And he could see a series of fires raging in the city itself where enemy shells had found vulnerable targets. How long could the poor bastards hold out? Lt General Sakai, the Japanese field commander, had already sent his peace envoys across the Straits under a flag of truce to demand the Colony's surrender, but the Governor, Sir

Mark Young, had sent the emissaries packing in no uncertain manner. But as a realist, Hamilton could not help wondering what sort of defense the troops could put up in the face of such overwhelming enemy numbers. Brave words were no substitute for bullets.

Mannon joined him on the bridge and together they surveyed the grim scene in silence. There were still no signs of any other British warships waiting to challenge an enemy attempt to cross the narrow Straits which separated Hong Kong from the mainland New Territories. It was becoming increasingly clear that only *Rapier* stood between the Colony and Japanese occupation.

'Harbor launch five hundred yards on port bow, sir.'

Hamilton was the first to pick out the small tender patrolling along the southern side of Quarry Bay. It was flying a White Ensign from its stern and he could just distinguish the skeletal outline of a two pounder in the bows. The stranger was moving purposefully across the black water with a crisp wave curling from its sharp stem.

'Searchlight!'

The duty signalman swung *Rapier's* reflector towards the picket-boat and switched on the power. The silvered beam danced quickly across the water and then trapped the mysterious patrol craft in its stark glare like a moth caught in the light of an electric torch. Hamilton focused his glasses and Mannon heard him suddenly laugh.

'Okay, Jenkinson, you can switch off. Stop engines. Bring me alongside, Cox'n.'

So the prophetic joke had come true. Admittedly Snark wasn't sitting in a rowing boat with a service rifle across his knees and snarling in defiance at the invaders. But Hamilton's fight hearted appraisal of the post-captain's character hadn't been *that* far from the mark. With most of the Navy's remaining surface ships cruising to the south of the island in anticipation of a seaborne attack, Snark had rapidly improvised an inshore defense force to cover the Straits. The tender, an old steam-driven pinnace dating back to the Victorian era, had been hastily daubed with grey paint and fitted with an equally ancient gun. And, with a scratch crew of Royal Naval personnel drawn from shore-duty ratings working in the dockyard offices and administration officers, Snark was imposing his own private blockade in defiance of the overwhelming odds facing him from across the mainland side of the narrow moat.

Hamilton climbed down the iron rungs on the outside of the conning tower and made his way onto the fore-deck casing as the wooden picket-boat bumped against *Rapier's* exposed ballast tanks. Snark was standing on the gunwale and, as the two vessels came together, one of the submariners reached across the help him over the slippery plating to the deck.

'What the deuce are you doing here, Hamilton?' Snark barked belligerently. 'I thought you were ordered to Singapore a week ago.' He glared at the lieutenant. 'Lucky for you I recognized the boat. In another couple of minutes we'd have taken you for a Jap sub and opened fire.'

Hamilton tried to repress a smile. The picket-boat's antiquated pea-shooter would have been next to useless - any self-respecting Japanese submarine would have blown him out of the water inside thirty seconds. And Snark knew it. But it wouldn't have stopped him from trying.

Snark growled to himself in the darkness. He was glad to have *Rapier* back, although he had no intention of admitting it. 'The situation is hopeless,' he announced bluntly. 'But the Navy will go down fighting.' He nodded towards

Rapier's deck gun. 'I reckon you could do some satisfying damage with *that,*' he added wistfully.

Despite his customary mistrust of authority, Hamilton recognized an unexpected determination in Snark's attitude. The old boy was due for retirement in twelve months and, as an administrator, he couldn't see further than the nose on his face. But he was a born fighter and a natural leader. And Hamilton had to admire his guts.

'Please regard *Rapier* as coming under your orders, sir.' He could not help feeling slightly amused at the formality of the phrase in the circumstances. With the enemy poised on the northern shore, the crash of exploding shells reverberating across the bay, and the night sky fit by fires still burning on both sides of the narrow straits, two naval officers were quietly deciding the appropriate lines of seniority and command in the approved regulation manner, with a total disregard for the chaos and confusion that surrounded them on all sides. To the impartial observer it was highly incongruous - but very British.

'Thank you, Lieutenant. Your offer is appreciated.'

Snark smiled thinly. 'But I think you will probably do better if I give you a free hand.' He paused for a moment. 'Let me put you in the picture. I've organized a make-shift flotilla of small boats to cover the narrows opposite Kowloon. We can't use our bigger ships at the western end of the Straits - the enemy has artillery batteries dug in every hundred yards along the Kowloon waterfront. *Firefly* is covering the eastern approaches down to Lye Mun Point and Gandy's Second Flotilla is patrolling Junk Bay. My boats will be keeping an eye on the harbor area down as far as the Sulphur Channel and that leaves our most vulnerable point - Quarry Bay and the Taikoo shipyard - wide open. If you can maintain a standing patrol in that area during the night, we should have all sectors covered against a landing attempt.'

Hamilton nodded. 'You realize that I'll have to dive at dawn, sir,' he pointed out. 'I daren't risk remaining on the surface in daylight.'

'Quite understood, Lieutenant. In any event, *Rapier* is far too valuable to lose. After submerging I suggest you withdraw eastwards and remain in the vicinity of Lam Tong Island. The Japs won't try a daylight attack across the Straits, but they might launch a seaborne assault. If you're lying off Lam Tong you'll be protecting our eastern flank, while *Circala* and *Tern* are guarding our southern and western coasts.' Snark drew himself up straight as he brought the discussion to an end. 'Good luck, Lieutenant. You can rely on the rest of us coming to your support if you need it.'

Hamilton saluted and escorted the captain to the port side, where the men waiting in the steam pinnace helped him safely down the slippery ballast tanks and onto the gunwale. Someone had painted HMS *Dreadnought* in large black letters on the side of the antediluvian tender and Hamilton could not resist a smile as he saw it. No doubt Snark disapproved of such levity, but he had the wisdom to ignore the wanton desecration of his beloved government property. And Hamilton concluded that the old post captain was probably secretly pleased by this unorthodox demonstration of his men's high morale.

Black coal smoke and a shower of dancing red sparks erupted from the tender's spindly funnel as she went astern to clear the submarine and then, with her White Ensign snapping proudly in the breeze, she chugged away until her outline was swallowed up by the darkness.

'Half-ahead together.' As *Rapier* began moving

forward Hamilton glanced at Mannon. 'There'll be no sleep for us tonight, Number One. And we'll have to miss our grub.' He stared out over the starboard side at the opaque blackness that cloaked the mainland. The fires had mostly died away and the darkness added a furtive secrecy to the enemy's preparations. 'I wonder what the bastards are up to?'

'Could we risk going inshore for a quick look, sir?'

'I suppose we might get away with it if we were to make a high speed run down the coast on the surface,' Hamilton said thoughtfully. Like Mannon he found the challenge difficult to resist. And the depth of the water precluded a more cautious submerged approach. 'To hell with it - let's try it!' He turned to Blood. 'Cox'n steer towards those fires on the airfield. When we're half a mile off-shore turn east and follow the coast.'

The fact that Hamilton's impulsive decision would probably bring *Rapier* under fire did not seem to unduly worry the phlegmatic Ernie Blood. The old veterans had seen it all before - and survived. Having sailed through the Dardanelles with Martin Nasmith's *E.n* in 1915 and escaped a steam submarine disaster in the twenties, the coxswain was a fatalist. If his number came up this time he'd had a good innings. And he did not believe in meeting trouble before it arrived.

'Aye aye, sir.'

Rapier's bows began to swing to starboard as Blood spun the helm and Hamilton searched the darkness ahead for enemy patrol ships.

'Ring down for maximum speed, Number One.' He moved to the front of the bridge and leaned over the screen. 'We're going to take a run down the coast, Morgan,' he shouted to the gunner's mate. 'Keep trained to port and load up with HE. If we see anything worth shooting at I'll give you the word.'

'Deck gun, aye aye, sir.'

'Keep your eyes peeled, look-outs! And sing out if you spot anything. But concentrate on the water - I'll watch out for shore targets.'

'I thought this was a recce run, sir,' Mannon reminded him quietly. Hamilton's preparations suggested a rather more active role.

'Well, I've changed my mind, Number One. No point in half measures. If we spot any landing craft I intend to blow 'em out of the water. It's about time someone remembered that attack is the best means of defense.'

'Turning to starboard, sir,' Blood reported.

The barrel on *Rapier's* deck gun swung to the left as the coxswain brought the submarine parallel to the northern shore and Hamilton began surveying the mainland through his binoculars as he searched for signs of enemy activity. He knew he was taking a gamble, but the element of risk involved would be reduced to the minimum by the priceless advantage of surprise.

There was certainly plenty going on. Army trucks were creeping along the roads in long straggling convoys and, at odd intervals, Hamilton could see small groups of tents where Japanese soldiers were setting up camp. Other troops were busy clearing the debris of burnt-out aircraft at Kai Tak, so that the landing ground would be ready to receive their own planes at dawn. An engineer unit was hard at work repairing a small road bridge under the inadequate light of storm lanterns that flickered fitfully in the off-shore breeze.

'Something's going on over there, sir!' Mannon reported suddenly. 'Fine on the port bow - about a thousand yards.' Hamilton lowered his glasses and found the deep shadows that had attracted Mannon's attention. Raising the binoculars he focused on a group of seven or eight small pontoons lying in the water. Moving his search to the left, he could see a dozen open trucks unloading more of the flat bottomed craft and a number of Japanese soldiers working like beavers in the dim glow of carefully shaded lamps.

'Stand by for gun action! Target red-two-zero. Landing craft.'

'I've got them, sir. Range eight-hundred.'

'Confirmed. Ten rounds rapid, Mister Gunner!'

The first shell burst on the shingle and spat fragments of jagged stones in all directions like shrapnel. The second struck a pile of pontoons waiting to be lowered into the water and flames leapt skywards as the wooden hulls ignited. Hamilton could hear the confused orders and counter-orders as the officers tried to bring the panic-stricken troops under control and he saw a large truck spinning its rear wheels in the damp earth as its driver made a frantic bid to get clear.

Rapier's third shell slammed into the cab of the lorry, where it exploded and sent up a sheet of vivid white flame that lit the entire area like a parachute flare. It revealed a scene of utter chaos- burning trucks, smashed and broken pontoons, and men running wildly in all directions to escape the murderous and unexpected attack from the peaceful darkness of the sea. Hamilton felt the adrenalin surge into his blood as the primitive excitement of battle gripped him.

'Steer inshore, Cox'n. Let's give the Lewis guns a chance. Is 500 yards enough, MacIntyre?'

The machine gunner grinned cheerfully and raised an

upturned thumb. 'Aye, that'll be fine, sir,' he confirmed in a thick Glaswegian accent.

'Open fire when you're ready '

He heard the sharp click of the bolt as MacIntyre tucked the butt of the Lewis gun into his shoulder and sighted the shadowy figures scrambling for cover. *Tak-tak-tak-tak- tak... tak-tak-tak-tak....* A line of tracer bullets ripped into the darkness and the screams of the soldiers carried back across the black water like the cadences of dying banshees. MacIntyre jerked the machine gun to the left and opened up on a group of Japanese struggling to climb aboard an escaping truck.

The devastating attack was all over in less than sixty seconds. Caught by surprise and with no weapons to hand, the enemy troops were unable to reply to the fusillade of high-explosive shells and machine gun bullets, and *Rapier* ran clear of the shingled beach without so much as a scratch. As the target area passed astern, Hamilton carried out a hurried post-mortem in the ruddy light of the burning lorries. At least two trucks had been hit and a dozen pontoons totally destroyed while, sprawled on the shingle, over twenty motionless bodies testified to the killing power of MacIntyre's Lewis gun. It had been a highly successful hit-and-run raid even though it had not completely knocked out the enemy's improvised embarkation point. A number of pontoons remained undamaged and, as he ordered Morgan to check fire, Hamilton could see the soldiers cautiously emerging from behind cover to assess the damage.

Rapier's skipper now faced three choices: to circle around on the engines and return for a second strike, to switch over to the motors and go astern for a repetition of the bombardment, or to earn on eastwards in search of fresh targets. If he returned for a second attack, the enemy would be on the alert and he might not be so lucky. He made his decision without a moment's hesitation.

'Maintain course, Cox'n. But stay about a thousand yards offshore- I don't want to run aground on the shoals.' As Blood acknowledged the order, Hamilton leaned forward over the bridge screen. 'Good shooting, lads. I'll see if I can find you some more targets.'

'Looks as though the Japs were planning a landing for tonight, sir,' Mannon observed as the skipper rejoined him on the port-wing of the bridge.

Hamilton shrugged. 'Possibly. More likely tomorrow - they've no artillery in position. And they'll need gun support if they attempt a crossing.'

'Landing craft ahead!'

Morgan's warning shout put a stop to further specula-tion and both officers peered anxiously into the darkness. This time it was Mannon who found the target first. 'Eleven o'clock off port bow, sir! Eight-hundred yards. Boats moored to a small landing stage.' His glasses swung to the left. 'And a number of trucks parked behind the trees.' Guided by the first officer's directions, Hamilton picked up the new target without difficulty. The enemy concentration was consider-ably larger than the previous one and most of the pontoons were already in the water loaded to the gunwales with fully equipped combat troops. Mannon was right. The Japs *did* intend to cross the Straits tonight!

'Gun action! Target red-two-zero... range eight-hundred. Fire! Fire! Fire!'

It was impossible to miss, and every salvo found its mark as *Rapier's* gunners poured shell after shell into the crowded target area. To an impartial observer it was little more than sheer bloody carnage. But to Hamilton and his men, already sickened by Japanese atrocities in China and Malaya, it was a just and rewarding vengeance on an enemy that asked, and gave, no quarter.

A fully laden pontoon reared like a startled horse and threw its cargo of soldiers into the sea as a near miss exploded close under its stern. Another vanished in a sheet of blinding flame as Morgan's men scored a direct hit on a box of ammunition. A third swung violently to starboard and collided with its companion. Within two minutes, the sea was strewn with wreckage, equipment, floating bodies, and struggling men. MacIntyre sighted his machine gun into the confusion and took deliberate aim at a group of soldiers staggering waist-deep towards the beach, bringing them down with a long sustained burst that ripped the night air with the sound of tearing calico. The water turned bright red as it lapped gently over the shingle and then fell back to leave the huddled remains of the dead soldiers on the wet stones; like grotesque black starfish thrown up and abandoned by the sea.

A concealed machine gun opened up from behind the trees and heavy caliber bullets thudded against the thin steel plating of the conning tower. MacIntyre swung his Lewis gun towards the source of the firing and answered with a quick burst that quickly silenced the opposition.

'Hard a'starboard!'

Mannon had to grab for the bridge rail as Blood gave the submarine full right rudder. He looked towards the bows. Hamilton must have eyes in the back of his bloody head!

In a wild bid to escape the holocaust on the beach, three motorized pontoons had started their outboards and were heading away from the shore towards the center of the Strait, in the hope that sea-room would bring safety. A bubbling white wash curled from their square sterns as they increased speed. Mannon could see the soldiers hanging on for grim death as the flat-bottomed landing craft bounced and jolted across, the smooth water.

'Steer at them, Cox'n!' Hamilton shouted to Blood. 'Ram the bastards!'

Rapier's sharp steel bows cut the leading landing craft in half and it vanished beneath the black water within seconds. The broad sweep of the starboard ballast tank struck the second pontoon a glancing blow that splintered the frail wooden hull like matchwood. It tilted on to its beam-ends, hung precariously for a few moments, and then turned over. MacIntyre's Lewis gun raked the sea as the survivors bobbed to the surface and his trigger finger did not relax its pressure until every man was dead.

The last pontoon in the line swerved sharply to starboard to avoid a similar fate and then swung purposefully towards the avenging submarine while the soldiers tried to bring their machine gun to bear. But with less than twenty yards to go, the clumsy flat-bottomed craft caught the full force of *Rapier's* bow wave and it reared up as a wall of cresting water swept under its blunt snout. Lacking the stability of a properly designed boat, it capsized in an instant and flung its occupants into the sea.

Most of the soldiers were dragged under by their heavy combat equipment and drowned within seconds, but three threw themselves forward with fanatical determination and tried to gain a grip on *Rapier's* slippery hull plating. The officer leading them was quickly swept away by the wash and his screams rent the night air as the propellers caught him.

'No prisoners!'

The submariners reacted to Hamilton's grim order without hesitation. Morgan grabbed an iron stanchion, ran along the fore-deck, and smashed it down on the hands of the first Japanese as he tried to haul himself to safety. Ryuji Kamisaka screamed but, ignoring the agony of his broken fingers, he continued to cling on with his left hand. Morgan struck again and the army corporal fell back into the sea with an anguished cry, drifted helplessly astern for a few brief moments, and then raised his arm and vanished beneath the surface.

The second soldier had already pulled himself up onto the fore-deck casing by the time Walker arrived in the bows and he received the seaman's boot in his face for his efforts. Losing his grip, he fell backwards into the water with a loud splash and disappeared.

The excitement was over before *Rapier's* men had had time to consider what they were doing. The skipper had given an order and responding to discipline they had carried it out. No one questioned whether it was lawful. And no one mentioned the Geneva Convention. It had been a matter of kill or be killed. In the heat of combat, personal survival could be the only consideration....

'*Destroyers to starboard!*'

'Check fire! New target three thousand yards on starboard bow - stand by!'

In the confusion of a night battle it is easy to make a mistake and Hamilton wanted positive identification before he ordered *Rapier's* deck gun to open fire. The approaching ships were unlikely to be British - but, he readily admitted it was an outside chance, they could be American.

'Three ships in line ahead - estimated speed twenty-five knots,' Mannon reported as he watched the approaching destroyers through his glasses. 'No lights.'

The crashing roar of an exploding shell astern rocked the submarine violently and Hamilton glanced back quickly at the shore. In the flickering glow of the burning trucks he could see a Japanese field gun on the shingle beach with another being manhandled alongside it. The heady self-confidence created by their two easy successes quickly disappeared in the face of this new danger. Suddenly everything had gone sour. And, if the approaching warships proved to be Japanese, the enemy had the submarine trapped between two fires!

'Reverse course, Cox'n. Steer west and make for mid-channel. I'm going to need diving room.' Hamilton leaned over the engine room voice pipe. 'Maximum revs, O'Brien! Pull out all the bloody stops!'

'Engine room, aye aye, sir.'

Having replaced the plug of the speaking-tube, Hamilton joined Mannon as *Rapier* heeled over sharply and swung onto her new course.

The leading warship had closed to 2,500 yards and not even the darkness could disguise the knuckled bow and cranked funnels of a typical Japanese destroyer. Yellow flame stabbed from her for'ard gun turret and, as the fierce crack of cordite echoed across the sea, two uncomfortably well-placed shells exploded close under the stern, throwing up towering geysers of dirty brown water.

Hamilton seemed unconcerned by the unexpected accuracy of the enemy fire. With calm professional detachment, he noted the color of the water thrown up by the bursting shells and turned to Mannon. 'They've stirred up the mud, Number One,' he observed casually. 'And that means we haven't enough depth of water for diving.'

The next salvo brought four shells whining down on the fleeing submarine, but Blood's expert handling of the helm kept *Rapier* out of immediate danger and Hamilton could feel the vessel jinking and twisting as the coxwain tried to throw off the enemy's aim. He leaned over the for'ard bridge screen. 'Secure from Action Stations, Mister Gunner. Get below!' Two more explosions rocked *Rapier* to starboard arid the crumbling fountain of water thrown up by the bursting shells fell on the exposed bridge like a shower of heavy summer rain. 'Stand by Diving Stations! First Officer and Coxwain to remain on the bridge. All hands below!' Hamilton moved to the voice pipe. 'Stand by to take over lower steering. What's the depth of water, Pilot?'

Scott checked the echo sounder on the starboard bulkhead. 'Thirty-five feet, sir.'

'Thank you, Pilot,' Hamilton turned to Mannon. 'No chance of diving yet, Number One. I'm not going to risk sticking the old girl's nose in the mud.' Crouching down on his knees, he opened the signal locker and fumbled inside. 'Are they gaining on us?

'Yes, sir - range down to two thousand.' Mannon sounded a little puzzled. 'The rear ship seems to be firing at something to the south.'

'Perhaps it's bombarding Taikoo,' Hamilton suggested as he continued his search of the locker.

'I don't think so - the shells are falling too short. Hang on... I can see another ship. Looks like a gunboat.' Hamilton found what he wanted and straightened up holding a couple of large cylindrical canisters. Tucking them under his arm, he raised his binoculars to find out the cause of Mannon's excitement.

The jaunty outline of a China gunboat, its light grey paintwork merging into the misty background of Victoria Island, was barely distinguishable in the bad light. But the large battle flag fluttering from the pole mast and the black smoke belching from her tandem funnels abaft the wheelhouse made it impossible to mistake her purpose. Flame flashed from the muzzle of the for'ard gun as she challenged the destroyers.

'It looks like *Firefly,* sir!'

'I wouldn't be at all surprised, Number One,' Hamilton agreed calmly. 'Only an idiot like Harry Ottershaw would take on three destroyers. They'll blow him out of the water with a couple of salvos.'

'Do we go about and give him support, sir?' Mannon asked.

Hamilton shook his head. 'No - and Ottershaw wouldn't thank us for it if we did. He's only shown himself in order to draw the Japs away and give us time to find deep water. If *Rapier* turns back, we'll both be done for.' He flipped open the cover of the voice pipe. 'Control Room-take over lower steering. Stand by to dive.' He snapped the lid shut and turned to Blood. 'Diving stations, Cox'n. Get below.' Ernie Blood moved to the upper hatch. He was sorry to miss the fun. But on the other hand, he preferred to be a live hero rather than a dead one and he wholeheartedly endorsed the skipper's unpalatable decision.

'One of the destroyers is resuming chase, sir.' Mannon warned from his vantage point at the rear of the conning tower. 'The other two are closing on *Firefly.*'

As Hamilton glanced astern to check the situation, he saw flame suddenly leap mast-high from the gunboat's superstructure as a salvo of enemy shells crashed down and exploded behind the wheelhouse. The little ship shuddered under the impact of two more direct hits but, seemingly undeterred by the punishment she was taking, *Firefly* defiantly maintained course towards her two powerful antagonists and a well-aimed shell from the for'ard gun forced one of the destroyers to turn away.

Hamilton moved to the engaged side of the bridge, jerked the fuse of the smoke candle, and threw the spluttering canister into the water. It was a device issued to submarines for service as a distress signal - the smoke from the canister floating on the surface indicated the location of the sunken vessel to rescue craft hurrying to its assistance. At that precise moment *Rapier* was certainly in distress and, in the circumstances, Hamilton felt justified in putting the emergency canisters to a more immediate and practical use. Ripping the paper from the second cylinder he tossed it into the water to join its companion.

'Depth of water, Mister Mannon?'

The first officer moved to the voice pipe to transmit the question to the control room below and waited while Scott checked the echo sounder.

'Forty feet and shelving, sir.'

'Very good, Number One. Get below. Diving in one minute.'

Baffled by the improvised smoke screen, the pursuing destroyer reduced speed and stopped firing.

There was a brief respite and then an unlucky gust of wind suddenly cleared a gap through the smoke to reveal the fleeing *Rapier* barely a mile away. Hamilton heard a salvo of shells screaming towards the defenseless submarine. A near miss kicked *Rapier* to port and, before the submarine had fully recovered, Hamilton was hurled across the bridge by the blast of a second shell bursting close under the starboard ballast tank. The brilliant white flash of the explosion dazzled his eyes and he fumbled blindly for a handhold.

Then, just as suddenly, the unpredictable breeze changed direction again and closed the gap in the smoke screen, bringing another short but vital reprieve from the enemy guns. Seizing his opportunity, Hamilton clambered down into the upper hatch and pressed the diving klaxon.

AHOOA...AHOOA...AHOOA.

Rapier was already sliding beneath the surface by the time he reached the control room and a quick glance at the dials showed that Mannon had used his intelligence and put the submarine into a shallow dive so that if, by ill-luck, they struck the muddy bottom of the Straits, it would only a glancing blow.

'Propeller noises approaching, sir,' Murray reported from the hydro-phones.

'Slow ahead both motors - level at forty feet.'

Hamilton made no attempt to stop engines and shut down for depth charges - the water was probably too shallow for the destroyer to use underwater weapons without placing herself in equal danger. It was a gamble worth taking. Every single minute counted and, once Rapier could reach the area covered by the shore batteries, she would be safe from further attack. Not even the most fool-hardy enemy captain would put his ship at risk against shore guns....

The submarine suddenly jolted sideways as if struck by a giant hammer, light bulbs shattered, gauge glasses cracked, and cork insulation wafted down from the deck head seams like fine brown snow. Ten seconds later, as the men were picking themselves up off the deck, the angry rumble of a violent explosion echoed like distant thunder against the hull plates.

'Either that was bloody close,' someone murmured 'or the Japs are using fucking big depth charges!'

The force of the concussion had blown the main fuses and there was a general sigh of relief as the emergency lamps glowed to life. Hamilton cast an anxious eye at the dials and felt reassured by what he saw. He rubbed a large bruise on his left buttock, where he had been thrown against a valve wheel.

'I don't think it was a depth charge,' he said quietly. 'It sounded more like a ship blowing up.' He turned to Murray crouched over his hydro-phone equipment. 'Where's the destroyer now?'

'Passed directly overhead just before the explosion, sir. HE suggests she's turned south towards Victoria....' Murray paused, listened intently and carefully moved the knurled knob of his apparatus. 'Still turning, sir. Now headed east towards Junk Bay.'

'Periscope depth!'

'Up-helm 'planes - level at thirty.'

The two coxswains eased the big diving wheels to the left and watched the red needles of the depth gauges swing upwards.

'Thirty feet, sir!'

'Reverse 'planes... keep her level, Cox'n.'

'Up periscope!'

Hamilton grabbed the handles and pulled them down as the thin stalk of the 'scope poked above the waves. He circled quickly until the upper lens was bearing towards the stern. The water suddenly drained from the angled glass and he found himself staring into the soft darkness of the tropical night, with a canopy of stars twinkling against the black velvet vault of the sky above the horizon. He picked out the stern of the destroyer disappearing in the general direction of Lye Mum Point and then carried out a swift 360 degree search of the surface to make sure there were no other enemy warships in the vicinity.

He could just make out the shapes of the other two destroyers circling off the coast to the east - their searchlights sweeping the surface as if looking for something. He switched to the high magnification lens for a closer inspection of the scene and watched the third destroyer join its companions. Working in formation, the three warships quartered the area off Taikoo like restless hounds prowling outside the lair of a runaway fox. Then, as a signal lamp flashed from one of the destroyers, they formed up in line ahead. Gathering speed, they steered eastwards towards the open sea. Hamilton watched them vanish and then surveyed the empty waters of Quarry Bay once again.

'Down periscope.' He turned away as the column sank back into its womb under the deck. '*Firefly's* gone,' he announced unemotionally. 'The Japs were searching for survivors but I doubt if they found any. Must have been a direct hit on the magazine. That would account for the explosion we heard.'

No one spoke for a few moments, but they all knew *Firefly* had deliberately sacrificed herself to ensure their escape. It was Mannon who finally broke the brooding silence with an epitaph that voiced the thoughts of every man in the submarine's control room.

'I reckon Harry Ottershaw deserves a bloody Victoria Cross.'

Hamilton leaned his elbows on the table while he studied the chart. Snark wanted him to patrol off Lam Tong Island during the hours of daylight and that meant a long sweep past Larama Island and then a run to the east keeping south of Victoria Island itself. It was tempting to cut through the channel via Deep Water, Repulse, and South Bays. But once the sun had risen, he had little doubt that Japanese air patrols would be scouring the inshore areas in search of any remaining British warships still afloat and he wanted to proceed on the surface to save *Rapier's* batteries.

'Urgent damage report, sir.'

Hamilton straightened up as O'Brien came through the bulkhead hatch into the control room.

'What's the trouble, Chief?'

'Starboard bunker leaking, sir. Clayton's been checking the oil level and it's dropping steadily even though the engines aren't running.'

Hamilton felt a cold finger trace slowly down his spine. O'Brien was worried about the loss of fuel and the consequent reduction in *Rapier's* effective range. Hamilton's fear was more immediate. With oil leaking from the damaged bunker, the submarine was leaving a trail on the surface which, once spotted, would bring every available enemy ship and aircraft zeroing in for the kill. If he came to the surface and radioed *Rapier's* exact position to the Japanese flagship they'd be in no greater danger!

'How much fuel in the other bunkers, Chief?'

'About forty tons, sir.'

'Well that's sufficient for the moment. Pump all the remaining fuel in the damaged tank overboard immediately.'

O'Brien hesitated. It was not in his nature to question orders, but he wondered whether the skipper realized the consequences of what he had just said. 'But if we do that, sir,' he pointed out, 'we won't have enough fuel left to go *anywhere*. I can plug the leak inside an hour or so. It's better than losing ten tons by opening the taps.'

'And until you do, Chief,' Hamilton said coldly, '*Rapier* is leaving a trail of oil on the surface that'll bring the entire Japanese Navy upon us in about the same time! It's sunrise in thirty minutes. If we're not at least five miles clear of that slick by dawn we won't live long enough to see another. Pump the bunker clear as ordered, Mister O'Brien.'

'Aye aye, sir.'

Hamilton returned to the chart table, pulled open a small drawer, and took out a slip of paper on which was written the latitude and longitude of a rendezvous point. He passed it to Scott.

'I want to be at that position by noon, pilot. You'll have to deduct an hour while we heave-to so that O'Brien can plug the leak. Can you do it?'

Scott glanced at the position shown on the slip of paper, gauged the distance on the chart, and nodded.

'I think so, sir. Although it will mean running at least half the distance on the surface at maximum speed.' The navigator frowned down at the chart. 'There's only one thing, sir. That fix you gave me is in the middle of the China Sea - there's no land within two hundred miles. What the hell are we going to find when we get there?' Hamilton smiled enigmatically. 'Wait and see, Pilot. Wait and see. Just lay on a course - I'll produce the rabbit out of the hat.'

NINE

The big trading junk looked innocent enough to the casual observer. The large rush-matting sails rippled in the breeze like blinds fluttering behind an open window and she was making barely two knots. The Chinese characters daubed on her flat stern indicated she was from Macao, but she carried no other mark or figures of identification - a not unusual state of affairs with native sailing vessels. But there was something about her that puzzled Lieutenant Furutaka and, after a short period of indecisive hesitation, he took the bull by the horns and called the captain to the bridge.

Commander Aritsu's expression boded trouble as he came up the companion way. He liked his junior officers to be self-reliant and made no attempt to conceal his annoyance as Furutaka pointed out the junk and explained his misgivings. Aritsu snarled impatiently, raised his binoculars, and examined the mysterious stranger for himself.

For the river people of China, their boat is their home. They have nowhere else to live and the larger sea-going junks often support two or three families extending, on occasions, to three generations, complete with all their worldly possessions and livestock. As the deeply laden vessels dip past with their leeside gunwales almost under water, it is often difficult to see what possible room could be left for commercial freight in the face of its superabundant human cargo. The men work the sails and steering, the women cook, wash clothes amidships, or idly gossip in the stern; chickens cluck importantly from bamboo coops strung from the rigging, and innumerable children of all ages play in whatever free deck space is left.

And, as Aritsu's experienced eyes quickly detected, *that* was the oddity which had puzzled his officer-of-the-watch. The junk moving slowly across *Suma's* bows only had three people on deck!

'Lower away the sea boat, Lieutenant. And send over a boarding party to check her papers.'

Suma's cutter was already swung out and ready - a normal precaution when a warship is operating under combat conditions in a designated war zone - and the boarding party of six armed seamen under the command of a young Korean sub-lieutenant climbed down into it, as the deckhands lowered it into the water and released the falls.

Responding to the signal flag fluttering from the destroyer's halyards - the square of yellow and blue bunting -indicating the letter *K* - the junk had come to an untidy stop and was waiting dead in the water as the cutter approached. The flag letter *K* in the International Code meant *Stop Immediately* and Aritsu showed little surprise at the junk's prompt obedience. The native seamen plying their trade along the Chinese coast knew nothing of such matters as signal codes and international conventions, but experience had taught them that any warship flying the yellow and blue flag intended them to stop. And failure to obey could mean a shot across the bows or a brutal shelling, depending on the mood of the naval commander - and his nationality.

The crew of the junk made no attempt to resist as the cutter came alongside and disgorged the boarding party. They stood in the stern neither helping nor hindering, seemingly unconcerned by the unceremonious visitation. Aritsu watched through his binoculars for signs of hostility, but the three Chinese seamen accepted the invasion with disinterested docility.

Sub-Lieutenant Mihoro looked quickly to right and left as he swung over the low side of the junk, but he could detect no obvious signs of concealed weapons and, raising his arms imperiously, he sent the boarding party for'ard to search the bows, while he and the petty officer went aft to question the crew.

The junk's cargo, carefully protected from the weather under heavy tarpaulins, covered every available inch of the deck space and Petty Officer Kino swore sharply as he stubbed his bare toe against something hard. Lifting the edge of the tarpaulin, he bent down to examined what was underneath and let out a soft but expressive hiss of surprise.

'Over here, sir!' he called to Mihoro.

Ordering the two armed guards to come aft and cover the Chinese crew, the sub-lieutenant joined Kino amidships. The petty officer's bayonet sawed through the securing ropes and, throwing back the tarpaulin, he showed the officer the cargo of black steel barrels hidden beneath the covers.

Oil!

Mihoro thought quickly. Unlike the petty officer he could understand English, and his eyes narrowed as he read the stenciled white letters on the side of each barrel - Diesel Oil. De Gama Oil & Wharfage Company, Macao. Well, the junk was outward bound from Macao right enough. But where to? Chinese sailors were notoriously wary of deep-sea voyages and were normally only happy when hugging the coast. Yet this particular junk was steering a course that was taking it out to the middle of an empty sea, the nearest land to the south, Borneo, was over a thousand miles away.

Getting to his feet, Mihoro glanced suspiciously at the three Chinese seamen standing meekly in the stern under the guns of the guards and spoke rapidly to Kino. The petty officer nodded and called Teishu down from the bows where he was checking another group of similar barrels. The seaman saluted as Kino gave him his instructions and, climbing on to the gunwale, he began semaphoring to the destroyer with his arms.

Seitaka, *Suma's* Yeoman of Signals, raised his telescope and read off the message. He passed it on verbally to Aritsu who was waiting impatiently at his side.

'Sub-Lieutenant Mihoro requests you go aboard the junk, sir. He says he has found a large number of oil barrels-diesel oil.'

The impatience vanished from Aritsu's face. He was suddenly alert. Diesel oil - fuel for warships. *Enemy* warships. What a stroke of luck. He could not only destroy the enemy's supplies but, if he was able to establish the rendezvous position for the refuelling operation, he could also lay an ambush and sink the warship for which it was intended. The normally taciturn commander was actually smiling as he ordered the bosun to lower away *Suma's* motorboat.

Aritsu sniffed the air suspiciously as he climbed over the side of the junk to join Mihoro and the boarding party. Ignoring the three prisoners, he slowly walked down the length of the deck and examined the serried rows of barrels.

The last doubts vanished from his mind by the time he had completed his inspection. Much as he would have liked to seize the junk as a prize and bring the captured oil back to Whampoa in triumph, it would interfere with his other plans, and after a short pause, he ordered Kino to unseal the barrels and tip the fuel into the sea. Better to destroy the stuff and leave himself a free agent, he decided. He turned to the Korean sub-lieutenant.

'Bring the prisoners to me.'

Prodded forward by the bayonets of the guards, the Chinese sailors shuffled their way down from the poop to the well deck amidships where Aritsu was waiting.

'Which of you is the Captain?' he asked in fluent Cantonese.

Chen Yu moved forward half a pace and bowed. Aritsu stared at him in silence for a few moments - his deep-set eyes boring into the Chinaman's brain, as if laying bare the innermost secrets of his soul.

'Where are you taking the oil?' he snapped.

'Palambang, sir.'

'Liar.'

Chen Yu bowed in acknowledgement but made no reply. He stared down at the deck and remained silent.

'You are in the pay of the British.' Aritsu made the question sound like a statement of fact. 'You are being paid to refuel British warships.'

'No, sir. Not being paid, sir.' Chen Yu answered truthfully.

Mihoro had disappeared through the hatch into the tiny cabin under the poopdeck and, as Aritsu pursued his interrogation, he suddenly emerged carrying a number of navigation instruments - instruments of a sophistication and type not normally found in a primitive Chinese sailing vessel...

Aritsu paused in mid-question, took one of the instruments from the sub-lieutenant, and examined it carefully. He smiled to himself as he saw the official British Admiralty mark stamped into the brass casing.

'Lies are of no avail,' he told Chen Yu ominously as he held the sextant up in front of his face. 'Give me the information I want and no harm will come to you. Where is your rendezvous position with the English warship?'

Chen Yu made no reply and the commander snapped a swift order in Japanese to the guards. Picking the Chinese skipper up by the arms, they threw him down across the opened hatchway leading to the hold and held him firmly, so that the lower part of his left leg was placed at an angle across the empty space- the limb being supported at thigh and ankle by the rigid coaming surrounding the hatchway.

'A crippled Captain is of no use to a healthy crew,' Aritsu said quietly. 'Tell us the rendezvous co-ordinates.' Chen Yu stared up at him with wide, terror-filled eyes.

Aritsu nodded and one of the sailors slammed the butt of his heavy service rifle down on the Chinaman's shin. There was a dry cracking sound of splintered bone and Chen Yu's leg snapped like a piece of rotted wood. Blood oozed through the cotton material of his trousers where the broken bone protruded through the flesh. He remained silent for a moment and then shrieked like a wounded animal as the pain reached his brain.

'The other leg, Suka,' Aritsu ordered unemotionally. He waited for the sailors to rearrange the Chinaman over the hatchway, so that his right leg stretched out in readiness for the same treatment. The agony of the movement brought more screams, but the commander's expression remained completely impassive. Bending forward, he stared down into Chen Yu's perspiring face. 'Tell me the position or you will never walk again.'

Chen Yu compressed his lips defiantly and the rifle butt descended for a second time. The Chinaman's body lifted in a rigid arch and his mouth opened in a soundless scream. An eternity of pain passed in a fraction of a second before he fainted. Aritsu straightened up. He took no pleasure from the torture. It was a barbaric necessity. He turned away slowly.

Wan Fu saw the movements and knew it was his turn next. Pushing the guards aside he leapt for the poop rail, swayed uncertainly for a moment, and threw himself into the sea. Sub-Lieutenant Mihoro reached the side almost before the Chinese seaman hit the water and, dragging a revolver from the holster at his hip, he took careful aim and continued firing until the chamber was empty. By the time Aritsu arrived at the rails, Wan Fu's lifeless body was floating face-downwards in the blood-stained sea.

'A pity,' he commented blandly. 'He would have been useful. You must learn the art of self-discipline, SubLieutenant. You Koreans can only think of killing.' Mihoro flushed angrily. The torture of Chen Yu had stirred a primitive evil in his subconscious - a latent sadism inherited from his Mongol ancestors which had remained dormant for many generations. He considered Commander Aritsu, like most professional Japanese naval officers, was too soft.

'We still have one more prisoner, sir,' he reminded the senior officer. 'Why not leave that one to me?'

Aritsu felt sickened by the brutality he had already ordered, but he did not allow his revulsion to deter him from what he saw to be his duty to the Emperor. And much as he wanted to wash his hands of the whole filthy matter, he felt a certain reluctance to give the sadistic Korean officer a free hand. He watched Wan Fu's body drift slowly astern while he decided what to do. Then, turning away from the rail, he walked back to the well- deck amidships.

Ignoring Mihoro's offer he looked at Kino and nodded. 'Bring the other prisoner to me, Petty Officer. I will continue the interrogation.'

As the men of the boarding party advanced towards the stern the surviving Chinese seamen made a wild dash for the side, but this time the guards were on the alert. Two of them moved to cut off his line of escape while the third reached out and his strong hand twisted in the prisoner's hair. He pulled hard and an unmistakable feminine scream of protest rang out. Two more guards closed in quickly, seized the woman's arms and hauled her bodily down the wooden steps of the poop, as she fought and struggled to escape.

Mihoro stepped forward as they dragged her before Aritsu. Without waiting for permission he grasped the pris- oner's sweat-soiled cotton shirt and ripped it off with a savage jerk. He looked at the smooth flawless body and saw the small high breasts tipped with dark nipples. His eyes glistened cruelly and the tip of his tongue passed across his upper lip in anticipation.

'The top half seems to be a woman, sir,' he leered at the grinning sailors. His hands fumbled at the cord holding up the baggy cotton trousers. It came undone and he watched them slide down to her ankles. 'And the bottom half undoubtedly is as well.' He stepped back to admire the view.

'That is enough, Sub-Lieutenant!' Aritsu snapped sharply. 'You are an officer - not an animal. Control your- self.' The commander stepped closer to the prisoner. There was something familiar about the girl. He stared at Chai

Chen who rewarded his interest by spitting in his face. Mihoro lunged forward and struck her across the cheek with his clenched fist, but Aritsu pushed him away with an angry gesture.

Suma's captain seemed flustered by the insult. He wiped his cheek with a handkerchief. 'Yes... of course. Your step-father is Dominguez Alburra. That would account for the De Gama Oil Company's name on the barrels.'

Ignoring the dictates of modesty, Chai Chen wriggled like an eel to break free from her captors; but the guards merely tightened their grip on her arms and her naked body arched with pain. 'You go to hell, pig!' she hissed at him.

Aritsu accepted the epithet with a smile as the girl's identity triggered his memory. The Japanese Intelligence Agency in Macao had kept him well-informed and very little escaped their notice.

'But, of course... Lieutenant Hamilton.' He did not miss the momentary flicker of fear on the girl's face as she heard the name. 'He saved your life when your launch was bombed. And, as I understand it, he has been a constant visitor to your step-father's home.' Aritsu paused, to give Chai Chen time to digest the fact that he knew rather more about her activities than she might have expected. 'That is why you are carrying diesel oil - *to refuel the English submarine!*'

Chai Chen knew it was useless to lie. She shivered and, as if suddenly conscious of her nakedness, squeezed her thighs together as she saw the sailors looking at her body. Lowering her head, she stared down at the deck.

Mihoro's impatience exploded with a savage snarl. Before Aritsu could stop him, the sub-lieutenant stepped forward and, motioning the guards to hold her securely, he raked his clawed hands along the girl's rigid body. Chai

Chen endured the indignity in silence until the probing fingers found a new and more subtle way to hurt her, and the Korean smirked with complacent satisfaction as he heard her soft whimper of disgust.

¹Leave her alone, Sub-Lieutenant!'

Mihoro retreated reluctantly. The expression on his face was like that of a child deprived of its favourite toy. He stared at his erstwhile victim and his eyes glittered at the memory as he saw the ugly marks left by his fingers. Aritsu swallowed back his anger, regained his composure, and steeled himself for the distasteful task that lay ahead.

'It is useless to resist,' he told Chai Chen quietly. 'Nothing can save the English submarine. If you tell me the rendezvous position I might be able to persuade Lieutenant Hamilton to surrender. There is no other way in which his life can be saved. But I am powerless to help him unless I know where the refuelling is to take place.' Chai Chen continued to stare at the deck and Aritsu made one last despairing effort to persuade her. 'If you continue to remain silent I will be forced to hand you over to the Sub-Lieutenant. And if I do, you will undoubtedly suffer a great deal of unnecessary pain. Make no mistake about it - your obstinacy will be broken in the end and you will tell me everything I want to know. Why not be sensible?' Chai Chen raised her head slowly. She stared at Aritsu as if judging the sincerity of his offer and then glanced at Mihoro. She turned away with a shiver as she read the cruelty in the Korean's face.

'I know nothing,' she said simply.

Aritsu closed his eyes for a brief moment as if suffering a spasm of physical pain. Then, with a stiffly formal bow, he walked to the side where the motorboat was waiting to take him back to *Suma*. Mihoro followed him like a dog eager to be loosed in search of a rabbit.

'You may proceed with the interrogation of the prisoner, Sub-Lieutenant,' he instructed the Korean. 'Report to me when you have obtained the information. You have precisely thirty minutes to achieve your object.'

Aritsu acknowledged Mihoro's salute and climbed down into the motorboat. Settling himself in the stern, he placed his fingertips together in an attitude of prayer and tried to come to terms with his conscience, as the launch reversed away from the junk and turned its bows in the direction of the waiting destroyer. The commander sat in contemplative silence for several minutes and then, as if forcing himself to perform an act of penance for his sins, he turned his head and stared back at the junk.

He could not see what Mihoro was doing, but Chai Chen was already tied spread-eagled and naked against the side of the deckhouse and the steel blade of the bayonet which the Korean was holding in his right hand glistened in the sun. Aritsu shuddered as her first screams echoed across the water.

HAMILTON WAITED until the hands of the control room clock settled exactly on 11-59, before easing himself out of his canvas chair and moving to the center of the compartment. The heat and humidity inside the submarine was unbearable and, in spite of his earlier warnings to the crew, his hooked fingers scratched relentlessly at a patch of inflamed and itching skin around his waist. He felt tired and dirty, and was acutely conscious of the unpleasant odour of the stale sweat clinging to his unwashed body.

Despite the personal discomforts, however, Hamilton

was still optimistic and he was well satisfied with the efforts of *Rapier's* crew. Even Villiers, the young fourth hand, had turned out to be an unexpected asset. During a recent tour of duty with the Diplomatic Corps in Tokyo, he had made frequent trips to the Japanese island of Kuro to observe and learn the secrets of the pearl divers - and it was this knowledge which Hamilton had made good use of.

With Villiers' ability to dive and remain underwater for upwards of two minutes at a time with no more specialized equipment than a heavy stone and a primitive nose-clip, it had proved possible to repair the damage to the fuel tank while the submarine lay stopped on the surface during the night. Admittedly with the tools available, it was a rough and ready job - canvas and a wooden plug - but it was adequate for the purpose. And as a result Hamilton had been able to reach the pre-arranged rendezvous without forcing *Rapier* beyond her normal cruising speed. With fuel supplies dwindling by the hour, economy was an all- important consideration...

'12 o'clock, sir,' Scott reported from the chart tables. 'We should be in exactly the right position according to the DR plot.'

'Well done, Pilot. Up periscope!'

The men in the control room watched expectantly as Hamilton carried out a quick preliminary sweep of the horizon, and waited quietly while he worked his way slowly around the full circle. It was apparent from the tension in his hands and the set of his shoulders that the rendezvous vessel was nowhere in sight; but the expression on his face gave nothing away as he closed the steering handles with a decisive snap and stepped back from the column.

'Down periscope!' He turned to Scott. 'Are you *quite* certain of our position, Pilot?'

'Yes, sir. I took some star sights an hour before dawn.

Even allowing for an unexpected alteration in the wind, I'd guarantee we're within a mile of the position you gave me yesterday.'

Hamilton rubbed his chin thoughtfully. Despite his outward skepticism, he had complete faith in Scott's ability as a navigator. So, for the moment, he could only assume that Album's supply vessel had not arrived. Unless - and he tried to keep the suspicion out of his mind - something had happened to it.

'What direction is Macao, Alistair?'

Scott checked the chart. 'North-east by east, sir.'

Hamilton waited for five minutes, raised the periscope again, and drew another blank. He was certain that Alburra would not let him down, but where the hell was his ship?

'Stand by to surface. Duty Watch to close up - negative deck party.' He glanced at Scott apologetically. 'It's not that I doubt you, Alistair, but I want another sun sight.'

Scott grinned understandingly and reached for his sextant. Then, moving across to the conning tower ladder, he waited to follow the duty watch up on deck.

'Surface!'

'Up helm 'planes! Blow main ballast and close all vents!'

'Ten feet, sir.'

Hamilton started up the ladder, unclipped the upper hatch, and pushed it open. The normally clean-tasting sea air seemed slightly tainted with oil fumes but he put it down to the fuel leak from the damaged bunker and, dismissing it from his mind, hauled himself up on to the bridge. Picking up his glasses he carried out a quick preliminary sweep of the horizon, while the look-outs hurried to their positions on the port and starboard sides of the conning tower.

'What do you make of the oil slick, sir?' Scott asked casually, peering over the side as he lifted his sextant from its case.

Hamilton glanced down at the sea. The surface of the water was streaked by oil and, for a few moments, he assumed it must be coming from *Rapier's* own damaged tank. A more careful examination, however, revealed that the rainbow tinted trail stretched well *ahead* of the submarine's beam. So it *couldn't* be leaking fuel from the bunker. At first he thought it must mark the grave of a recently sunken ship, but the slick was too long and narrow - and the oil seemed fresh rather than dirty. He called Scott over for a discussion.

A detailed search with their binoculars revealed that the slick was spreading over a wider area to the south, rather than to the north and, significantly, it seemed to be thicker on the surface ahead of the bows where it had apparently had less time to disperse. Having compared notes, they agreed that the slick was following the direction of the wind which was blowing astern and from the south. Consequently, the source lay somewhere to the north. Any further speculation was abruptly ended by a sudden shout from the port look-out.

'Ship hull down and dead ahead, sir!'

Hamilton put the binoculars to his eyes and saw the ungainly sails of a large junk peeping coyly over the rim of the horizon.

'Full ahead together! Deck parties to stand by.'

But even as *Rapier* increased speed towards the distant vessel Hamilton could feel his optimism slowly evaporating. The oil on the surface boded bad news and the fact that the junk was drifting *before* the wind and *away* from the rendezvous position suggested that something was seriously wrong.

By the time *Rapier* had drawn close to the drifting vessel, the black slick polluting the surface was thicker and the acrid fumes rising up from the sea was making the eyes of the men on the bridge of the submarine smart and sting. Streaks of oil were now clearly visible down the sides of the junk and the flapping rudder showed she was not under control.

'Foredeck party topsides at the double.'

By the time Morgan's men had emerged from the gun tower and assembled on the foredeck, less than a hundred yards of oil polluted water separated the two vessels. *Rapier* was lying broadside on to the wind and Hamilton had to brace himself against the motion of the submarine as his binoculars scanned the abandoned junk for signs of life. But the decks were empty and the scattered oil barrels clattering noisily against the bulwarks and sliding from one side to the other as the boat rolled in the swell, warned him that disaster had already struck.

The deserted junk posed no apparent danger, but Hamilton knew the value of caution. It was tempting to assume that the abandoned vessel was harmless - but he remembered the Royal Navy had often employed a similar ploy during the Kaiser war when their deadly Q ships hunted Germany's U-boats to death by masquerading as innocent merchantmen. And, despite the evidence of his own eyes, he wanted to make sure he was not walking into a trap. Bending over the voice pipe he ordered the helmsman to circle the junk at half-speed.

Rapier moved slowly across the stern and started to pass down the lee side of the abandoned vessel, while Hamilton continued to search the deck and upperworks for some sign of the crew.

'Christ Almighty! What the hell's *that*...?'

Hamilton broke off his examination of the poop as he heard Scott's shocked exclamation. A chilling undertone of horror in the navigator's voice sent an involuntary shiver down his spine and he turned his attention to midship section of the junk. The blood drained from his face as he saw the reason for Scott's incredulous shout.

A naked body was spreadeagled against the side of the deckhouse. It hung suspended like a limp starfish, the wrists and ankles secured by ropes to the four corners of the primitive wooden structure, with the head drooped forward and the exposed flesh covered with hundreds of crawling flies. The breeze blowing the tangled black hair across the face made recognition impossible, but a quick inspection with the binoculars revealed that it was the body of a woman.

Hamilton's hands trembled as he lowered the glasses. Although it was impossible to see the woman's face, he knew instinctively that it was Chai Chen. Bringing his emotions under control and taking a deep breath, Hamilton stepped away from the rail and moved towards the voice pipe.

'Stop motors... slow ahead starboard.' *Rapier's* bows swung towards the junk and he leaned over the for'ard screen. 'Morgan! I'm going alongside. Use a grappling hook to secure for boarding.'

Returning to the starboard wing he waited for the submarine to drift closer. He forced himself not to look at the obscenity of the tortured girl stretched rigidly against the side of the deckhouse and he concentrated all of his attention into the task of bringing *Rapier* safely alongside the abandoned junk.

'Stop starboard motor... slow astern both. Full starboard helm.'

Morgan balanced himself on the edge of the ballast tank, swung the weighted rope like a cowboy with a lasso, judged the distance with an expert eye, and let go. The grappling hook soared up from the deck of the submarine, landed squarely over the weatherworn bulwarks in the bow of the junk, and the line pulled taut as the deck party hauled in the slack.

'Line secured, sir.'

'Take over, Alistair. Keep her close alongside.' Hamilton swung his leg over the conning tower coaming and shinned down the iron rungs to join the gunner's mate and the men waiting on the foredeck. 'Well done, Chief. I'm going aboard first. Once I'm safely over I want you and two men to follow and back me up.'

Clinging to the life line, Hamilton edged gingerly down the slippery slopes of the weed-encrusted ballast tank, balanced himself precariously at the water's edge and carefully gauged the swing of the submarine as the two vessels drifted together in the wind. At exactly the right moment, he leapt across the narrow gap, grabbed for a handhold, and hauled himself up the slab side of the junk onto the deck. Pausing at the rail, he signaled to Morgan to follow and then made his way along the oil-stained deck towards the wooden shelter amidships.

As he came around the side of the deckhouse and saw Chai Chen's body at close-quarters for the first time he stopped, held on to the rail for support, and was violently sick in the scuppers. Wiping the back of his hand across his mouth and steeling himself forward he started to unfasten the ropes Mihoro had used to secure his victim in position.

Chai Chen was dead. And the ugly cuts and burns on

her body showed that her death had not been easy. Hamilton tried not to look as he freed the ropes binding her wrists and ankles and lowered the pitiful remains of the girl onto the deck with a gentle compassion surprising for a man with his reputation.

'Anything I can do, sir?' Morgan asked as Hamilton found a length of ragged canvas with which to cover the body.

Rapier's commander knelt beside Chai Chen in silence and it was not until the gunner's mate repeated the question that he came out of his reverie.

'Thanks, Chief - I can manage. But there's one thing you can do. Most of the De Gama Company's junks are fitted with old Packard automobile engines - I remember Alburra telling me about them during one of my visits. I daresay this one's the same as the others. See if you can locate some cans of petrol. Bring one to me and use the others to soak the decking and upperworks.'

Morgan returned a few minutes later to find Hamilton still kneeling beside the makeshift shroud. He put a two gallon can of Amoco on the deck in front of the skipper and then made his way to the stern to help the other submariners sprinkle the remaining gasoline containers over the weather worn woodwork of the junk.

Hamilton rose slowly to his feet, unscrewed the brass cap of the can, and tilted the container so that the inflammable spirit splattered over the canvas sheet covering Chai Chen's body. When it was completely empty, he threw it into the scuppers and made his way back to the poop. There was nothing more he could do - nothing except to swear revenge on the barbarous savages responsible for the atrocity. The expression on his face was carved from granite as he approached the *Rapier's* gunner.

'Did your men find anyone else aboard, Chief!'

Morgan nodded vaguely towards the bows. 'Only an old Chinaman. His legs looked like they'd been broken with the butt end of a rifle. He was dead too.' The Welshman paused for a moment at the memory of Chen Yu's agonized death mask. 'What sort of bastards could torture an old man and a girl, sir?'

Hamilton's face lost none of its grimness. 'I don't know, Chief. But if I ever find them...' He left the threat unfinished. 'Get your men back to *Rapier*. I can't risk staying on the surface any longer.'

Restraining an impulse to go back to the girl, Hamilton walked to the port side of the junk and waited while Morgan and the two sailors jumped on to the submarine's foredeck. Then, having prised the grappling hook out of the bulwarks, he leapt across the narrow width of water separating the two vessels, and joined them.

'Get below, Chief and secure the gun hatch. We'll be diving in a couple of minutes.' Tossing the hook for Morgan to catch, he made his way unhurriedly down the foredeck, swung himself up the rungs on the outside of the conning tower, and dropped on to the bridge. 'Stand by to dive ... all hands below!' He bent over the voice pipe as Scott and the look-outs slid into the hatchway and went down the ladder into the control room. 'Slow astern both motors. Full port rudder. Call all hands to diving stations, Number One.'

'Aye aye, sir. Standing by.'

As *Rapier* went astern and backed slowly away from the junk Hamilton walked to the signal locker behind the binnacle, unfastened the watertight door, and took out a Very pistol. Slipping a cartridge into the breach, he snapped it shut, and moved to the starboard, side of the bridge. He waited until the submarine was safely clear and then, aiming carefully at the base of the tall bamboo main mast, he squeezed the trigger.

The signal cartridge hissed across the water and struck a pile of petrol-soaked sacks where it came to rest, buzzing and sizzling like an angry bee as the fuse burned down. The sudden flash of the flare ignited a pool of gasoline in the shadow of the deckhouse, there was a violent explosion, and within seconds the entire deck from poop to bows was a soaring mass of roaring flames. Hamilton lowered the pistol and watched. He was not a religious man but, alone on the bridge with no one to see, he lowered his head in silent prayer...

'I don't suppose we'll ever know who was responsible, sir,' Mannon observed quietly as Hamilton clipped the lower hatch and came down the final rungs of the ladder into the bright sanity of the control room.

'I don't suppose we will,' *Rapier's* commander agreed grimly. 'But I'm quite certain about one thing - only the Japs would have done something like that. And from now on any enemy ship we meet up with will be sunk without warning. Furthermore, no prisoners will be taken.'

Mannon made no reply. The skipper had been through a bad experience and the black mood would soon pass. Most of the *Rapier's* crew had heard what had happened on board the junk and Chai Chen's relationship with their captain was common knowledge. His reaction was understandable in the circumstances.

'Where to now, sir?' Mannon asked in an attempt to change the subject and to direct Hamilton's mind towards other matters. Brooding would only make things worse. 'O'Brien says we've less than half capacity in the bunkers. If we can't get hold of some more fuel our maximum surface range will be down to two thousand miles at the most.'

Hamilton nodded. Although his expression had lost none of its grimness he seemed to be thinking rationally again.

'We'll make for Charlotte Island to begin with, Number One. The TGM reports only four torpedoes left so we'll have to go to the island to load up the spares. And at the same time, we can top up our water and stores. After that we go hunting for a tanker.'

'But supposing the Japs have already found the island, sir?'

'I doubt that they have, Number One. Only *Rapier's* officers know about it...' He paused for a moment as he remembered. 'And of course, my Portuguese friends.'

'They might have forced the girl to tell them,' Mannon suggested.

Hamilton's face blazed in anger. He swung round as Mannon put the question and, for a brief moment, the submarine's executive officer thought that the captain was going to strike him. Hamilton controlled his fury with superhuman effort.

'If they had forced her to talk she would have told them about the rendezvous and we would have walked straight into an ambush. The fact that the Japs merely threw the oil overboard and then left the area shows she kept her mouth shut.' Hamilton shivered as he recalled what Chai Chen had suffered to protect *Rapier* and her crew. His shoulders bowed suddenly and, without another word, he turned on his heel and made his way to the privacy of the wardroom to be alone with his thoughts....

TEN

'Charlotte Island dead ahead, sir!'

Hamilton made his way forward to take over the periscope for the final approach and he carefully focused the low wedge of land in the center of the upper lens. The island resembled a saddle placed astride the blue rim of the horizon. The hummocked hill at the western end formed the pommel, while the gradual upwards slope to the east, ending with abrupt suddenness in the cliffs at Mi Lim Point, completed the illusion. To the south, and nearest to the submarine, the encircling arm of the palm-studded sandspit elbowed the sea aside to enclose a fine natural harbor within its protective grasp.

'Stand by Diving Stations. Slow ahead both motors.' He checked the bearing of the hill against the gyro repeater. 'One point to starboard.'

It was a familiar routine. At least once a week for the last two months *Rapier* had nosed her way past Taichee Rock into the secluded bay and then slid under the camouflage nets covering the tiny inlet on the west side of the lagoon, to begin unloading the torpedoes and stores which Hamilton had carefully spirited out of Hong Kong in readiness for a situation such as this.

A line of red painted floats marking the fishing net suspended beneath, was clearly visible as *Rapier* edged within three miles of the island - innocent enough at first sight but, in fact, deliberately laid by the submarine's crew during their first survey visit to mark an area of treacherous shoals to the southeast of the island.

Hamilton carried out a standard sky-search for hostile aircraft and then moved back from the 'scope. 'Take over the watch, Sub,' he told Villiers. 'I want a few words with Roger in the wardroom. Give me a shout as soon as you see the starboard channel marker.' He grinned. 'You'll find it on the north shore of the entrance - it looks like a pile of stones with an empty barrel on top.'

Despite the seemingly carefree way in which Hamilton had selected and prepared *Rapier's* secret hiding place he had, in point of fact, tackled the scheme with considerable thought and a surprising attention to detail. Scott and his two assistants had used the submarine's rubber dinghy to survey the anchorage on *Rapier's* first inspection visit to the island and, on returning to the boat, the navigator had drawn up an accurate chart complete with cross bearings and depth soundings. Then, in consultation with Hamilton, an approach course was plotted and where the natural features were non-existent, artificial navigation marks had been put down - an untidily piled heap of stones on the beach or perhaps a section of bark carved from an old palm tree lying in a prominent position close to the shoreline.

Villiers took his place at the periscope and watched the island sliding past on the port side, while Hamilton rifled through the chart-table drawers in search of the maps he needed for his Council-of-War with Mannon, Scott and O'Brien.

'Can't see Betty Grable coming down the beach to welcome us ashore,' the young reservist joked to pass the tedium of *Rapier's* slow approach. 'I hope you blokes remembered to bring the map showing where the treasure was buried.'

The men on duty watch in the control room grinned. Villier's casual attitude made a change from the skipper's customary dour concentration or Mannon's pedantic attention to detail.

'As long as you can't see Errol Flynn swinging about in the trees I don't mind, sir,' Venables retorted from his seat at the diving panel. 'I don't fancy having any competition when I meet all them hula-hula girls!'

Villiers winked broadly at the chief ERA and then returned to his solitary vigil at the periscope. Suddenly something caught his attention and he flicked the lever of the high magnification lens.

'Hey! Scotty! I thought you said those two volcanoes were extinct?'

Hamilton looked up sharply. 'They're as dead as dodos. I've been up and inspected the craters myself. Why?'

The grin on the sub-lieutenant's face faded. He stared through the lens again to make sure he wasn't mistaken. 'There's black smoke coming up in the direction of the more northerly one, sir.'

Hamilton put the charts down on the table and took over the periscope. He stared at the smoke, scanned along the length of the island, and then returned the lens for a more detailed examination of the northern sector. Villiers' report - and it was a natural enough error - had been wrong in locating the smoke as rising from the extinct crater of the squat volcanic hill dominating the lagoon on the left hand side of the island. It was, in fact, coming from a wooded area at the base of the hill and less than half a mile from the north shore itself. It was impossible to determine the exact location, because the fire was spreading rapidly through the dense undergrowth, but Hamilton felt his mouth go dry as he realized that somewhere in the midst of the smoke and flames, was *Rapier's* carefully prepared base camp and storage depot. Was it just a spontaneous bush fire - or had the enemy discovered their secret?

'Down periscope! Stop motors. Are you getting any HE, Glover?'

The hydro-phone operator slipped the pads over his ears and moved the knobs of his listening apparatus. He shook his head.

'No HE, sir. Just the surf breaking on the beach.'

'Try an Asdic probe.'

Glover swivelled his seat to the right and transmitted a series of sonar pulses that *pinged* sharply in the loudspeaker above his cabinet. 'No contacts, sir!'

'I reckon this is when we could do with one of these new-fangled radio location sets,' Hamilton grumbled quietly to Mannon. 'But I'm certain about one thing - if there is an enemy vessel in the vicinity it must be anchored or else we'd have picked up its engine noises on the hydrophone.' He paused to consider his next move. 'Slow ahead both motors. Stand by Torpedo Room. Up periscope.'

The fire was still burning and the northerly breeze was sweeping the dense smoke out across the lagoon, where it hung above the water like a heavy sea mist. *Rapier* glided silently inshore while Hamilton carried out a detailed examination of the anchorage. Satisfied there was no enemy ship in the lagoon he turned the lens towards the entrance. This time there *was* something - a small boat chugging slowly towards the shore from the direction of Taichi Rock.

'Close up Attack Team! Steer one point to port... blow up all tubes!'

Hamilton could well understand the reluctance of an enemy commander to enter the lagoon. Its waters were uncharted and treacherous and he would have had no time to survey the depths or locate any hidden reefs. In addition, no sensible captain would want to find himself trapped inside a virtually landlocked harbor in the event of a surprise attack. And this appreciation of the enemy's reasoning led him to one inevitable conclusion - a conclusion backed by Glover's failure to pick up any HE and his own inability to sight the ship through *Rapier's* periscope. The intruder must be anchored in the lee of Taichee Rock.

Swinging the eye of the upper lens to starboard, he waited tensely as the submarine moved into the area which would enable him to see what was lurking on the inshore side of the gaunt, granite rock. Yard by yard, more of the northern face of the rock became visible and then, suddenly, the dark grey paintwork of a Japanese warship came into view.

'Enemy destroyer anchored between Taichee Rock and the island. Small boats going ashore,' he reported back to Mannon and the other men in the control room. 'Estimated range two miles...'

'Someone must have given us away to the Japs,' Mannon said bitterly. 'It would have taken them months to find this place.'

'Steer zero-six-five. Reduce to half power. Open bow

caps.' Hamilton waited to complete his instructions and then glanced at Mannon. 'No one's given us away, Number One,' he said sharply. 'Chai Chen realized she would die whether she talked or not. She must have told them about the island in order to put them on a false trail.'

'I can't see anything false about it, sir,' Mannon objected. 'If the enemy has destroyed our storage depot *Rapier* will be about as battle-worthy as a bloody canoe without paddles.'

'Perhaps so - but, in my opinion, she was trying to lead us to the men responsible for her death. And that destroyer anchored under the Rock *proves* it. If she'd told them the truth the Japs would have ambushed us when we arrived at the refueling point. And the reason they didn't do so is because they did not know we were planning to meet the junk at sea.'

Mannon shrugged. 'I'm not denying the girl's courage, sir. She may not have told them about the rendezvous, but she certainly seems to have given away the secret of our supply base. And while I don't blame her after what they did to her I'm damned if I can see any advantage in it.'

'In that case, Number One, I'll spell it out to you,' Hamilton said coldly. 'If Chai Chen had told the Japs about our refueling plans, *Rapier* would be lying on the bottom of the South China Sea by now because they would have caught us by surprise. She knew, however, that once we found the junk we'd be very much on the alert.' So she told them the oil was being shipped to the island - it would have sounded a plausible enough story. As a result, the Japs are still under the impression that they have surprise on their side and they're hiding behind Taichee Rock waiting to jump us when we arrive.'

'But Chai Chen was obviously thinking several moves

ahead. She realized we'd make for the island and she knew, also, that we'd be prepared for trouble after finding the junk. So by telling them about the replenishment base she made sure that retribution would follow within a few hours. And, in addition, *I* would know that the officer commanding the Japanese ship waiting at the island must be the man responsible for her death.'

Mannon made no immediate reply. Hamilton's theory was a little too trite for his liking. And it involved a hell of a lot of supposition. But whether the skipper was right or wrong there was no disputing the fact that, on the balance of probabilities, the man who had tortured Chai Chen to death was the captain of the destroyer now anchored off the island. Any other explanation would be stretching the long arm of coincidence a trifle too far.

'You're probably right, sir,' he agreed reluctantly.

At that precise moment Hamilton was not particularly interested whether Mannon agreed or not. He wanted revenge. And no one was going to stop him from carrying out his self-appointed task. He picked up the telephone to the bow compartment.

'Is everything ready, Number Four?'

'Bow Compartment, aye, aye, sir,' Villiers reported. 'Doors open and tubes flooded up. Standing by.'

'Well, keep your fingers crossed that we don't miss. They're our last four torpedoes and it looks as if our reserves have already gone up in smoke.' He cradled the phone on its hook and nodded to Bushby. 'Up periscope!'

He found the enemy destroyer almost immediately. The dark grey warship with its strangely cranked funnels and knuckled bow was lying broadside on to the submarine in an almost perfect attack position. Hamilton felt a sudden surge of adrenalin pump into his bloodstream as he recognized the sleek silhouette. It was *Suma*. The man he was hunting was Aritsu!

Hamilton controlled his excitement and mechanically wiped the damp sweat of his hands on his trousers. The range was down to eight hundred yards. This time he had no need for the back-up support of the Attack Team- with a stationary target course and speed were irrelevant and there were no problems of deflection or aim off. All that counted was the accuracy of his eye and steady nerves. Moving to the attack 'scope he ordered it to be raised and carefully brought the anchored destroyer into the center of the graticule sights.

'Stand by to fire. Fire One... Fire Two... Fire Three... Fire Four...'

A slight increase in air pressure inside the control room indicated that the tubes had been fired and the four green warning lights on the for'ard bulkhead display glowed brightly in confirmation. Glover bent over his box of tricks as he listened for the sound of the whirring propellers.

'Torpedoes running, sir!'

'Hard a'port, helmsman! Stand by to surface. Close up for gun action... *surface!*'

'Up helm 'planes! Close vents and blow main ballast!'

Although Mannon rapped out the routine commands with disciplined obedience, he was puzzled by Hamilton's decision to surface. Most submarine commanders dived deep immediately after a torpedo attack in anticipation of the enemy's counter-action. And if the skipper had miscalculated, it seemed foolish to invite a fight on the surface when the odds would be all against the submarine. Perhaps Hamilton had allowed his excitement to override his natural caution.

The muffled clang of the vents being slammed shut

coincided with the shrill scream of high-pressure air as the ballast tanks were blown clear. Acting on his own initiative, Mannon decided to increase speed so that the submarine would make a more difficult target when she emerged on the surface.

'Group up - full ahead both motors!' He glanced at the dials and saw that the bows were rising too sluggishly.

'Blow Q!'

'Ten feet, sir!'

'Stand by for gun action!'

'Come on, lads,' Morgan urged the gun crew. 'Up you go!'

Hamilton had just unclipped the upper hatch and thrown back the heavy steel cover, when the blast of the explosion nearly hurled him from the ladder. He hung on grimly, as a vivid flash lit the sky and a thunderous roar deafened his ears. A second detonation followed a moment later and then a third. Pulling himself up through the narrow opening he hurried to the starboard side of the bridge.

The dying echoes of the three thunderous explosions were still reverberating back from the sheer north face of Taichee Rock and the screaming protests of the gulls disturbed from their nests added to the confusion. *Suma* had been struck fair and square amidships and the second torpedo had broken the destroyer in half. The stern section was already sinking beneath the surface and, as he stared at the awful spectacle, Hamilton saw the bows tilt upwards, hang suspended for a few seconds, and then slide back beneath the sea with a sibilant hiss of quenched white-hot steel. Wreckage and bodies bobbed aimlessly in the water and a cloud of steam hung wraith-like above the surface to mark *Suma*'s grave.

'Machine guns to the bridge! Reduce to half-speed!'

MacIntyre and Davidson came up through the hatch clutching their cumbersome Lewis guns and Hamilton sent them to their battle-stations in the port and starboard wings. Then, raising his binoculars, he searched the floating wreckage for survivors. But the torpedoes had done their deadly work almost too efficiently. *Suma* had gone down in less than half a minute and those members of the crew who survived the first torpedo had died in the water, their ribs smashed and their lungs ruptured by the pressure wave radiating outwards from the second explosion.

'Boat approaching on port side!'

Hamilton swung round to focus his glasses on a small rowing cutter emerging from the entrance to the lagoon. The sailors on shore had obviously heard the noise of the explosions and were hurrying to the scene in search of survivors.

'Target red-eight-zero!' Hamilton shouted to Morgan. 'Open fire!'

Rapier's deck gun traversed to port and the layer's arms pumped like pistons as he reversed the elevation wheel to depress the barrel. The loader slammed the first shell into the breech, closed the block, and pulled down the locking lever.

'Loaded and ready Chief!'

But Morgan hesitated. Pitching steeply as its bows met the swell of the sea beyond the sheltered waters of the lagoon, the cutter thrust forward as its crew strained on their oars. The boat was less than five hundred yards off the submarine's port beam and the Welshman's keen eyes could make out every detail.

'They're not armed, sir,' he shouted up to Hamilton.

Rapier's captain examined the cutter through his binoculars. There were four men at the oars and the fifth, a petty officer, was at the tiller. Hamilton studied him closely and saw the holstered pistol at his hip.

'They're carrying guns, Mister Morgan. Open fire!'

Years of discipline had destroyed Morgan's initiative. He knew that the men in the cutter were carrying only side- arms. They posed no threat to the submarine and intent on the task of finding survivors, they wen; showing no hostility towards *Rapier*. He knew too that in his present mood for revenge Hamilton would not rest until every single member of *Suma's* crew was dead. But he had been given an order by a superior officer and it was not for him to question it. He turned back to the men working the deck gun.

'Fire!... Reload!'

The first shell fell short by twenty yards and exploded harmlessly in the sea ahead of the cutter. Morgan saw the petty officer glance at the splash of the bursting shell and then concentrate his attention on the steering again. Ignoring the threat of *Rapier's* gun the oarsmen continued to row steadily towards the spot where *Suma* had gone down.

'Up ten... fire! Reload!'

The shell exploded with a blinding flash as it struck the starboard gunwale of the cutter. Jagged splinters of red- hot steel scythed through the men bending over the oars and simultaneously, the tiny boat disintegrated. Only the petty officer survived and, as he bobbed to the surface some twenty yards astern, two ugly triangular dorsal fins darted through the water. Hamilton lowered his glasses and leaned his elbows on the conning tower rails as the sea around the struggling man was suddenly ripped into a frenzy of boiling foam. The petty officer let out a single despairing shriek as he vanished from sight and a circle of bright red blood rose to the surface....

'Coxswain to the bridge! Stand by to transfer steering to upper position.' Hamilton waited for Ernie Blood to come up through the hatchway and take his position at the helm. 'Obey telegraphs - full ahead together. You can take her into the lagoon, Chief.'

Fifteen minutes later *Rapier* was snugly berthed under the camouflage netting, with her bow and stern tied up to the makeshift wooden jetty the submariners had constructed the previous month. However, nothing else remained of their carefully prepared hiding place. Both of the bamboo huts had been torn down. The aqueduct which Scott had designed to bring fresh water down from the hill had been destroyed and only the smoldering ashes remained of the wooden crates containing the victuals, stores, and spare parts which had been so laboriously trans-ported from Hong Kong a few weeks earlier.

Hamilton looked at the heartbreaking remains of his labours unemotionally. He consoled his disappointment by admitting it had been a crazy idea from the outset. And yet, although everything had gone wrong, he had no regrets. Without torpedoes, his grandiose plans for a lone marauding sweep of the South China Sea in search of enemy shipping would have to be set aside. And now, deprived of its oil reserves, *Rapier* had barely enough fuel to retire to a safe base. Tightening the gun belt around his waist, he made his way down the rickety bamboo gangway and joined Mannon on the jetty.

'O'Brien has found one of *Suma's* motorboats hauled up on the beach, Number One, and that means there are still some survivors hiding ashore. I intend to remain here until every last man is dead.'

'The Japs are trained in jungle fighting, sir,' Mannon pointed out. He disliked his continual role of devil's advocate but as *Rapier's* executive officer he considered it his duty to underline the difficulties. Hamilton's unreasoning thirst for vengeance made him blind to any defects in his plans. 'Most of our lads hardly know how to aim a rifle.'

But Hamilton was not listening. 'The motorboat suggests there's an officer with them, and there's just an outside chance it's Aritsu.' He turned to Mannon. 'How many men can be made available for a search party?' he asked sharply.

'Every man in the ship's company has volunteered for shore service, sir. But as we only had ten rifles aboard I've had to prune them down a bit. They're waiting over by the trees.'

Hamilton strode over and gave the hurriedly constituted landing party a cursory inspection. Individually they looked tough enough and, despite Mannon's pessimism, he knew that three of them had obtained marksman badges. It was a rough and ready little army, but Hamilton considered it adequate for the task he had in mind. The enemy was unlikely to be better armed and, judging by the size of the destroyer's diminutive tender, he felt confident he had superiority in numbers. Even so, like most sailors, he felt slightly uneasy at the prospect of fighting ashore. His knowledge of military tactics was limited to a fortnight's course at *Excellent* and the uninspiring contents of the *Royal Naval Handbook of Field Training* - most of which was devoted to the niceties of parade ground drill and ceremonial occasions, although he could vividly recall a bloodthirsty photograph demonstrating 'withdrawal of bayonet after kill on the ground.'

'Take five men and search the north hill, Number One.

The remainder will go with me to cover the southern section of the island.'

'What happens if we find them?' Mannon asked. Hamilton stared at him impassively. 'Don't ask bloody silly questions, Number One. If you find them- kill them.' 'But suppose they surrender, sir?'

Hamilton unholstered his revolver and broke it open to check that the cylinder was fully loaded. 'The Japanese do not surrender, Mister Mannon,' he said coldly. 'To lay down their arms when they are still capable of fighting would be regarded as an act of dishonour.'

'Not always, Lieutenant...'

Hamilton spun around as he recognized the voice. His right hand swung up and his finger tightened on the trigger as he saw Commander Aritsu, another officer and two ratings emerge from the trees and walk slowly down the beach towards him. Aritsu's hands were stretched out in front of his body and he was bearing his sheathed sword.

'Stop where you are, Commander!' As *Suma's* captain obeyed the order, Hamilton turned to Mannon. 'It could be a trap. Search the bushes. If you find anybody hiding... shoot them!'

'There is no one else, Lieutenant.' Aritsu told him quietly. 'I regret to inform you that we are the only survivors.' He bowed stiffly, 'Permit me to hand you my sword.'

Hamilton flicked the safety catch of the Webley as the Commander took a pace forward. 'Stay where you are! Throw the sword on the ground.'

Aritsu hesitated for a moment and then obeyed. Hamilton lowered his revolver fractionally. Although he had *Suma's* captain at his mercy, he intended to take no chances. His brain worked quickly as he considered what to do with his unexpected bonus. According to the book, he should take all four of them prisoner and hand them over to the proper authorities when *Rapier* returned to base. But as things stood at the moment, he could not even be certain that the submarine would ever succeed in reaching a friendly harbor, and with a shortage of stores and fresh water he saw no reason for carrying any extra passengers. He had little doubt what the fate of his men would be if they fell into the hands of the Japanese in similar circumstances.

'I should take you back and have you charged with war crimes, Commander.'

'You found the junk then?'

Hamilton parried the question. 'I always thought that an officer of the Imperial Navy was a man of honor. Having seen what you did to the crew I realize I was wrong - the Japanese are nothing but a race of sadistic barbarians!' Sub-Lieutenant Mihoro had not spoken since Aritsu had led the survivors out to surrender. His small black eyes watched the English submarine commander with the chilling intensity of a mongoose stalking a snake. It was apparent from the expression on his face that he had no respect for *Suma's* captain and Hamilton's accusation stirred him to life.

'You are directing your insults at the wrong man, Lieutenant! Commander Aritsu had no part in the affair. *I* carried out the interrogation of the crew.' His eyes blazed suddenly, as if defying Hamilton to do something lo him. 'Is this correct, Commander?'

Aritsu shook his head. 'Any action taken against prisoners is my responsibility. When I saw the oil drums I knew they were intended for your submarine. It was my duty to obtain information. Mihoro was merely the instrument who carried out my instructions.'

Realizing that he had just signed his own death warrant, he bowed politely and composed himself with dignity to await Hamilton's inevitable order.

'I appreciate your candour, Commander. Perhaps I was mistaken in saying you were a man without honor.' Hamilton stared hard and deep into Aritsu's eyes as he put the question. 'Did you tell your Sub-Lieutenant how the interrogations were to be carried out?'

'No... I left him to do whatever he thought fit.'

'He was too weak!' Mihoro spat defiantly. 'He went back to his ship so that he did not have to witness what happened. He is not fit to serve the Emperor.'

Hamilton switched his attention to the Korean. His eyes were completely expressionless as he looked at him, and his index finger was trembling on the trigger of his revolver. 'You are the one who interrogated Chai Chen?'

'If you mean the girl - yes. *And* I succeeded. She told me all about the island and your plans to use it as a secret refueling base. She was stubborn - but I consider myself to be an expert in such matters...

Hamilton's right arm came up before Mannon or anyone else could stop him.

The sudden crack of the revolver sent the birds wheeling into the sky with fright, and Mihoro clutched his stomach as the heavy caliber bullet threw him backwards into the sand. Forcing himself up onto his knees, he stared wide-eyed at the British officer, and then folded forward. It was a slow and agonizing way to die, and the Korean's body threshed wildly as he tried to staunch the blood with his hands. Hamilton waited a brief moment and then fired again. Mihoro jerked as the bullet struck his head and then, suddenly, he was still.

Every eye was on Hamilton as he turned towards Aritsu

and the Japanese Commander braced himself in readiness. Yet, even in the face of death, his expression remained as impassive as ever and he held himself with quiet dignity.

Hamilton lowered the gun and bent forward. He said nothing but, picking up the sword, he walked towards Aritsu and handed it to him hilt-first.

The Japanese officer understood the gesture. He bowed politely, took the weapon from Hamilton's hands, and bowed again. Unable to control his emotions any longer, he began to weep silently, the tears trickling down his cheeks as he struggled to find the right words.

'You are a chivalrous man, Lieutenant Hamilton,' he said very quietly. 'I pray that my ancestors will look kindly upon you and protect you in battle.'

'Thank you, Commander. I appreciate that you were only doing your duty as you saw it. The ways of Japan are something that we in Europe will never fully understand.' Hamilton paused for a moment. 'Although I know you would never countenance the barbarities employed by your Sub-Lieutenant to obtain information, you have acted in accordance with the traditions of the Imperial Navy by accepting responsibility for what happened because you were the senior officer. You must therefore die - but you may die with honor.'

Aritsu bowed his acknowledgement. Getting down on his knees in front of the lieutenant, he pulled open his bush shirt and unfastened the belt of his uniform trousers. Hamilton swallowed his instinctive revulsion and steeled himself to witness the barbaric, yet strangely noble, ceremony Aritsu was about to perform. *Seppuku* - ritual suicide.

Grasping the hilt of the sword with both hands the Japanese directed the point of the blade against the center of his stomach, closing his eyes as if summoning up the spiritual strength he needed to perform the act, and with a sudden powerful jerk of his arms, rammed the sword into his body. He uttered no sound despite the agony of the self-inflicted wound and, closing his eyes, he moved the blade upwards to make the first vertical incision.

Hamilton felt the bile rising in his throat but, out of respect for the ancient traditions of a brave man, he forced his unwilling eyes to watch. Blood was already welling from Aritsu's belly, and the grey-mauve mass of his intestines protruded obscenely from the wound as he centered the point of the sword for the second cut. Mills, the young cockney able seaman from Poplar, who had never even seen a chicken have its throat cut, suddenly rolled his eyes and collapsed on to the sand in a dead faint. The other submariners looked away from the horrific spectacle and prayed it would soon be over. Only Mannon, like his skipper, stood firm and faced it out.

Aritsu paused before the second incision, opened his eyes, and looked up at *Rapier's* captain. His lips moved but it was impossible to make out what he was trying to say. Then the blade cut to the right, was dragged painfully back to the original point of entry and sliced to the left.

The commander paused for a moment, raised his eyes to the sky, and then collapsed face-forward on to the blood soaked sand - the weight of his body forcing the sword deeper into his vitals. His hands clenched in a spasm of unendurable pain and, in accordance with the ancient traditions of the ritual, Hamilton stepped forward and ended Aritsu's agony with a single shot through the back of the skull.

Hamilton lowered his head briefly and then, emerging from the almost catalyptic trance which had gripped him during the ceremony, pushed the revolver back into the holster at his hip. He had had a surfeit of killing and Arit-su's death had blunted his hunger for revenge. He was suddenly sick of the whole useless waste of war.

'Take the landing party back to the boat, Number One. I want to get away from this damned place before we all go raving mad.'

Mannon passed the order to the petty officer in charge and, as the men lifted the unfortunate Mills to his feet and helped him back to the jetty, the submarine's executive officer nodded towards the beach.

'What about the seamen, sir?'

Hamilton shook his head. He had not forgotten the two Japanese sailors. But he had had enough of death for one day. 'Leave them here, Number One. They can either stay on the island until the Japs send a search ship out - or they can try to make their way back to the mainland in the motorboat.'

Zibuki and his companion stared questioningly at the two British officers as they approached across the narrow stretch of sand. Both men expected to be shot out of hand, and with characteristic fatalism they offered no resistance. The taller officer spoke to them in English, but the language meant nothing to them. They waited for the guns to be unholstered, aimed and fired. The officer spoke to them again, but when they did not respond he shrugged and turned away.

Hitiose Zibuki showed no emotion at the unexpected turn of events. He watched the officers walk slowly back to the submarine and said something to his comrade. Crossing the beach to where Aritsu was lying, they knelt down and began to gather pieces of driftwood to build his funeral pyre

O'Brien was waiting inside the control room as

Hamilton and Mannon came down the ladder. He was holding a sheet of paper in his hand.

'I've been checking the fuel reserves as you requested, sir. It doesn't look too good.'

Hamilton took the notes and glanced down at the figures. 'How far to Singapore, Alistair?'

The Navigator bent over the small-scale chart with his ruler. 'Just under fourteen hundred miles, sir.'

'And Darwin?'

Mannon looked up sharply as Hamilton put the question. Australia! What the hell was the skipper up to- a conducted tour of the British Empire?

'About double the distance, sir,' Scott reported. 'It wouldn't be a straight run - we'd have to go around Borneo, down through the Celebes Sea, and south via the Molucca Straits. Then...

'Alright, Alistair, that's enough. I know what a map of the East Indies looks like.' He turned to Mannon. 'Can you see any objection to Australia, Number One?'

'No, sir. Other than the fact we don't have enough fuel and your last orders were to report to Singapore.'

'I'm glad you reminded me, Roger. I'd forgotten all about that,' Hamilton said equably. 'But the situation is different now. Hong Kong had surrendered and the Japs are already spearheading a new offensive into the East Indies. They've landed in Sarawak and Brunei. With virtually no naval forces to oppose them, I anticipate attacks on Java and Sumutra within the next two weeks. And judging by the speed of the enemy advance through Malaya, I'd say Singapore will have fallen by the end of the month. I have no intention of returning to Singapore and finding myself in a repeat performance of the Hong Kong shambles. As I see it, the whole of Australia is wide open to a Japanese invasion.

There are virtually no naval forces south of New Guinea and the Americans are, for the moment, too busy defending themselves. If we were able to operate out of Darwin, *Rapier* could be Australia's first fine of defense against a Japanese attack.' He glanced across at O'Brien. 'Could we make Darwin, Chief?' 'Depends on how much power we might need, sir. A couple of severe storms or a detour to avoid enemy patrols and we certainly wouldn't. If Scotty can plot the shortest course' to Aussie and we make use of the motors on the surface whenever we can, we *might* just make it. If you want my personal opinion, sir, I'd say it was touch and go.' Hamilton smiled. 'In that case, gentlemen, it's go!'

COMMODORE HASLITT GOT up from his chair, walked across to the window looking out across Fort Hill and Boom Jetty, and flung it open. His office was without air-conditioning and after twenty-two days at sea with only one change of clothing and minimal washing facilities Hamilton did not exactly smell like a fresh spring rose. But with three week's growth of beard and eyes red-rimmed with exhaustion Hamilton was past caring about personal appearance. The luxury of a hot bath, clean clothes, and a good night's sleep could come later. His first duty was to report his arrival to the Darwin SNO.

The Commodore returned to his desk and sat down. The sea breeze wafting through the opened window was having the required effect and he sniffed the clean salt air appreciatively, like a medieval judge smelling his nosegay as he passed through the City streets on his way to the Law Courts.

'You realize, of course, Lieutenant, that the C-in-C (Far

East) had been searching the length and breadth of the
Pacific for you for the past five weeks.'

'I'm sorry, sir, but our transmitter was on the blink and I
wanted to save the batteries in case we ran out of fuel and
had to finish the trip on our motors."

'So you said earlier, Lieutenant,' Haslitt commented
drily. 'But you still haven't explained why you did not
report to Singapore as ordered. The Admiralty will
undoubtedly require your explanation.'

'The situation was very confused, sir.' Hamilton could
not help wondering if the Commodore would be quite so
pedantically calm if he'd experienced the first shock of
Japan's blitzkrieg into South-East Asia. In the circumstances he decided that he would be excusable. 'We were
picking up radio reports, sir. I was under the impression that
Singapore had fallen. In view of that, I decided to make for
Australia.'

Haslitt did not seem very convinced by the explanation
but he accepted it without comment. At that precise
moment, his greatest desire was to get Hamilton out of his
office and into a hot bath and clean clothes. The post
mortem could come later.

'I must admit I am disappointed with your lack of
success. It will all have to appear in your written Report of
Proceedings, of course, and no doubt the Admiralty will
have a few observations to make. But what you've been
doing with yourself for the last six weeks or so is a mystery
to me. You were the only British submarine in the entire
area and yet all you succeeded in sinking was one bloody
little destroyer!'

Hamilton said nothing. Staring at the blank wall behind
the Commodore's desk, he recalled the night battle in the
narrow straits between Kowloon and Hong Kong, the

destruction of *Firefly,* the fate of the refueling junk, and those last terrible hours on Charlotte Island. It was something Haslitt would never understand in a thousand years.

'And another thing, Lieutenant,' the Commodore continued. 'The Foreign Office is after your blood for infringing Portuguese neutrality. Your private arrangements with that damned Macao oil merchant could have international repercussions.'

A picture of Chai Chen's naked body splayed out and roped to the side of the deckhouse flashed into Hamilton's mind. He wondered what *she* would have thought about Portuguese neutrality and International Law. Or, for that matter, Sub-Lieutenant Mihoro. Not that his own actions had been above reproach, and he was curious to know how he was going to explain the Korean's execution and Aritsu's suicide. Suddenly he realized he didn't care any more.

'I'll let you have a full written report in the morning, sir. May I have permission to return to my ship?'

'Permission granted, Lieutenant.'

Hamilton saluted, turned, and walked wearily towards the door. He could not help wondering what the future held for him now. Perhaps he should resign his commission. Or volunteer for service with the Commandos. Anything that would enable him to fight the enemy without the hampering restrictions of rules, regulations and laws. And yet not even total annihilating victory could ever repay the debt owed to people like Chai Chen and Harry Ottershaw, or to Captain Snark and Chen Yu. A sudden shout from the Commodore made him pause in the doorway.

'By the way Hamilton, you can ship your half-stripe. The New Year promotion list came through a couple of weeks ago. You've been made up to Lieutenant Commander. Congratulations.'

But the door was already shut and Hamilton was making his way down the stairs towards the harbour. Haslitt shrugged. Rum sort of a bloke, he concluded. But that was the trouble with some of these upper-yardmen. They might be officers, but one could hardly call them gentlemen....

A LOOK AT: NO SURVIVORS, THE U-BOAT SERIES

Mutiny or murder. These were the stark choices that confronted Kapitan-Leutnant Konrad Bergman. To go against the discipline and training that had been instilled in him from youth and disobey an order. Or to carry out the Fuehrer's command and destroy his own comrades in an act of cold-blooded premeditated murder.

As commander of a U-boat, Bergman had always greedily accepted his orders, lusting after each of his kills with the relentless energies of a primitive predator. Now the harsh realities of war were proving to be somewhat different from the romantic dreams of his youth. But it was too late to change his destiny now.

AVAILABLE NOW ON AMAZON

ABOUT THE AUTHOR

AUTHOR EDWYN GRAY specialized in naval writing, and has occasionally written short stories.

Born in London, Gray pursued his education at the Royal Grammar School, High Wycombe. After reading economics at the University of London, he went on to join the British civil service.

Gray began his career as an author in 1953, writing for magazines. His first novel was published in 1969, and he became a full-time writer in 1980.

Find Edwyn Gray at:
https://wolfpackpublishing.com/edwyn-gray/

www.ingramcontent.com/pod-product-compliance
Lightning Source LLC
Chambersburg PA
CBHW022110240626
47153CB00007B/2316